Endings

ENDINGS

Her Sweet Revenge Series - Book #4

Mimi Barbour

Sarna Publishing

Contents

Dedication
xi

Praise
xii

Also author of...
xiv

Chapter One
I

Chapter Two
9

Chapter Three
13

Chapter Four
17

Chapter Five
22

Chapter Six
30

Chapter Seven
34

Chapter Eight
46

Chapter Nine
48

Chapter Ten
50

Chapter Eleven
57

Chapter Twelve
63

Chapter Thirteen
67

Chapter Fourteen
74

Chapter Fifteen
81

Chapter Sixteen
86

Chapter Seventeen
91

Chapter Eighteen
100

Chapter Nineteen
108

Chapter Twenty
113

Chapter Twenty-one
119

Chapter Twenty-two
123

Chapter Twenty-three
128

Chapter Twenty-four
134

Chapter Twenty-five
141

Chapter Twenty-six
147

Chapter Twenty-seven
152

Chapter Twenty-eight
156

Chapter Twenty-nine
162

Chapter Thirty
165

Chapter Thirty-one
174

Chapter Thirty-two
179

Chapter Thirty-three
185

Chapter Thirty-four
198

Chapter Thirty-five
203

Chapter Thirty-six
212

Chapter Thirty-seven
217

Chapter Thirty-eight
229

Chapter Thirty-nine
235

Chapter Forty
241

Chapter Forty-one
243

Chapter Forty-two
249

Chapter Forty-three
260

Chapter Forty-four
268

Chapter Forty-five
272

Chapter Forty-six
280

Chapter Forty-seven
284

Chapter Forty-eight
290

Chapter Forty-nine
297

Chapter Fifty
305

Chapter Fifty-one
310

Afterword
317
Faith
319
Faith - Chapter One
321
Special Agent Kandice
328

The Vegas Series
332
A word about the author, Mimi Barbour
335
Contact Me
337

Dedication

I'm dedicating this series to my father, who we lovingly refer to as Papa John. This man has been a huge influence throughout my life. He's a smart, energetic, affectionate and very wise ninety-two-year-old man who is still going strong – likes to brag that he's only taking one pill a day. He's legally blind, but no one can tell from the way he gets around. Whenever he appears in the dining room at his lodge, people light up, and the jokes start flying.

This man brightens the day for everyone around him, and it thrills me to be his very fortunate daughter. To dedicate this new series to him is my way of telling the world that without his calm guidance and constant example, I'd never be the writer, the wife, the mother or the successful, happy woman I am today.

I love you, Papa John!

*Sadly, I lost my wonderful Papa John in 2018, and in his memory I wrote a book using him as one of the characters. It's called Special Agent Charli. So far, he seems to be reaping the best comments in the book's many reviews. Amazon Universal link: http://mybook.to/SpecialAgentCharli

Praise

"The happy ever after story for Cass. But so many uneven steps to get to happy. As usual Mimi delivers a excellent book with great characters, good plot, twist and turns and loads of excitement. You are drawn into the book in minutes. Back with familiar characters.
Excellent book that you cannot put down till the end." ~ *Reviewed by Shirleen*

"What a great end to Cassi's story! I could not put this book down until I found out how her story ended and if she finally got the truth she searched so hard for about her brother's killer. Needless to say, Mimi did not disappoint! If you haven't read any of the books in this series, you must start with book 1 and read them in order. You will not be disappointed." ~ *Reviewed by Laura*

"This series is so, so, good it should be a movie or a tv series. Mimi Barbour is a excellent writer. I have several thousand books downloaded and I purchased her books. Good writing and fast pace that makes these books impossible to stop reading. Love your writing." ~ *Reviewed by Pat*

"Ms. Barbour has done a magnificent job with

this series. A happy ending for a story with unexpected twists. A thoroughly satisfying read." ~ *Reviewed by Colorado Avid Reader*

"What an absolutely brilliant ending to Cassi's story. In typical fashion with this series, could not put this book down. There were so many twists and turns and unexpected events that I was holding my breath in some spots, the anticipation of what was to come was so intense! So pleased we will also get to read Faith's story! I can't get enough of these characters." ~ *Reviewed by Bella*

Also author of...

***Most of Mimi's books can be found FREE on Kindle Unlimited!!
Universal Links used for your Amazon address.
***

~*~*~*~
The Vicarage Bench Series
— Spirit Travel at its Best! —
She's Me (Book 1)
He's Her (Book 2)
We're One (Book 3)
Vicarage Bench Anthology (Book 4 – Books 1-3)
Together Again (Book 5)
Together for Christmas (Book 6)
Together Always (Book 7)
***

Angels with Attitude Series
— Angels Playing Cupid! —
The Angels with Attitudes Anthology (Books 1-3)
My Cheeky Angel (Book 1)
His Devious Angel (Book 2)
Loveable Christmas Angel (Book 3)
A Wonderful Life (Book 4)
Mischievous Christmas Angel (Book 5)
***

Elvis Series

— Make an Elvis Song a Book! —
She's Not You (Book 1)
Love Me Tender (Book 2)

***

Vegas Series
— Action–Packed Thrillers! —
Vegas Series – Complete Boxed Set
Partners (Book 1)
Roll the Dice (Book 2)
Vegas Shuffle (Book 3)
High Stakes Gamble (Book 4)
Spin the Wheel (Book 5)
Let it Ride (Book 6)

***

Undercover FBI Series
— Popular & Compelling! —
Special Agent Francesca (Book 1)
Special Agent Finnegan (Book 2)
Special Agent Maximilian (Book 3)
Special Agent Kandice (Book 4)
Special Agent Booker (Book 5)
Special Agent Charli (Book 6)
Special Agent Rylee (Book 7)
Special Agent Murphy (Book 8)
Special Agent Sophia (Book #9 – to be released
in May 2020)

***

Holiday Heartwarmers Series
— Truly a Christmas favorite! —
Holiday Heartwarmers Trilogy

Please Keep Me (Book 1)
Snow Pup (Book 2)
Find Me a Home (Book 3)
Frosty the Snowman (Book 4)
Love of my Life (Book 5)
A Perfect Storm (Book 6)
***

Her Sweet Revenge Series
— She's unstoppable! —
Retaliation (Book #1)
Justice (Book #2)
Resolution (Book #3
Endings – (Book #4)
Faith (Book #5)
Leni (Book #6)
***

Single Title Series
He's My Baby (Book #1)
Christmas Runaway (Book #2)
Because You cared (Book #3)
Daddy's Mine (Book #4 – to be released in
March 2020)
***

The Best in Romance Series
Red Hot Divas (Book #1 Box Set)
Hot and Handsome (Book #2 Box Set
***

Other Titles
I'm No Angel
Hotshot Cowboy

Big Girls Don't Cry

The Surrogate's Secret

Mimi's Mix (Box Set)

'Tis the Season (Box Set)

Hearts, Flowers & Romance (Box Set)

Love, Christmas (Multi-author Box Set)

Unforgettable Romances (Multi-author Box Set)

Sweet and Sassy (Multi-author Box Set)

Unforgettable Heroes (Multi-author Box Set)

Unforgettable Christmas (Multi-author Box Set)

A Christmas She'll Remember (Multi-author Box Set)

Snowflakes and Christmas Kisses (Multi-author Box Set)

Unforgettable Valentine (Multi-author Box Set)

A Valentine She'll Remember (Multi-author Box Set)

Unforgettable Suspense (Multi-author Box Set)

Unforgettable Danger (Multi-author Box Set)

Unforgettable Trouble (Multi-author Box Set)

Unforgettable Weddings (Multi-author Box Set)

A Wedding She'll Remember (Multi-author Box Set)

Sweet and Sassy Brides (Multi-author Box Set)

Love, Christmas 2 (Multi-author Box Set)

Sweet and Sassy Suspense (Multi-author Box Set)

Unforgettable Thrills (Multi-author Box Set)
Unforgettable Passion (Multi-author Box Set)
A Romance She'll Remember (Multi-author Box Set)
Sweet and Sassy Cinderella (Multi-author Box Set)
Unforgettable Power (Multi-author Box Set)
Daring Protectors (Multi-author Box Set)
Unforgettable Charmers (Multi-author Box Set)
Sweet and Sassy Baby Love (Multi-author Box Set)
Sweet and Sassy Heroes (Multi-author Box Set)
Unforgettable Intrigue (Multi-author Box Set)
Unforgettable Christmas Dreams (Multi-author Box Set)
Sweet and Sassy Holiday (Multi-author Box Set)
Christmas Shorts (Multi-author Box Set)
Unforgettable Temptations (Multi-author Box Set)
Doctors in Love #2 (Multi-author Box Set)
Cute but Crazy (Multi-author Box Set)
Unforgettable Joy (Multi-author Box Set)

***

Website: http://mimibarbour.com

Chapter One

Surrounded by the people she most cared about, Cassidy Santino handled the police interrogation about Trace McGuire's disappearance as best she could. Considering her heart was shattered into small painful fragments, she held her cool rather than following her instincts to crawl into a corner and scream out her pain.

Detective Michael Kowalski, Trace's new partner, cared about her anguish. She could tell. But the gleam of seriousness in his questions belied his gentle tone. Another Vegas officer she didn't recognize, totally businesslike, stood taking notes. The two men had arrived at her house after her boxing match with Ariana Swift.

Unable to think cohesively, she'd let Rusty and Arlene play hostess for her, passing out coffees, showing everyone to chairs, shielding her as best they could.

Hurting, bruised, the punishment her body had taken earlier finally catching up with her was nothing compared to the utter devastation of her thoughts, her fears. How could she focus on their stupid questions when all she wanted was Trace?

Here.

Now.

Holding her.

Protecting her from the horrible pain.

Michael, bald and oddly handsome, leaned closer. As Trace's new partner, a Polish man with a reputed sense of the ridiculous, he wore a serious expression. It gave no clue to the quirky personality Trace had earlier described. Perched on a chair next to her, he reached for her hands to stop them from mangling each other and to gain her attention.

"Cassi, I'm sorry for your distress, but we really need you to answer these questions." His green eyes searched hers, providing support and strength. "Okay?"

"Okay. Yes. What do you need to know?" She connected with him and her eyes focused on his.

"I was at the hospital to see Trace and left before you arrived. In between, he had a visit from Sam." He nodded at the man slouching in a tipped chair next to the wall.

"Yes, Sam Smith, my co-worker at the Lipstick Club downtown."

"Right. Sam told us that he spent a very short

time in the room after you arrived."

"I caught him telling tales to Trace and scared him away." Her sad grin toward Sam let everyone know how well they got on. "After that, Trace and I were alone." Her mind fled back to the wonderful moments they'd shared when Trace had told her for the first time that he loved her, had put it in words. *"You're so blasted beautiful, you're the temptress. I'm just the poor sap who's crazy in love. All I want is for you to get naked and join me here in this son of a bitchin' bed so I taste your skin and feel you next to me."*

A sob broke. Wrangling her hands free, she lowered her face into them, shaken, distraught... terrified.

Arlene Montgomery, Rusty's protégée, leaned forward from the other side of Michael. Her harsh tone was anything but cordial. "Look, you moron, she's upset and you're questioning her? Man, you guys suck. She just got the crap beaten out of her in a ring by the US Featherweight Champion, and then she finds out her boyfriend has been kidnapped. Give her a break."

Michael responded quickly, his face was only inches from Arlene's. Sparks ignited between them. His expression became deadly serious.

"Look, lady. Trace is my partner. I care about the guy. And I need to know whether Cassi saw anyone loitering or hovering around when she went into his room or when she left. It's important.

So, either sit back and be quiet, or I'll have Officer Grady escort you out."

Rusty, who'd been the coffee maker, interrupted and saved the day. "Arlene, come into the other room and help me make up a bed on the couch. I'm not leaving Cassi here by herself, not when there's crazies around kidnapping people. Christ knows who's next."

Cassi heard the exchange and Rusty's words filtered in. The older man still looked as shaken as he'd appeared in the hotel's bar area after they'd left the dressing room. Now she had a suspicion as to why. He thought she was in danger. The sweet idiot wanted to protect her. She adored the old man for putting her welfare first.

"I'll be okay, Rusty. You don't need to stay."

"Ain't no discussion going on here, toots. I didn't ask, did I?"

Cassi saw his lip jut out and caved. "I'm fine, Arlene." Without realizing she'd touched the prickly girl, she patted her arm. "Please go and help Rusty."

Her dark-haired sparring partner scanned her face to see if she was telling the truth, and it still took a moment before her defender stood down. With a last glare at Kowalski, she followed Rusty and disappeared down the hallway.

"I'm sorry, Detective Kowalski. I'm a mess."

"Please call me Michael. I understand completely, Cassi, but we need this information.

If there's anything you can think of that will help us, any lead you can give us, I'd appreciate it immensely."

At this point, Sam coughed to get her attention. The telling look he sent vocalized better than words that she needed to get it together. She nodded at him and turned to Michael who held a small pad in his hand, waiting.

Her mind drifted back to the hospital. She'd been in a daze. Her thoughts absorbed with the coming fight. Plus, her determination not to lie to Trace had been a paramount worry and had kept her from focusing on the world around her. Trace had still been under the impression that Arlene would be in the ring.

"No, I'm sorry. I had just a short while with him. Rusty expected me to get to the casino early, and I wanted to stop and see Arlene first before leaving the hospital. Turns out, she'd discharged herself, and so I left."

"Trace told me that he'd given Dani Andino a fairly strict warning that he would be coming for her. Any leads there?"

Fuck! Her heart dropped to the floor and lay there quivering like a dying goldfish escaped from its bowl. *Dani!* Her mind whirled.

"Cassi?" Michael didn't miss a thing.

"She was at the fight. I saw her. You said Trace was taken during that time? She couldn't have been two places at once."

"Since it was two men who wheeled him out, I didn't suspect she'd be there. Just wondered if any of her men might have been hanging around the hospital, and you recognized them."

"How do you know there were two men?" Cassi shot the question at the surprised detective.

"We have it on video. But the men were dressed like surgeons with face masks, hats, and gowns so they can't be identified."

She shook her head, then stopped because the crushing torture on the inside of her scalp pounded unmercifully. "God, I wish I could help you but I truly don't remember anything. I was kind of focused on the coming fight."

Dani!

"No doubt. Look, is there anyone else you think might have had reason to kidnap Trace? Has he mentioned anything to you about being worried or followed?"

"Trace didn't talk about the job. And he only worried about me and my working at the club. But you're correct about one thing. He did have a run-in with Dani Andino there a few days ago. Plus, he was shot at the warehouse, right? So, he must have made even more enemies when the police interrupted their drug delivery. Did he hurt one of their members and now others are getting retribution? It's what they do, you know. They're all about payback. You can ask Sam about that. He's been around them longer than me."

Michael glanced briefly in Sam's direction but turned back to her. "A good suggestion, we're looking into it. One of the *Armas* members was killed in the shootout when Trace was wounded. We're talking to anyone who knew him and his family."

"Which member?"

"We haven't been able to identify him, just his gang name, Gunner."

"I don't remember him."

"Another man also died before we got there, shot in the back. Harry Sneed. Did you know him?"

"A little. He stood up against Pete for being disrespectful to the boss. That was the last time I saw him. And it was the night of the warehouse shooting."

"We heard about that. Talked to Pete yesterday but got nothing. Certainly not enough to lay charges, but some hinted he had it in for Harry and could have shot him in the confusion. Ballistics has the bullets at the lab and we'll try to match them to Pete's gun. Of course, there's no witnesses who'll step forward."

The chatter finally got to Cassi. She stood and hovered over her interrogator. Angry and frightened, her voice rose. "You've got to find Trace. Who knows how long they'll hold him as a prisoner? Oh God, they'll kill him, won't they?"

"I don't know, Cassi. I'm thinking if they wanted

him dead, they'd have killed him at the hospital and saved themselves all the effort of stealing him away in a van."

"Not if the person who wants him dead intends to do the job herself."

Dani! It has to be Dani...

Chapter Two

"Rusty, you can stop checking on me every minute. I promised you I wouldn't try to sneak out again, and I won't."

Rusty's outline in her open doorway slumped, and he stepped fully into the bedroom. He still wore his pants paired only with a black T-shirt that had seen better days.

She patted the mattress next to her. "Come on and sit with me. I can't sleep anyway; I've just been lying here worrying, remembering Trace and what a good man he is."

"I know. I could hear you in the other room."

"Hold it! I never said a word. And I'm all cried out for now. My eyes are so swollen, they ache like the dickens."

Rusty disappeared into her washroom only to reappear a few moments later with a cold wet facecloth he placed on her face. "Here. This will help. No, leave it there." He slapped her hands away.

"I'm just adjusting it, Rus. It feels wonderful. Thank you. And I appreciate you staying with me."

"Even though I stopped you from sneaking out earlier?"

Her sigh was loud and quivering. She lifted the cloth to look at him. "I wanted to question Dani, but since I don't know where she lives, it was kind of a stupid idea. Sam was in his car out front anyway. The minute he saw me, he shooed me back inside. And Arlene has the spare room door open and she's watching me like a hawk. Truly, you guys have me so imprisoned, I've given up trying to escape."

"It's for your own good, kid. We heard your voice when you suggested to Detective Kowalski that Dani could be behind Trace's disappearance."

"When the notion popped into my head, I never even stopped to think."

"We kinda figured that. It took three of us to hold you back from leaving right then. Thank goodness you stopped when Arlene stood in your way."

Cassi folded the damp padding and dropped it on her night table. Then she leaned back against the headboard. "I couldn't tussle with her after seeing her bandage." Cassi revisited earlier where she'd pushed away from Michael with intentions of going after Dani right then and there.

Something had snapped. All she could think of was getting into her car and finding the boss, begging for Trace's life if necessary. She'd promise anything in exchange for his safety... anything.

"Hey, brat. You in there?" Rusty interrupted her musings. "You can't go off half-cocked like that. The police are trained to deal with these kinds of situations. You aren't."

"Yeah, I know. But what have they done about all those crazy gangs like the *Armas* and *Soldados* that run rampant in the streets. Selling whatever shit they can get their hands on and no one stopping them. It's criminal. You have to agree, Rus."

"Calm down, Cass. You're right. Of course, you are. But the police do the best they can with the laws and the manpower they have. Most times they win."

"And as many times, they lose. Trace got shot a few nights ago, remember?"

"Yeah, yeah. I know. And we can play this game all night, but the fact is there're laws. And if we go breaking them, we're as bad as the criminals." His hand snuck out to push the hair from her face and tug it behind her ear.

"Quit hiding on me. I want your word that you won't do sumpin' crazy tomorrow. I couldn't bear it if I lost you too, Cassidy Santino. And... when Trace gets back, he'll need you waiting. You've got to stay safe. Promise me."

Cassi's heart dropped. There were fibs, and then there were real lies. She'd always prided herself on being a person who told the truth no matter what. Ever since Raoul died, that rule had drastically changed.

But there were lines one couldn't cross. Lying to Rusty, her favorite person in the world, the man who'd been her safety net her whole life, well, that's where she had to draw the line.

"I can't make that promise, Rusty, because I won't lie to you. But I will swear to be as careful as I can if I'm in a dangerous place. Will that be enough for you?"

"Not nearly enough. But it's all I'll get. I can tell by the mulish look on your face, little girl. You could never fool an old fool like me. So, just give me this. Come to me if you need anything. I'm here for you, you know that."

Cassi leaned into his open arms and took the solace he willingly offered. Unlike the old man's normal ways, he initiated a hug and for her that was like balm to her wounded spirit.

When the tears flowed, she let them. His gnarled old hands gently soothed and his soft kisses on her hair lessened the misery to where it was bearable.

Chapter Three

Trace didn't know what time of the day or night it was. They'd nabbed him before he'd put on his watch. Funny thing about not being able to tell the time, it could drive a person seriously batty.

The damp cellar they kept him in had no windows and the only light he had was the one dim lightbulb hanging from the ceiling close to the stairs. Circling the areas he could reach had become his goal. Counting the rounds, he drove himself to beat his total from his last stroll.

It took ten steps to do a full circle. To have it make sense, he'd pulled his mattress into the center of the space and used it to walk around. Exercising, he'd made one hundred and fourteen rounds before he became weak and had to flop down.

Taking careful sips from the bottle with an inch of water still in the bottom, he'd surmised that he'd spent about fifteen hours chained up alone with no one hassling him, not certain if that boded well for him or not.

He'd sure as hell like to know what the fuck they – whoever they were – wanted with him, and why they'd dragged him out of the hospital. But until someone came, he'd stay in the dark – literally.

Flexing his muscles, his arm hurt like a son of a bitch, still he sensed that the healing had started. No infection had invaded the wound, thank Christ. Other than it needed time to knit together, at the moment, it was the least of his worries.

When his head began to itch, he lifted his arm without thinking and the padlock holding the two ends of the chain together smacked his chin, reminding him it was time to work on loosening the steel ring.

Every so often, he'd go over and smash the padlock against the ring protruding from the solidly drilled plate on the wall. His goal to loosen the bolts or even break off the ring would free him. Unfortunately, after his many attempts, it hadn't budged at all.

Suddenly, the door at the top of the stairs opened and light shone down halfway. Chained to the wall, his limit was four feet from the stairs which meant that whoever came into his space could stay out of his reach. Unless they were there to harm him...

Adrenalin started pumping. Tensing, his muscles hardening, fists forming, he waited.

The man who appeared wore a black balaclava and stopped on the third step from the bottom. He carried a bag which he threw at Trace. Then he spit out one word. "Asshole."

After he disappeared up the stairs, a door slammed, and a bolt slid into place.

As he left, Trace bellowed. "Hey, come back. My bucket needs emptying."

In the distance, Trace distinctly heard, "Fuck you, man."

Knowing he was alone again, he went to his mattress and sat. Slowly, he opened the bag and found another bottle of water and a sandwich wrapped in cellophane, two pieces of buttered bread, ham and cheese. Nothing else. But it would keep him alive.

He ate slowly, savoring every mouthful, knowing it could be his last meal. Once he'd finished the first half, he carefully wrapped the other portion and slid it into the bag. Then he allowed himself a small guzzle of water, finishing the first bottle and dipping into the second one. The taste was a bit off, probably old or from the tap. But at least he knew one thing; they weren't going to starve him.

Laying there, holding the plastic in his hands, he began to wonder if it could be used to make a tool, something to open the locks on the cuffs around his wrists. This became an all-consuming notion before he fell asleep.

He didn't see the door open or the tattooed man

slip down the stairs, carry out the bucket, and replace it with another.

Chapter Four

"Sam, it's me. Can we meet?"

"Sure, princess. I was on my way over there anyway. Where do you want to go?"

"How about the café near Rusty's gym where we met before? I'll be there in half an hour."

"See you then."

After Sam hung up, Cassi headed for the coffee pot and caught Rusty and Arlene in the kitchen, their heads together at the table, filled mugs in front of them both.

"What are you two planning in here?" Cassi saw them flinch and knew they were up to something.

"Hey, brat. You shouldn't sneak up on an old guy like that? Almost gave me a heart attack."

"Don't play dumb, Rusty, or change the subject. You two have a secret, and I want to know about it. I saw your face last night after the fight, so what's wrong?"

Rusty fidgeted with his mug and then looked to Arlene for help.

"It's nothing, Cass. Just so you know, you look like hell. Your eyes are puffy and red."

"I know what I look like, so quit changing the subject. It's not nothing. What?"

Another look passed between Rusty and Arlene and suddenly she broke.

Slamming her sore hand on the table, she winced from the pain. "Ow, shit! Okay, okay. Ariana's manager tried to set some new restrictions for Rusty last night, and our friend told the prick to screw himself."

"What kind of new restrictions?"

Rusty piped up. "He says Ariana will only fight you for the title match, not Arlene."

Arlene's sour look perfectly expressed her feelings. "The bastard laid down the ridiculous rule after the reporters put out that José Santino was your father, and that he'd held the middleweight championship for as long as he did. They won't list me with her. They want Santino's daughter. Hell, I didn't know your dad was a boxer."

Rusty interrupted. "He was one of the best. The man had a will of iron and never let anyone take anything away from him."

"Until the booze became more important than the win." Cassi couldn't hide her scorn.

Rusty's good eye drilled into her spite, and she

backed down. "He won a lot of matches, even made a comeback. But it didn't guarantee him a good life, did it? Fighting is hard on a person's body and messes with their brains if they get hit enough times."

"So you know, I'm not my dad or Raoul. It's never been my dream."

Arlene nodded, but she couldn't keep the spite out of her anger. "The bitch wants revenge and to get you in the ring again. This time for real."

"They can't do that. Can they, Rusty? Isn't there rules against this kind of manipulation?"

"The bit-witch can do whatever she wants. It's her title. She has to fight to keep it. But it's her choice as to who'll be her opponent."

Arlene cut in. "Plus, her manager's a pussy and lets her run the show."

Rusty nodded sadly. "In the meantime, we can get Arlene other fights. Once she gets better known, the public will demand to see the two of them together. I'm thinking, over time, the pressure will work."

Cassi looked from one to the other and put her hands on her hips, her defensive stance obvious to anyone with brains. "I'm not fighting her again."

"Wouldn't ask you to, kiddo. Shouldn't have put you on the spot in the first place, it wasn't fair."

"After what you did, the sleaze reneged on her promise to set up a match with me anyway." Arlene slapped her hands on the tabletop once more and again she winced and cussed under her breath. "Ariana can't be trusted. Hope her tits fall off."

Cassi burst out laughing, shocking everyone, herself included. "Arlene, I never knew you had a sense of humor."

"Who's joking?" A grin belied her words, and Cassi appreciated the girl's support and Rusty's too.

"Both you watchdogs saved me from going mental last night, hanging in here, playing night guards. It means a lot."

"Babysitters is more like it, stopping you from making a big mistake." Arlene winked at Rusty. Her ringing phone stopped her teasing, and she left the room.

"I'm good now, Rusty. In fact, I have to meet Sam in a little while. Then I'll probably stop at the gym for some exercise."

"I heard you on the phone. Thought you were talking to Kowalski." Rusty was questioning her in his own, non-prying way.

"I was, earlier. He had nothing new. They've ruled out the likely leads, but they have everyone on the street paying attention. He's sure they'll get more tips. Today, they're interviewing the staff and those individuals who left the hospital around the same time to see if anyone remembers anything, a license plate maybe."

"What's the chances?"

"Little to none, but it relieves me to know they're

willing to go that far to find some—"

"Trace of Trace?" Rusty's grin slid off and he muttered, "Sorry."

Before she could answer, Arlene returned to the kitchen. The pain on her face had Cassi moving in to steady her and wrap her arm around the shuddering shoulders. "Arlene, what happened?"

"My uncle died early this morning. My aunt fell asleep in a chair by his bed and when she woke up, he'd passed. She's terribly upset. I have to go."

"Of course, you do. If there's anything Rusty or I can do to help either you or your aunt, call us. You hear?"

Rusty piped up, his face concerned. "Yeah, brat. We're here for you."

Lips quivering, eyes full, Arlene stepped away from their circle. She stared first at Rusty and then toward Cassi. The faint words she spoke were hard to hear and even harder to understand. "I'm sorry about Trace, Cass. And... about everything." Before they had a chance to question her, she ran out of the house and the front door banged behind her.

Left behind, a gigantic question lighting the airwaves, Rusty surveyed Cassi and when she shrugged, he did too.

Chapter Five

Waiting at the café, Sam made sure he sat at the back booth where he had a complete view of the place. The same waitress who'd flirted with him before sidled up and flashed him her your-my-kind-of-man smile.

"What'll you be having, handsome?"

"Bring me a big breakfast and a coffee." He kept the menu for Cass and stopped her when she reached for it. "I have a friend joining me, but I won't wait. You can bring my order as soon as it's ready."

"Comin' right up, sugar."

"Nope. I take it black."

She laughed, and he saw her teeth were her best feature, white and straight. He winked, and she giggled.

Once alone, Sam traveled back to the night before. He'd watched Cassi closely. Expecting her agonized mind to clear while being questioned, he'd waited for her thought processes to kick in.

Anticipating her reaction, she hadn't disappointed. As soon as she'd arrowed in on Dani being the possible culprit, she'd lost it.

Cassi in fighting mode had shocked the two police officers so much, they'd stepped away. But he knew her well. When she'd flipped, he'd known how to stop her – him and Arlene.

Truthfully, he didn't blame her. The first person he'd thought of for Trace's disappearance was Dani too. After all, she'd had the most to gain by him being out of the picture, both with Cassi and earning back her boys' respect.

After she'd pulled the big meltdown the other night, there'd been a lot of bellyaching. Pissed that they'd had to deal with the problem at the warehouse alone, the men had grumbled, and he'd heard them.

He had no doubt that when the rival gang, the *Soldados*, showed up followed soon after by the cops, taking orders from Pete made most of the members cringe.

He'd heard stories from some of the boys who'd driven with Pete to the warehouse. He'd openly mocked the big, muscled Harry Sneed who'd put him in his place at the bar before they'd left. Livid, he'd ranted and whined to the others.

Sam knew, sure as shit, that wouldn't have won him any kudos with those guys. Harry had been one of them and in the gang a lot longer than Pete. Then, during the battle, Harry getting killed led to questions. Except no one had any answers.

Earlier, Sam had quizzed Michael about the bullet and found out it hadn't come from any of the police service weapons. Which could mean one of two things? Either one of the *Soldados* killed him or Harry was shot by an *Armas* member. He had to ask himself – who?

Wouldn't surprise him at all if it turned out that Pete, being such a slimy prick, had shot Harry as payback. Sam had run into crazies like him throughout his career with the FBI. They were the psychopaths that had no scruples whatsoever.

Which led Sam to believe the bastard would shoot Trace with no regret either. But would he go to the trouble of hauling him away in a van first?

Problem was – Pete had been at the fight with Dani while Trace had disappeared. Not saying Dani couldn't have had some of the others nab him. He wouldn't put anything past his green-eyed jealous boss.

Sam checked his phone messages again like he'd been doing for the last few days, waiting for a message from his FBI handler. He hoped they'd broken into the files he'd copied from Dani's computer. They were in code, so it didn't surprise him they were taking longer to suss out the information.

Sam knew the minute Cass walked into the café. Three of the men from Rusty's gym called out their greetings. "Nice move last night, Cass. Glad you didn't let the bitch take you down. She's a dirty fighter and deserved everything she got."

"Thanks, guys." Cass grinned at them, and with a pure Cassi move they loved, she squeezed the held-up hand of the fellow at the end of the booth.

"Hi, Sam."

"Hey, Cass. How's it going?" He stared hard at her bruised face, but said nothing.

"Just putting one foot in front of the other. Have you talked to Dani? Did she really fire me the other night?"

"Shit, you jump right into the deep end, don't you? No – how are you? Is your ankle better where I dug my heel into it last night? Or your side where I punched you?"

Looking truly abashed, Cassi reached out to him and squeezed his arm. Her eyes soft, she flipped her hair so he'd get the full view of her regret. "You stopped me from being arrested. I owe you."

"Bloody right you do. Don't know why I keep you in line."

With her head tilted, she grinned sadly. "'Cause you're as nuts about me as I am about you?"

He chuckled. "See – you got me." He patted her hand and sat back as the waitress delivered his stacked plate. The smell of the bacon and eggs had him drooling, and he shoveled in the first mouthful and groaned.

"What would you like, Cassi?"

"Just coffee, Mona, thanks."

As soon as they were alone she watched Sam, her eyebrow lifted, questioning.

"Right. Dani. I ran into her at the fight, and she didn't look like a pissed off boss. Just the opposite. She seemed excited, kept saying as how you were her girl. She almost fell into the audience at the end when you decked Ariana."

"So, I'm going to work tonight. You, too?"

"Yep. Although, I don't know whether it's a good idea for you to show up." Dipping his toast into the yolk, he took another huge forkful of food.

"It's the only place I know where we might be able to get leads on Trace's disappearance. Some of the boys like me, Sam. I'm thinking to pull in some favors."

"Don't you go messing around, Cass. If Pete sees you, he won't like it, and he's a mean son of a bitch. He'd just as soon shoot you as talk to you."

"I've had first-hand experience with his sunny temperament, Sam. Remember? I'll be careful."

"Hell, woman, don't be careful. Be smart. Not like the other night when you decided to wander around places where you don't belong."

"I wondered when you were going to bring that up." Cassi looked disheartened, and he almost backed off. Then he decided her life teetered on the line, and she needed to take things more seriously around the club. Sometimes he got the feeling it was all a game to her.

"You do know those two would have shot you

when you showed up unescorted in the club's basement? Right?" He wanted to shock her.

Appearing calm rather than disturbed, she listened and then shrugged. "About now, I wish they would have."

Sam dropped his utensils onto the almost empty plate. They clanged and drew looks. He waved and grinned to show the boys getting ready to come over there wasn't a problem and turned back to her. "Don't be a complete idiot, Cass. When Trace is free and finds out you died to save him, how's that gonna make him feel?"

Tears gathered. She fought hard to stop the deluge. He watched her struggle. "You fall apart on me now, and so help me God, princess, I'll walk. It's time to grow up, be strong, play smart. Until there's a body, far as I'm concerned, the man is alive."

She nodded and swallowed. He waited. Finally, she spoke. "You want to know what I was doing downstairs?"

"I'm sitting on pins and needles holding my breath, sweet pea." His sarcasm did the trick.

She wriggled her head from side to side, let her shoulders slump and sighed loudly. "Okay. I went down to set up a video camera so I could catch Rodrigo on tape. I had intentions of blackmailing him. I wanted proof of him with the drugs and counting the money, maybe talking, giving orders to the men. Hell, I don't know. Anything that would give me ammunition – make him tell me the truth about Dani. If I could discover once and for all if she's the female at the warehouse the night they killed Raoul, then I can find some peace."

"My God, you're like a rabid she-dog with a bone. You won't let it go."

"Never."

"And if she isn't?"

"God, Sam. I don't know. What I do know is that they had to have reported to her after the incident. If it wasn't her, she knows who was there."

Sam thought about what she'd revealed, and a surge of excitement began to take shape. "If you do get any evidence, you know it won't hold up in a court of law."

"I know. I talked to Maria, Billy Duran's assistant. Then I decided I didn't need to threaten Rodrigo with the law. I could tell him I'd give it to the reporters who are always sniffing around, looking for a story. The law would have no choice then but to step in, right?"

Sam grinned, reached to stop her hands from mauling each other. "Did you set it up properly?"

"I got the guy at the store to show me. It's action activated."

"How many hours will it tape?"

Suddenly, she paled. "I don't know."

"Hey, princess. It's okay. I'll snag it after they do another big count when I know Rodrigo's involved."

"Thank you, Sam. So, you figure it's a good plan?"

"I didn't say that." He watched her face drop.

"On the other hand, I can't say it's a waste of time either. The more evidence we gather on any of those slimy assholes, the better."

Interrupting them, Cassi's phone rang and her eyes lit up with hope, only to dim after she answered.

"Sure, Maria, I can come by for a few hours this afternoon. See you then."

Chapter Six

Cassi left Sam at the restaurant playing nice with the waitress and went to the gym, realizing within minutes she had no energy, nor any desire to push her body. Still sore from the fight the day before, she made her way into the steam room where she encountered Doug, one of Dani's guys who periodically worked as an upstairs guard.

"Hey, Cass. Good fight last night. I bet on you getting a knockout and won a bundle."

"Sweet! I'd hate to be the reason you lost." She clung to the towel she'd wrapped around her neck and moved to sit on the steps across from him.

"Figured you'd be lying low and healing today after the beating you took from that bitch before shutting her down."

"I should be. But I couldn't stay away. Had to get out of the house. What's happening with you lately, still working the upstairs rooms?"

"Yeah. The boss's been riding us pretty hard. She's not been herself, hides out more and I've come across her having these wild coughing spells. I told her she should see a doc and she told me to mind my own effing business." Doug grinned. "There's been a lot of unexplained mishaps, and I guess they're getting to her."

"Like what? Using too much of her own product?" Cassi made a funny face to lessen the insult.

"Sure, there's that." Doug grinned back and then shrugged. "But it's more about all the strange shit happening. The *Soldados* are squeezing her out, and she can't take the hint. They want their territory back. Since we moved in on them, Dani's been undercutting prices, pushing crap and making life difficult. Now, after the last two raids, I think her distribution source from L.A. is fed up with her. She's worried they'll cut her off."

Cassi perked up and listened carefully to everything he said. "You're saying that the *Soldados* were here in Vegas first, is that right?"

"Sure, they've been here for years. Had the streets to themselves and played things pretty straight. They didn't mess with the cops and the cops basically left them alone."

"Yet, they're breaking the law."

He stared at her as if to see whether she messed with him and when he saw her sincerity, he answered respectfully. "Cass, no matter how you look at the drug culture, most people who use the shit need it to stay alive. Their demand has to be met. Even the law officers accept that reality. But it's how that business is carried out – that's what matters. The *Soldados* have heart. *Las Armas* are a bunch of misfits who don't give a shit."

Cassi needed him to continue, so she kept talking. "I don't understand. I mean, working in the bar, I hear things. It's hard not to."

"No doubt. The men get pissed and blab like fools."

Cassi had no intention of agreeing in case he stopped sharing. "After the club got shot up, a lot of guys were shaken. Can't blame 'em."

"Sure, some of us were wounded. A few even died. That'll throw anyone into a spin. But the *Soldados* attacked the club in retribution for what some of our stupid idiots did, going off half-cocked and killing two little girls when they shot up the dude's house. Dani recruits youngsters who have no manners, no loyalty and no brains. As long as they get their money and drugs, half of them would shoot their own mamas. Anyone would take exception to that kind of slaughter. Mandala had no choice but to come back in the same way, gun down the club."

Nausea struck Cassi. Knowing people who thought so little of life and held it in such low esteem as to drive by and shoot no matter who was inside, sickened her. "I guess I shouldn't be shocked, Doug. Except I am. To me, it's like a movie. I guess I grew up pretty sheltered." She used the towel wrapped around her neck to wipe off the sweat while Doug added another cupful of water to the coals and the steam flared.

He reclined on the cedar slats and covered his eyes with an arm. "No, Cass. You're normal. It's the rest of us who are bent. I don't know how I ever got caught up in this crazy shit. One thing I do know, you did me a favor, patched me up that night, and I don't forget. You're good people, honey."

"Thanks, Doug."

As if his words affected him, he shot up and left, the door closing behind him. Cassi shook her head, thinking how strange these hard-hearted devils were. They could kill a man in cold blood, but some never forgot a good deed.

Left alone with her thoughts, they zeroed in on Trace. She'd called Michael again on the way to the club, and he had little to add. The ongoing investigation had hit some dead ends, but they weren't giving up. Every cop on the beat, driving a car, and behind a desk, was willingly putting in overtime. Something would break soon. He'd get back to her.

She lifted the towel and wiped the sweaty tears from her cheeks. Time to move, because as soon as she found herself alone, all the yearning for Trace and the pain of remembering he was in danger attacked her like a swarm of creepy-crawlies picking her skin raw.

Chapter Seven

Glad to have someplace she needed to be, Cassi showed up at the Sampson and Little law office just after two in the afternoon.

Cassi waved to Gladys, and following her gesture, she went in through the open door to Maria's office. Once there, she plopped into the only chair not piled high with files. "Hi, Maria, I'm glad you called. I needed a distraction."

"What's happening, Cassi? I figured you might be sore after the fight, but you look in worse shape than I expected." Maria stared at Cassi and her eyes narrowed. "Damn, girl. You look like hell."

"Good description. It's how I feel. Someone I care about has gone missing, and the police are looking everywhere. So far, no luck."

"Is he in danger?"

Suddenly alert, Cassi asked, "How did you know it was a he?"

Smiling, her grin rueful, Maria answered, "Because unless you're gay, I can't imagine you being that heartbroken about anyone but a sweetheart."

Satisfied, Cassi pushed her hair behind her ear. "You're right, of course." Before she could say more, Billy arrived and the quiet of the office became instantly disrupted.

"Hey, sweetie. Glad to see you." Billy swooped in for a cheek kiss and held her chin in place. "Your face looks better than I thought it would."

"Hey!"

He smiled.

"I used makeup to cover the worst." Not surprised that Billy didn't pick up on her heart pain, she let it go.

"That's my girl. Never let 'em see your wounds. Did Maria tell you that we've got a pre-trial motion with Judge Dover for tomorrow? I want to get Mary's charges reduced to manslaughter. I'm hoping that the prosecution's been swayed by the media and accepts that it'll be difficult to make murder one stick. If he doesn't and Mary walks, that could ruin his budding career."

The noise of Maria's cell phone disturbed their conversation and she dove for it. By moving so fast, she knocked over the pile of papers it perched on and the phone flipped to the floor next to Cassi.

She bent to pick it up and noticed the lit number. Saying nothing, hiding the shock, she passed it over and watched as Maria checked the caller and shut it down.

"That's why I called Cassi, Billy. She offered to help with research and I have some cases that need to be checked. I thought she could read through them to find any references to the Morgan case in Philadelphia."

"Hey, good idea. It's similar enough we might be able to persuade the judge that it has merit in Mary's situation."

Cassi kicked in, "The Morgan Case?"

"At the request of a father, a boy shot his mother because she was suffering terribly in the last stages of Pancreatic Cancer. The kid was only ten and the dad didn't figure they'd charge him as a criminal."

"What happened?"

"The police charged the dad. Got a little crazy because of the circumstances and tried to stick him with first degree murder, which didn't take. The judge ruled it a homicide and the dad got ten years and walked after seven."

"That's horrible. I feel sorry for the kid."

Billy stared at her in a strange way. "You must see what that dad went through, putting his kid up to it? No sympathy for him?"

"Not even a little. If he wanted his wife to be at peace, he should have done the dirty deed himself." Not hearing her words, Cassi sensed the shock from the other two as they looked at her in horror. "What?"

"I'm just glad you're not on the jury, that's all." Maria passed over the files she wanted Cassi to read. "You've just convicted our client."

Cassi thought back over her words and grimaced. "Sorry."

***

"Come to dinner with me, Cassi." Annoying and insistent, Billy wouldn't let up.

She didn't want to go and tried every which way to refuse but the silly man wouldn't take no for an answer. "Okay, just dinner. I have to work later."

"That's one of the things I want to talk to you about. You want to take your own car?"

"Uh huh."

"Right, I'll follow you to the old place by Rusty's."

"I was there already once today. We can walk to the diner down the street if you want."

"Fine. Let's go." Even though Maria looked up as if waiting for an invitation, Billy said nothing. Uncomfortable, Cass let the moment pass. On the walk there, she questioned him. "Why didn't you ask Maria to join us? I felt rude just walking out on her."

"Because we're strictly co-workers now, and I don't want to change that."

Now? "Yet you brought her to the fight last night."

"I didn't bring her. I gave her a lift."

"Come on, Billy, a playboy like you without a

girl. I don't believe it." Wanting to lighten the mood, Cassi teased her old pal and didn't like the results.

"Baby doll, there's only one girl I'd change my single status for, and she's not interested." His tone said it all. So did the arm he wrapped around her waist to hug her close.

Reacting before she could stop herself, Cassi pushed away and slapped at his hand. "Quit flirting with me."

"See? She's not interested, and she keeps breaking my heart."

Cass stopped. She searched his eyes and saw the truth. He was sincere.

"I'm really sorry, Billy."

"Yeah, honey, me too. Come on. I can still buy you dinner."

Soon seated at a table for two next to the window, shyness caught hold and made it difficult to look at the man across from her. Instead, she watched the pedestrians rushing to catch the corner bus. Harried, absorbed in their phones, completely unaware of each other, everyone moved like robots.

"Hey, none of that. I'll deal with my infatuation, Cassi. If you react this way when we're together, it'll spoil everything."

She searched his eyes and saw a sincere plea. "You're right. We've been friends too long to let that happen." Relief hit her at his calm acceptance, and she relaxed.

Interrupted by the waitress who took their orders, they sat with drinks in front of them. Cassi sniffed the aroma of an Italian restaurant and felt her stomach revolt. Forced to be here didn't mean she'd have to eat. All it meant was she'd let her old ways prevail by allowing him to coax her into doing something she didn't want to do. When would she learn not to put the needs of her men folk over her own?

"Honey, I want to know why you look like you've lost your best friend. I haven't seen you like this since Raoul died."

Shifting her head so her hair fell into place to cover part of her face, she picked up the knife and toyed with it. Not sure how much she wanted to reveal, she decided to stick to a partial truth. "A friend of mine's gone missing. We have no idea where he is. And I'm terrified he's in danger."

"Who?" Billy's tone suddenly meant business.

"Detective Trace McGuire, the man working on Raoul's case."

"I see." His gray eyes darkened in a way she'd always hated. Probably because they'd turned that way during times when he'd been unsympathetic and self-absorbed. That piercing glare brought an automatic reaction she squashed. His moods were no longer important. She saw his dislike of Trace and wondered how they knew each other enough for Billy to hate him so.

"Why did you want to talk to me tonight, Billy? You practically dragged me to the restaurant."

"It's about you working at the Lipstick bar. It's a dive, Cassi, and from this moment on, it isn't safe."

"What do you mean? How do you know?"

"I keep tabs on some old acquaintances on the street. They share stuff. Things are happening behind the scenes, baby. You need to stay away from that joint." His no-nonsense tone sent shivers of apprehension running wild over her tense body.

"I'll be careful."

"Not enough. It's dangerous. Trust me, Cassi. I'm serious."

His expression presented an unarguable truth. The man knew what the hell he was talking about, and he meant every word he said.

"It'll only be for a short time, Billy. Then I'll quit. But for now, don't ask me. It's the only place I know where I might find the truth."

"For crissakes, what truth?"

"About who killed Raoul."

"You still fixating on that?" Billy's sour expression showed his disapproval. "He's been dead for some time, Cassi. And he wouldn't want you to be in danger to find his killer."

"Maybe. But you said it yourself. He's gone, and I'll do what I need to. There's still one person running free who either did the deed herself, or was there and saw it happen. Until I find her and learn the truth, I can't rest." Cassi heard her words and doubt started to creep in. *Was she too fixated on this goal? Who would it really help in the end when they learned the truth?* Billy interrupted, and she shrugged off her misgivings.

"What if I told you the woman is too powerful for you to mess with?"

Sparks ignited. Riveted, she froze and watched his closed face. "You know who she is?"

"I've heard rumors. She's out of your league, trust me."

"Maybe, but no one is more powerful than the law, Billy, you should know that. If she killed Raoul, she broke the law and I want her to pay."

"Oh, she'll be paying all right – for her crooked, backstabbing treacheries. It's the law of the jungle that'll get her in the end."

"You're talking about Dani Andino, aren't you?"

The waitress arrived at the worst possible moment and Billy's hand gesture said it all. No more talking.

"Let's eat" were the words he muttered.

Sickened, revolted by the smells, never mind the food, Cassi had to leave. "I'm sorry, Billy. I can't. Guess I'm still recuperating from the fight. I'll connect with you soon."

Bolting from the table and the overheated, heavily scented restaurant; she left and walked quickly to her car. Before she reached the vehicle, a Hummer pulled alongside, and Sergio Mandala motioned for her to get in.

Before he had a chance to order or cajole her to obey, Cassi slid in next to him in the back seat and whipped around. She asked, "Why are you in touch with Maria Delgado?"

She watched as Sergio filtered her questioned, deciding what his response should be. Hedging, he finally asked, "How the fuck do you know I called Maria?" Okay, this Sergio scared her. He'd assumed his gang-boss persona. This dude meant business. But bending to him was no longer her style.

Deciding only the truth would suffice, she answered. "Because I memorized your number. Because she dropped her phone, and I picked it up when it was ringing. Because I'm curious. Pick any of the above."

For a moment, she thought he'd take offense at her sass. He didn't. Chuckling, he slapped her knee without hurting her. "You're too smart for your own good, my friend."

"And you haven't answered my question." She breathed a sigh of relief over his softened attitude.

"You mean the question you've got no right to ask. That question?"

Put in her place, Cassi said, "Yes." And refused to back down.

In silence, he scanned her face and saw by her expression that his truthfulness meant a lot to her. "Shit. You get away with too much, Cassi. I have no idea why I let you. All right, stop looking at me like that. I'll tell you this and no more. Maria and I go back a long way. She's a smart woman, someone that's better to be friends with than enemies."

"Enemies? For heaven's sake, the woman's a lawyer."

"And her brother in L.A. is a very powerful man, partners with one of the biggest cartels in Mexico."

Suddenly, a shaft of light began breaking through. "And he's your supplier?"

"Never mind. Stop digging." His eyes drilled her to obey.

Absorbed in her own world, working out the obvious, she ignored him. "Uh huh. And she's your connection?"

"I said to drop it."

This time she caught the tone but pushed it with one more question. "Is she involved with the gang?"

Sergio shrugged. His hand squeezed her knee as a signal. "As you said, she's not her brother, she's just a lawyer. You don't get to choose what your relatives do. You should know that."

Somewhat mollified, she loosened her neck muscles and let her hand cover his. He had a point. "I'm glad." Sergio's gaze held secrets but to probe wouldn't be smart.

His hand released the tight grip and instead tugged hers to get her attention. "There's something you need to know. It's why I'm here. Why I stopped you tonight. I like to protect the people I care about before the shit hits the great big familiar fucking fan. I want you to stay away from the Lipstick Club from now on, Cass. I'm not asking you. I'm telling you."

"Stop it!" The words burst loose before she knew they would. Gulping, apprehensive, she still didn't back down. "I promised myself not to let anyone tell me what to do anymore. So, either make me understand the reason, or I won't listen."

"The reason! Okay, how's this? Because you could be killed."

Knowing a serious expression when it stared her in the face, Cassi stopped. "As of when?"

"What do you mean, when?" Exasperation rang in the voice of a man on the edge.

"I mean, I'm scheduled to work later. If you know that something is going to happen tonight, share specifics. Or tell me which day I should call in sick."

Sergio looked like he'd explode. His dark eyes were huge and dangerous. "You messing with me?"

"Quit yelling at me. It's a legitimate question. If you know there's going to be a – a situation, tell me when, and I promise, I won't work."

"Listen to me, Cassi Santino. If I have to take you into protective custody, you won't be the first. You need to stay home until you hear from me that it's safe. For crissakes, I'm not going to go into *specifics*."

"Okay. Fine. I'll stay home. I just need to call my

partner at the bar and warn him to stay away, too."

"You're kidding me, right?" His explosion this time scared her. "You can't tell anyone else. Just get in your car, get your pretty ass home and lock the door. Promise me."

"Fine. Okay." Cassi noticed that the Hummer had stopped around the corner from where she'd parked her car. "Before you drop me off, I have one more question. Do you have any idea of what happened to Detective Trace McGuire?"

"Who?"

"Never mind. Thanks again, Sergio. Take care."

"You, too, baby." His face softened slightly. But he didn't return her smile.

Chapter Eight

Trace had never been so bored in his life. He'd rather be fighting a mob war and ducking bullets than holed up in this dump where the air stunk from his open bucket and the damp cold leached into his aching muscles.

He did another ten laps around his mattress. Using the padlock, he then hammered at the ring as long as he could, hoping to see it budge. No such luck.

At first, he'd thought the noise would attract attention but after so many aggravating attempts where he smashed at the blasted steel and no one came, he had to accept the fact that either no one gave a shit how much noise he made because they couldn't hear through the thick stone walls, or there was no one else around.

He sensed the latter. Not one to delve too deeply into perceptions, he could swear that the surrounding energy came from his presence alone. Not questioning how he knew, he just did. Which meant whoever kidnapped him had locked him away and was keeping him alive without any intentions of hurting him. Or did he have that all wrong? Could be they intended to, only not yet.

Since he suspected Dani Andino was his warden, he could only wonder why the hell the bitch didn't just kill him and get it over with. Everyone knew she hated his guts.

Maybe even more than he hated hers.

Chapter Nine

From home, Cassi tried Sam's cell number more than once. Then she called the club and waited for him to answer. Most days, he started work before she did, and he'd eventually pick up.

Tonight, when she needed him to be there, it didn't happen.

What the hell is going on? First, she gets a warning from Billy and then from Sergio. Taking everything into consideration, it made total sense that a major event would happen soon. Therefore, how could she leave her bar-partner to face that danger alone?

She rang the number again. Still no answer. Finally, she called Michael.

"Hi, Cassi. I'm sorry. I don't have any new information for you. We've pulled in every favor we could, and no one knows anything. It's like he's disappeared into thin air. Man, I hate that cliché, but I truly have no other explanation."

Her heart dropped the same it did every time she talked to this apologetic guy. "I know you're doing everything possible." The word *but...* hovered between them. She swallowed the rising bile and coughed to cover up her emotions. "Look, I had intended to go into work tonight and dig around, see what I could find out, only I've been warned to stay away and not just once."

"Who warned you?"

The sharp edge of his tone rattled her. "Two people I trust who know others that live on the street. Have you heard anything?"

Hesitation filled the silence. She heard him breathing, and sensed he was thinking of what to say. "Don't lie to me, Michael. I need to warn Sam if there's a battle going to happen. I tried to get him on the phone, but he didn't answer."

"You don't have to worry about, Sam, Cassi. He's a smart man. If there's anything percolating, he'll know."

"That's not good enough. But thanks. Talk soon." She hung up and grabbed the keys to the Harley. Reaching into the closet for her helmet and leather jacket, she quickly donned her biker disguise.

Tonight, she needed to be incognito.

Chapter Ten

Taking Sergio's warning seriously, Cassi swung the bike into the bar's lot and parked on the darker side where not many others did. She saw the guard at the front and recognized a friend.

"Hi, Doug." Happy to see her pal, she relaxed somewhat. "Has Sam arrived?"

"Hey, Cass. Nope. And the boss is livid that neither of you are at work yet." He leaned in close so she could see his seriousness. "And... if I were you, I'd just take my pretty little butt and hightail it outta here before she does see you. The lady's ready to explode and you don't wanna be in her vicinity when she blows."

Relieved that her partner wasn't in danger, Cassi had to ask. "Do you know if Sam called in sick and got a replacement?"

"Nah, I don't know." Suddenly, the big man whipped her around, shoving her behind the corner of the wall. Just in time before the club doors smashed open and Dani, followed by the boys, a huge number tonight, came out of the club. The red-head stopped to cough and cuss, but just for a few seconds. Then she mounted her flashy Harley.

Noisy, quarreling, swearing, spitting little boys playing at being tough, they converged toward their bikes ignoring Doug as if he were invisible.

Roaring, gravel spitting, the bikes trailed Dani's. As did the black-as-night SUV with darkened windows and obscure rims on the wheels. It came from around the back of the building. Cassi watched as they reached the road and two bikes split from the rest – Dani's and Pete's went right followed by the vehicle while the rest turned left.

Her revved heartbeats slowed, and she tamped down on her frantic breathing. "Thanks, Doug. I really didn't want to deal with Dani just now."

"Don't blame you, Cass. Tonight for sure. She's got something stuck up her ass, called us all in and reamed so much shit down our throats, I'm still choking."

"Did she say why she's so pissed?"

"Hell, I wish. You know that crazy chick. She keeps her business to herself. Word is the old boss is breathing down her neck and spooking her. And the *Soldados* are making life uncomfortable too."

Since Doug had treated her well – intending to share, she admitted, "Truthfully, friends in the know warned me to stay away from the club tonight. I wouldn't have come except I couldn't find Sam to tell him. If it's dangerous for me, it's as bad for you and for him, right?"

"Sam can take care of Sam, Cass." His voice lowered. "And I'm fine. But you need to go home and be safe."

"Now that Dani's gone, can I at least go in and see if one of the girls working the bar heard from him? Then I promise I'm outta here."

"Yeah, sure. I'll watch over your bike. Don't push it though. Hurry in case she comes back."

"Thanks, I will." Cassi hustled into the joint and found her favorite waitress, Floss.

"Hi, Floss. You seen Sam?"

"Hey, Cassi, I'm glad you got here late and missed Dani. But you have to leave. She's looking for you and the bitch is spooked. She's furious about you being late."

"I heard. Look, I'm only here to see Sam."

"He's late, too."

"I know. Did he call in?"

"Nope. And, Cass, her anger has nothing to do with Sam. He's an okay guy but the boss isn't fixated on him. Honestly, my friend. She was screaming at everyone when you didn't show up on time."

"Me?"

"Yes, ma'am. Raged about how she couldn't depend on anyone, called her men a bunch of losers and ranted on about how they were useless when she wasn't around. She even dissed them about protecting their product and that she couldn't rely on them for nothing. Trust me, they didn't like it one bit, especially that psycho, Pete."

"What did all that have to do with me?" Cassi was stymied. "I don't even belong to the gang."

"Beats me. You should go. It's dead here now so us girls are handling things. Rodrigo says he'll shut the place down if it stays like this. I think he's spooked too."

"A friend warned me to stay away so I didn't intend to come at all except I couldn't get a hold of Sam. Look, Floss, maybe you should just leave."

"I will if Dani comes back. But as long as she's not here, I figure we're safe enough."

"Don't take any chances."

"I won't, Cass. You better get home and lock the doors. I'll call you if anything happens."

Cassi retrieved her bike and turned in the direction of her house. After everyone's warnings, she didn't feel safe anywhere.

***

What the fuck!

The front door of Cassi's house stood open and the lock had been smashed – as if it had been kicked in. The person who entered didn't worry about leaving it ajar.

Hesitating, Cassi listened and got the feeling that whoever had paid her a visit was gone. The house felt empty.

Hesitating, she slipped around to the back and

surveyed the kitchen through the window over the sink. The light had been left on, but it didn't appear anyone was there.

Suddenly, tingling awareness emerged. Someone had snuck up behind her. Her senses on high alert, prickles of apprehension warned her they were closing in. Before she could turn, she felt a gun in her back, prodding, pushing... hurting.

"I knew you'd get here eventually, bitch."

Recognizing the voice, Cassi began to panic. Knowing that to show her fear would only titillate the prick, she quashed it and made her voice hard. "Hey, Pete. Why'd you break into my house? If you'd have waited for me to get home, I'd have let you in like regular folks do for visitors."

"Shit, Cass. I didn't break in, Dani did. She's looking all over Vegas for you. Made me stay and wait for you here. We're supposed to take a trip to L.A. and the stupid bitch won't leave without you. The stoner's certifiable." When he stuck his face close to the back of her head, his stinky breath floated past.

His words made her relax somewhat. He wasn't going to hurt her, just hold her for Dani. At first, the idea made every sane notion in her head scream – Hell, no! But Trace's image, always close by, surfaced and stopped her from reacting. What if Dani had taken him? And by going along with her plans now, she'd be able to force the boss to admit what they'd done with him.

This could also be her last time to actually question Dani about the night Raoul had died. All these thoughts raged through her mind in the split second she'd hesitated from fighting off Pete and taking her chances.

Once she'd decided to step down, she slowly turned and faced her nemesis. "Okay. I'll go with you to see Dani."

Pete's beady eyes blinked. "You will?"

"Sure. She's the boss, right?"

"For now." Not trusting her, he added, "You gonna fight me, Cass? 'Cause I'd shoot you as soon as look atcha. Hell, I'd put a bullet into that sexy body you wiggle around the club and be glad to do it. Getting the men all excited, making them have stupid dreams. I hate women like you."

Sensing his building animosity and having no idea what she'd done to get him riled, she lifted her hands and spoke low. "Hey, down boy. I'm doing what you say. Just stay cool. Call Dani if you have to."

"Nah. I'll take you to her." He pulled a plastic tie wrap from his pocket, yanked her closer and before she could stop him, he had her wrists in a painful grip while he tightened the loop.

His hands made free with her chest as if he'd accidently brushed against her, but she knew differently. The pervert groped her.

Her voice full of anger, she called him on it. "Hey, asshole. Keep those hands to yourself unless you want me to tell tales."

"Shut yer yap. Come on. I have the SUV parked at the back."

"Where's your bike?"

His voice turned even meaner. "The stupid bitch made me trade with one of the others. Didn't want them to know where we'd be heading, and she figures I'll be des-creet." He snorted. "Des-creet, bullshit! She's scared shitless and doesn't trust her own men to protect her. She needs me, 'cause I'm her link to the big guy in L.A."

"You had to give up your bike? Man, that's gotta be a piss off."

"What's the piss off is that I had no choice. And it's all your fault."

"Christ, Pete. How can it be my fault?" Cassi faked hurt feelings.

"She wouldn't leave without you unless I promised I'd take you to her. The chick's nuts. Come on."

He hauled her with him to the back lane where farther down he'd parked the black SUV. Forcing her into the passenger seat, he slammed the door and took his place behind the wheel.

All the while, Cassi tried to imagine what the scene must have been like when Dani forced Pete to give up the only possession he cared about.

Man, oh, man. The shit's gotta be off the charts for this wacko to have stood down and taken her orders.

Chapter Eleven

Sam pulled up to the bar and noticed the lack of bikes out front or vehicles in the parking lot. As he approached the door, Doug appeared from the shadows, and he stopped to talk.

"Hey, man. Where's everyone tonight?"

"A bit late, ain'tcha, Sam?"

"About an hour. Had an appointment." Sam didn't apologize to anyone except Dani or Rodrigo, and only if forced.

Truth was – he got held up with his handler who told him they'd broken the code in Dani's files he'd managed to steal. Now they had access to her private records.

Unfortunately, they were poorly kept spreadsheets showing the amounts and dates she'd received product from China and recently from L.A. There were also entries of when and who they'd passed the drugs to. Those figures went back even before Vegas. They estimated more than a year where her scrawling, poor penmanship and unbalanced totals showed up.

Before Dani, the earlier sheets had been immaculate. Someone had known exactly what they were doing and the detailed accounts of the money they'd made while in L.A. had been staggering.

Unfortunately, the one problem they were up against was the lack of names. Only initials. And they didn't have a clue if those repeated scratchings represented people's identities or even their nicknames; could be groups or some suggested way to describe different products. It was all ambiguous, certainly not enough identification or proof to lay charges. And the biggest downer, the title for the large supplier in L.A. hadn't been revealed.

Frustrated, Sam kept in mind the one trap still feasible – Cass's video camera. If she'd set it correctly, and they were able to get the information they sought, better yet, have tape of Rodrigo incriminating himself, they'd have him by the balls.

Maybe then, they could force the prick into spilling his guts. Offer him witness protection. Who more perfect than the weak, slimy womanizer, like the club's manager?

"Sam! You okay, man? I asked you twice if you're going to work tonight or not." Doug's frustrated tone, barely controlled, cut through his daydreaming.

"Yeah! No!" He let out a stream of cuss words and then started again. "Look, sorry, man. I'm worried about Cass. Tried calling her to not come in, but she's not answering. Figured I'd stop by and see if she's arrived."

"She was here earlier. Came to warn you she'd heard rumors the club wasn't safe tonight. I sent her home. Now that Dani took off, I doubt there'll be any problems."

Ears perking up, Sam moved nearer, hoping Doug had more to say than the closed-mouthed mobster normally did. "You heard something?"

"Just that Mandala is on the hunt for Dani." Doug hesitated and then the words burst out as if the glue on his lips had melted. "There's a showdown gonna happen soon, man. It has to, right? They're fighting over the street drugs, and she doesn't have enough merchandise after that last hit on her warehouse. Instead of giving up Vegas or organizing a new shipment, she's got our guys attacking his street sellers and stealing their shit. Hurt a few real bad. A good boss don't lay down for crap like that. Man's after her now."

"What the hell? Is the lady nuts? And you say she took off. Where'd she go?"

"Don't know. She left right after her freakin' breakdown, screeching about you and Cass not being on time. And that's after she laid down the law, telling the boys to get out there and destroy anyone who stands in their way of getting her drugs. Crazy thing is, Cass got here just after that all went down, but I forced her to hide around the side until the boss left with the rest of the guys. She made me and a few of the others stay behind to guard this place."

"She clean out the basement?"

"Hell if I know."

"Okay. Thanks, man. Stay safe, right?"

"You too, bro."

Sam hurried to where he'd parked his truck and pulled a wheelie that sent gravel spraying in all directions. Heading to Cass's house, he prayed to find her holed up and waiting to hear from him.

His prayers weren't answered. When he saw the smashed-in door, his thumping heart dropped to the floor and lay there writhing in fear. *What the hell?*

Checking the place, he saw it had been broken into, yet nothing looked disturbed. That is until he found the picture Cass had of Trace on her bedside table smashed in a million pieces. Someone hadn't been satisfied to break the frame on the edge of the night table where slivers of glass still lay. Instead, they'd taken more satisfaction in grinding the heel of their shoe into it so the pieces were now totally crushed and the photo destroyed.

Dani!

He continued searching throughout the house and into the backyard. The light from the kitchen window illuminated the area enough for him to see a dark object lying on the ground. Her phone! He lifted it and pressed the activate button to find she'd left it on and recording.

"Yes! That's my girl."

He listened and his face darkened. He kicked the trunk of the cacti close by and after he'd listened to the end, he stamped his boot hard enough to break a piece off.

Son of a bitch! That girl gets into more trouble than anyone I know.

He pulled his own phone out and barked his request until Michael Kowalski answered on the other end.

"You're kidding me? That scumbag took her by force? I'll be right there. Don't move and don't touch anything." When Sam snorted his disgust, Michael remembered who he was talking to and backed down.

"Sorry. Didn't mean any disrespect. Be there soon."

"I can't hang around, man. I'll arrange for some of my guys to trail them and see if they can catch up with Pete's SUV. As you know, our mission is to uncover the L.A. connection so I'm hoping they'll lead me to him. But I'll be in touch. Oh, right, I forwarded you the recording Cass left."

"I see the message on my phone. Thanks."

Sam made a split-second decision. "But first, I'm heading back to the club to see if I can get anything out of Doug, the guy they left guarding the place. He's a good man and likes Cass. I'll call if anything comes of it."

"Good. I can use the help. This city is crazy tonight with gang shootings all over the place. Emergency is packed and more coming in every few minutes. I think the losers are snorting too much of their own freaking product, they've gone loco."

Sam shared his theory. "I suspect *Las Armas* are stealing from Mandala's crew. Even threats and beatings haven't stopped their customers from going elsewhere to get the shit they need. Dani's boys are now forced to take from those who have. I guess they're on the streets stealing merchandise from *Soldado's* sellers and that's a great big fucking no-no."

"No kidding. Crazy-assed woman. No wonder she's headed in the opposite direction."

"From what I hear, Sergio's seriously fed up with her. Far as he's concerned, there's only room for one club in this city."

"Where I'm sitting, at least he's good to his men and protects them. Not like her. She's taken a powder and left her guys facing the music alone."

"Yeah... and after you listen to that phone recording, you'll know she's taken Pete and now Cassi with her too."

Chapter Twelve

"Hey, Doug, I'm like the notorious bad penny that keeps turning up." Sam hoped his dumb joke would win some brownie points with the dead-panned man now facing him, arms-crossed and attitude blazing.

"Yeah. What's up now?"

No way of knowing for sure why Doug switched from being halfway decent to an asshole, but he suspected that he must have heard about the mess on the streets.

Though he'd been trying to quit, Sam pulled out his crumpled package of cigarettes, took one and held out the temptation to Doug. He'd seen the man with a butt in his mouth often enough to know him as a chain smoker.

Grudgingly, Doug accepted his offer and even bent for the offered light. "Thanks. I ran out a while back."

"I think you should know I went to Cass's house and found this out in the backyard. You wanna listen to it and then maybe tell me what the fuck's going on?" Sam passed the phone to Doug and waited. He watched the other man's poker face change from disgust to fury.

"Pete's got her."

"Looks like."

"The man's a sadistic prick."

"Yep. And... he's got her hogtied. Where's he taking her, Doug? What went on in the meeting earlier?"

Doug leaned back against the wall, his knees seemingly giving out as he slid down to a crouch. He took a huge pull from the cigarette and appeared to be making up his mind about what to say.

Sam knelt next to him. "Come on, man. This is Cass we're talking about. Pete'll hurt her 'cause he likes hurting women and Dani'll try doing worse. Those two need to be stopped. You gotta help me find her."

"I can't help you, man." Doug turned and let Sam see his sincerity. "Trust me, Sam. I would tell you if I knew anything. All Dani and Pete said was a bunch of crap like we were weak mothers and no good for nuthin'. That we let the *Soldados* take our deliveries, and we needed to pay them back, get out on the streets and take what was ours. She riled the boys up good, fed them enough booze and shit that by the time they left here, most were stoned stupid and out for blood. I was happy to be on guard tonight and that's the truth."

"Okay, then I need to talk to Rodrigo. He inside?"

"I don't know. He was earlier, but then he could have left out the back from down below."

"Right. Here's my number. You hear anything at all that might help me find our girl, you call me. I had to bring the cops in on this so most likely they'll be paying a visit. Hell, if I can get to her before they do, all the better."

***

Doug watched Sam head inside and waited until he was sure that Sam wouldn't hear him talking. Then he dialed from his phone's sideline number, the app he installed for making calls strictly to one person.

"Hey, boss, I got some news you ain't gonna like. Sam Smith, the bartender here at the club, just played me a recording from Cass's phone. Seems she dropped it on purpose after Pete Bradford forced her to go with him to meet up with Dani."

Doug held the phone away from his ear and waited for the swearing to slow down. "I'm sorry, Sergio. I done what you told me and kept my eye on her. She promised to go home, and she did. Bastard was waiting there for her. Said Dani wouldn't go to L.A. without her. That crazy chick made him give up his bike and use the van to collect Cass. He's pissed."

"Nah! But he tied her hands and then had his all over her. I heard her complain, so I know. She warned him off, and I think he listened. Sounds like he'll take her to Andino, but who knows where?"

Doug waited again for Sergio to calm down and answered him the best he could. "I called you about what they was planning earlier, right? They went after our guys on the street like I said they would. Now I wanna leave this joint and help out. Nothing's happening here. It's so dead, Rodrigo told the girls to shut it down at midnight."

Doug listened while Sergio ranted and then he spoke. "Okay, boss. See you at the old house. You want I should bring the sandwich?"

Chapter Thirteen

Sam headed inside to find Floss and the girls making free with the booze and partying at Dani's favorite booth near the bar.

"Hey, ladies. Have any of you seen Rodrigo? Is he in his office?"

Floss answered; her grin sliding after she recognized the bartender. "We were just taking a break, Sam. The place is dead. Rodrigo split a while ago and told us to hang in till midnight and then close it down unless things picked up."

"You know for sure that he's left?"

"Could be he's downstairs but upstairs is closed. Dani ordered the place shut down, saying the men would be too busy to spend any time there tonight. Just sayin', dude, she was some pissed earlier, especially when you and Cass were both a no-show."

"So I heard. Thanks anyway." Sam started to

turn away and stopped to add with a wink. "Don't let me spoil your fun."

Floss grinned and her face lit up before she added, "You know, Rod might be at the warehouse."

Sam snapped his fingers and then pointed at her. "You're right. I'll check downstairs first and if he isn't around I'll catch up with him tomorrow."

Sam made his way to the top of the stairs and waited, listening. Would Dani pull everyone out? Leave the place empty? Could they have taken the cash from the safes to store it elsewhere?

Made sense seeing as how Sergio would be after blood. And the most likely place to come under his wrath would be the *Las Armas* clubhouse. Unless he knew for sure that no one would be here. That made sense too. Why waste time and resources when it sounded as if he had his hands full in the streets.

Just to be sure he wouldn't run into a surprise, Sam called out. "Rodrigo, you down here, man? I need to talk."

He waited and heard nothing. The tomblike silence shredded his patience, and he moved down a few more steps until he could see around the corner.

Nothing.

Nobody.

Dark, empty and sinister, the room waited.

He turned on the light and paused for some

reaction. Again, he called out. Now was a good chance for him to check the video camera but something held him back. Instead, he pulled out the gun he'd retrieved from behind the bar and inched forward. When he got to the sorting table, he noticed a trail of blood on the gray linoleum floor.

Shit! Something's happened down here. Dread built inside him as to what he'd see if he went further into the recessed area behind this space.

Sweat broke out on his forehead and his armpits flooded. His training kicked in as he palmed the weapon in both hands and aimed it first one way and then the other, covering all areas while he stepped forward.

By the time he'd gotten to the far end of the room, on his right he could see the empty corridor where a small store room and an office shared space.

Disturbed yet steady, he decided to go to the left and check the older part of the building that looked like it had been built years before. Thick stone walls leading to that section of the old basement gave off a cold, moldy scent and the air chilled perceptively.

He knew they only used this area for a wine cellar and a beer locker. There was even a lower area that no one used at all. He stepped into the space and checked around. The kegs and barrels were lined up as he'd seen them last. Nothing looked to be out of place.

Because of what went on down here, he wasn't usually allowed freedom to come and go. If he needed stock, either Rodrigo organized for it to appear or Dani got one of the guys from down here to bring it upstairs. He'd only been here on a few occasions when the rooms were cleaned up and nothing was going on.

He pulled the switch to turn on the lights and slowly searched every inch before standing down. He went to the door he knew led to the lower floor, opened it and listened.

Nothing.

Dead space.

He backed away and decided since he was already here, he'd go to the office and stockroom, too. By the time he'd searched both of those areas and came up blank, he visibly relaxed and returned his gun to the waistline of his jeans. Then he moved over to where Cass had set up the clock camera and stood still.

The ingenuity of the chick delighted him. She'd hidden it in such a way that one would have to move aside the filthy baseball cap that surrounded it except for the face which was fully protruding from under the flap. Since the dust and grime on the old hat looked to have been building for some time, it seemed quite safe to leave things as they were.

Thanking the Gods he hadn't touched it, he

turned in time to see Rodrigo descending the stairs and heading his way.

"Floss said you were looking for me, Sam?"

"I was. Called out and got no answer. Thought you might be in the office so I came past the stairs knowing you'd catch me in the video if you were down here."

Sam could see the questioning look that Rodrigo still wore, and he knew then they would have video feed that could be accessed elsewhere in the building. It made sense to keep guard even if there were no men in the office down here.

"You'll think I'm crazy, but this place spooks me. And when I saw the blood, I got really concerned."

Rodrigo stiffened. "Blood? What the fuck? Where?"

Sam pointed to the edge of the table and then the floor. "Right here. Figured you might be hurt. Hell, with all the wild shit happening in the city tonight, nothing would surprise me. Who knows? Could be Mandala broke in. Hell, I don't know. My mind's creating all kinds of wild scenarios, fucking nerve-wracking."

"You looked pretty much in charge to me. In fact, you seemed to know exactly what you were doing, Sam." Rodrigo's calculating stare spoke volumes.

"Oh, you mean my gun-handling. Thank goodness we have it under the bar for times like this. I learned how to handle one when I was in the army. About the blood..."

Rodrigo pulled up his shirt to show a bandage on his right arm. "We were in a hurry to load up the gear and one of the crates scraped me. I forgot to clean up the mess. There's a bucket by the bathroom if you wouldn't mind mopping up. And turn off the lights when you leave."

Sam swallowed the retort that flew into his mind and forced back the impulse to wave his middle finger. Instead he nodded.

Rodrigo headed up the stairs and stopped. "By the way, what did you want to see me about?"

Sam couldn't believe Cass's welfare had slipped his mind, even for a few moments. He watched Rodrigo's reactions as he questioned him.

"I can't find Cass. I hoped you might be able to help. Do you know where she is?"

Rodrigo's confusion seemed real. "I have no idea."

"I went to her house earlier. After I saw the disturbance there, I got the feeling that Dani might have taken her by force. I know she was looking for her. Girls upstairs say she acted a bit crazy when Cass didn't show up for work."

Rodrigo's face blanched. He stuck his hands in his front pockets and then took them out again and waved them around to emphasize his words. "She's really losing it, man. I have no fucking idea where she is other than to say that her and Pete had some crazy idea to approach one of the contacts out west and try and make a new deal."

"Do you know who that dude is? I'll go after her, but I need a direction or better yet an address."

"No can do, Sam. Can't help you."

"Can't or won't. It's Cassi, Rod. She's in trouble."

"Sorry, man. Shut the place down when you're finished. See you tomorrow."

Fucker!

Chapter Fourteen

Soon after his call from Sam, Michael arrived at Cassi's. Before his team of investigators started the primary search for evidence, he surveyed the damage, which wasn't a whole lot. In her bedroom, he noticed the pile of glass around the smashed framed picture of Trace. He particularly noticed the boot mark destruction of the image. The utter maliciousness made him shudder and curse.

Could it be a sign that the person who destroyed this could have done the same to the real person? The thought crossed his mind and sparks of absolute fury lit his reactions.

Some crackpot had a real grievance against his partner. Thinking over all the dead ends they'd hit while trying to find the kidnapper turned his belly sour and made him reach for the antacids he'd stolen from Trace's desk. The material in the Santino files Trace had forced on him came in handy now. All the players he'd mentioned were character dancing around in his mind, real and with agendas.

Footsteps on the porch had him freezing, but when the chimes rang, he relaxed. Anyone wanting trouble wouldn't be ringing a doorbell.

He moved to answer and ignored the surge of blood to his extremities when he saw Cassi's gorgeous boxing friend waiting to be let in.

He sucked in his gut, straightened his shoulders and greeted the startled babe. "Hi."

Arlene looked stunned. Then she glanced all around him as if she looked for someone else. "Hi."

He didn't move, couldn't. Just stood and stared. His brain acted like a blue-screened computer. He did smile. Or was it that goofy grin his mom teased him about. The one that made him look like a ten-year-old when he'd discover she'd made a pot of perogies for dinner.

"Is Cassi here?"

His tongue rolled itself back into his mouth. Able to answer, he muttered, "Ahh... no."

"Okay? Look. Is something wrong? Why are you here?"

The porch's lit bulb highlighted her shining hair; tonight she wore it draped over her shoulders, wavy and flowing. He'd never seen her look this beautiful. Yet every time he'd been in her company, he would have laid money that this gorgeous knockout could win Miss America hands down.

"Why am I here..."

"Hey! That's my question. Are you okay, Detective Kowalski?"

"It's Michael, Detective Michael."

The grin she couldn't hide brought him to his senses. "Sorry, mind's elsewhere. Real busy. Crazy day. Just call me plain Michael."

"Will do, plain Michael. Now can you tell me where Cass is? Rusty didn't want her to be alone at night. I got here late but my aunt's still upset, and I didn't want to leave her until she settled."

"Like Florence Nightingale." He beamed at the thought of her kindness.

"More like a good niece. She and my uncle brought me up from the time I was a baby. We lost Uncle Phil early this morning and it's been a very taxing time for my aunt."

Big-hearted himself about family, Michael allowed his mask to drop and showed his compassion. Unconsciously, he started to reach for her and stopped. *Whoa, boy.* Instead he awkwardly patted her arm. "I'm so sorry. It's hard to lose someone you love."

Arlene searched his face and her mask faded enough for him to see her own pain. Eyes globby, chin quivering, forcing control, she answered in a weak voice. "My aunt took it hard. I was frantic about her sinking into a pit of depression, and I finally called a friend who's a nanny. She came right over with the baby and that did the trick. My aunt loves babies." Arlene moved closer, forcing him to let go of the door he'd held on to and back up.

"Why are you stalling? Something's wrong. Cass isn't here, is she?"

Gaining back the last brain cell that hadn't turned to mush, he nodded. "She's gone. And before you ask me where, we don't know."

"You can't tell me she left under her own steam. Not with Trace missing. No way she'd leave without knowing what happened to him."

This girl's tuned in, got her friend's number.

Having hit a dead end and seeing no other recourse than to share some of the information on the small chance that Arlene might know something, he waved her into the living room. Gesturing to the couch, he sat across from her. He needed to see her eyes. Hell, he liked looking at the woman, period.

"What I'm about to share is for your ears only. Keep it to yourself."

"Okay."

"Sam came here earlier to check on Cass, and he found her cellphone. She'd left it recording. Here, listen."

He passed her his phone and watched her reaction. Confusion appeared, followed by horror, only to be usurped by pure fear. "This Pete bastard has taken her to Dani? Why the hell would she let him?"

"No doubt, he had a gun. Rumor is he never goes anywhere without one and likes to threaten people with it."

"Still, I'm wondering if Cass wanted to get to Dani to find out what she knows about Trace. Remember last night when it took all of us to stop her? You know Cass, it's all about Trace... right? She adores him."

Michael raked his hands over his bald head and agreed. "I know she does, lucky prick. What I wouldn't give to have a woman love me like that."

Arlene stared him down. "No girlfriend, Detective?"

"Nope and it's Michael."

"Right, Detective Michael."

"You? Any boyfriends you'd put yourself in danger to protect?"

"Nope." She slapped her hands on her knees and stood, an obvious ploy to change the subject. "We have to find out where they went."

"Story goes, Dani needs to get back into the good graces of her supplier in L.A. Seems there's been a falling out. Some think she's headed that way."

"Of course! Okay, I know a little about that."

"You do?" Looking stunned, Michael waited.

Arlene stuck her hands on her slim hips, her low-riding jeans barely covering the detailed, colored tattoo of a rose. "You wanna judge me, go ahead. But I used to belong to *Las Armas* back when they were still based in Los Angeles. It's a long story, but when they moved the action here, my cousin found out about it, and he talked Dani into letting us swap places. Being a smart guy and someone she needed to help her control the gang, she agreed to let me go as long as I moved out of Vegas."

"Your cousin was Mani Abel." He didn't ask. He knew.

She nodded.

"And Dani didn't freak when you stuck around? I can't imagine she'd have left you alone when she found out you were still hanging out in this city?"

"At first, she didn't know. My uncle was ill, and I couldn't leave him. So, Mani warned me to use a disguise. I got a night job and changed my name. Only place I went during the day was Rusty's gym. By the time we ran into each other, she had a lot more on her plate than little ole me. I only hung out with the gang here in Vegas for a short time, but I do know some of the people and places they dealt with in L.A."

Michael's pulse revved up and he took out his phone to make notes. "Tell me their names and if you have the addresses and I'll follow up on the information."

"No can do."

"Excuse me." He knew the stunned look on his face must be obvious to her. "If you know something Arlene, you gotta tell me. We need to check every possible lead. Cassi's in danger. You get that."

"Sure. But I can't tell you what I don't know. I can show you but as far as names, they were never used, just aliases like Big Boss and Storekeeper. As for the addresses, I never kept note of them."

Michael thought for a minute and then made up his mind. "If I can get clearance, can you get away early tomorrow, and we'll fly down there. I'll be your puppy on a leash and you can show me around your old stomping grounds. Who knows, memories can be funny sometimes. You just might get lucky." As soon as the words left his mouth, they reverberated in the air and he blushed.

Of course, being an intelligent female, he saw her pick up on his discomfort. "Let's just concentrate on finding Cassi, Detective Michael. My aunt needs me, so it's hard for me to promise what time I can get away. I'll ask Faith to help out and get back to you. Will it be okay for me to call you?"

He watched her take out her phone and gave her his number. "Honey, you can call me anytime."

Chapter Fifteen

In a foul mood, Trace began strolling around his mattress, boredom making him crazy. He'd done so many push-ups and sit-ups, he felt like a robot. Next, according to his routine, he smashed his padlock against the steel ring in the wall as he'd done a thousand times.

Only this time a miracle occurred. The ring still hadn't moved but the padlock had miraculously sprung.

"Yes!" Using his other hand, he wrenched it open. Though still handcuffed, he was free from the chain securing him to the wall. He could move.

"Holy hell!" He actually did a little dance shuffle before rushing to the stairs and trying to open the door at the top.

"Shit!" It was firmly locked, with no handle facing his side. Someone had done a number on the door, replacing the regular knob with one fashioned to keep a person from being able to escape.

With his hands fisting and unfisting, he tried to remember how many hours it had been since the last sandwich drop. It was impossible for him to figure it out because they doped his water and he slept a lot. But since he'd finished eating the last one they'd brought, and he normally portioned it out well enough to last until the next one arrived, it should be any time soon.

He pushed the mattress against the wall and sat there waiting, listening, every nerve in his body awake and alert.

Did he doze? Shit! Someone was opening the door. As slick as a cat sensing danger, he slid his body against the wall closest to the stone stairs and prayed for the person to come down far enough so he could tackle and overpower him and make good his escape.

His jailer had a habit of descending only halfway and throwing the paper sack at him. He had to grab him before he knew Trace had gotten free.

With his heart thumping, painful and unnerving, he waited, counting the footsteps. When he knew the other man had reached as far as he would normally come, he let out a yell and threw himself at the legs and held on with all his might.

Caught off guard, the figure buckled and caved, both of them rolling to the bottom of the stairs and ending up in a skirmish – until a shot rang out. Thinking quickly, catching the other unaware, Trace wrapped his handcuff chain around the other's throat and dragged him toward the man with the gun.

"You let me go, asshole, or your buddy here's a goner."

"Hell, Trace. You're a cop. You don't kill people. Give it up."

Trace saw the person at the top of the stairs in shadow, a man, someone familiar and his hold loosened. "Why are you keeping me here?"

"For your own safety."

Shocked to the core, he stuttered his next question. "My own safety? Fuck, why?"

"There's a hit out on you. A guy called Neil Chrome. Ever heard of him?" The person at the top of the stairs sat on the first step and lowered his gun so it hung from his fingers between his knees. He added. "Let the man go, Trace. He's starting to be angry and I can't be responsible for what he'll do next."

Trace slowly loosened his hold. In a second, the guy turned to retaliate but the man in charge whistled. That stopped him. Instead, the hooded assailant kicked at the paper bag, releasing the smell of bologna and stomped up the stairs past his buddy, cussing his disgust.

Stunned, his brain racing in so many directions at once, Trace repeated the last words. "Neil

Chrome. Yeah, who hasn't heard of him? The man's a legend. He's made more kills than the Justice Department will acknowledge, and they have him down for over thirty. Who the hell would sic him on me, a lowly police detective?"

"My guess is someone who wants you out of the way so they can move in on your girl."

Startled into pure rage, unable to hide his emotion, Trace stiffened. Muscles in his arms formed from his fisted hands. He growled his reply. "Cassi? You think someone wants me dead so they can move in on Cassi? Fuck me, it's gotta be Dani Andino."

"Nope, don't think so, dude. Of course, I could be wrong, but that bitch's got too much on her plate right now to be worrying about you. On the other hand, she has flown the coop and taken your lady as hostage. Oh, and just so you know, Neil Chrome won't be bothering you anymore. We caught up with the prick earlier, gift-wrapped him and dropped him off at the police station with a note to your partner to keep him under lock and key until he hears from you."

"You're letting me go." Trace knew it to be true and didn't say it with a question mark at the end.

"Yep. You're safe for now. But Cass isn't. And I don't have the time right now to go to her rescue. Hell, I don't even know where they've taken her. All I know is that sick bastard, Pete Bradford, drove off with her, and we suspect he's under orders to take her to Dani in Los Angeles." Voice hard with his frustration clearly heard, the jailer continued, "Look man, your partner has more information than I do, she left a tape recording. You have a lot more techie resources too. You need to rescue her before she gets hurt. After all, the only reason she'd let that ugly snake take her is she believes Dani's holding you."

Trace started forward, his hands held out, his voice sounding like a man ready to kill. "Unlock me."

"No can do. Wait here for a few minutes until we leave and then you'll find some helpful stuff upstairs and a car waiting. You better save her, man, or they won't need Vince Chrome to come gunning for you. I'll do it myself."

Chapter Sixteen

While she rode her cousin Mani's Harley in the late hours, heading back to her aunt's, Arlene decided to take a short spin to clear her mind. Since it refused to stop thinking about the man who'd been waiting for her at Cass's house, she stopped trying to shut it down and let the visions come.

Detective Michael, as he'd referred to himself, intrigued her. Truth be known, he delighted her. Somehow, he'd drilled a small slit into a place she'd thought had been locked tight. A grin lit her face under the helmet and a little shake of her head followed. He was a nutbar, but a loveable one.

She hadn't been this attracted to a man since... forever. Mostly, guys tended to annoy her. Without regret, she normally walked away from them unless she was in the mood for a liaison and then it would only play out according to her rules –

short and sweet.

People thought it was a man's prerogative to take sex so lightly, but there were a lot of women today who felt the same, her included. No entanglements, thank you very much. Just a wham, bam, thank you, man. A giggle escaped, which relieved some of the stress she'd been under.

Worry for her aunt who'd completely fallen apart over her husband's passing, didn't let up. Though his death had been expected, distress had made Barbara weak and clingy.

Now with Cassi missing, she thought about Rusty and knew he would take her disappearance harder than any of them.

Add to that, the frustration of knowing Ariana Swift had no respect for her talent and only gave Cassi creds, pissed her off every time it crossed her mind – which was often.

All this shit strained her loyalty to Rusty and the unwanted growing admiration and concern for her missing sparring partner. Not comfortable digging into these unsettling emotions, Arlene forced her mind back to her aunt and the dilemma facing her for the next day.

As strange as it felt for Barbara to turn to her, for the first time in her life, she'd actually been needed and wanted by the woman who'd raised her. And it felt wonderful. Her aunt had cried in her arms, truth be known, they'd shared their tears in an embrace so wonderfully warm that Arlene had felt years of walls start to crumble.

Increased sensitivity in her aching hand forced Arlene to head for home. Though the infection from the cat bite had almost disappeared she knew better than to push the recovery. Rusty had warned her and whatever that old man said, she took as gospel.

Waves of affection washed over her, and another grin broke out. That old shit rocked her boat, no two ways about it. Somehow, without her being aware, he'd begun to mean a lot, almost equal to the respect and love she'd felt for the other old man in her life who'd mattered – her uncle – and that was huge.

Parking the bike in the backyard, she was shocked when she saw the garage light on and Barb in a shabby pink housecoat sitting at the work bench surrounded by open boxes.

"What are you up to now? I thought you were all tucked in for the night. I wouldn't have left you otherwise." Shocked by her automatic scolding, nonetheless, she felt confident enough to do so gently.

"Hi, Leni. I'm fine, dear. It's something your uncle said that's been nudging me. Do you remember? He wanted to be sure I didn't clear away all the old rubbish out here until you'd found the box of things your mother had left you the last time we saw her. It's gotta be here someplace." She rose to get another box from the pile stacked in the corner. "I've gone through most of this junk and it's worthless."

"Aunty, you're exhausted. Let me look. I promise not to throw anything away until you get a chance to check everything, but it's time for you to rest now. It's been a hard day. Making all the funeral arrangements and dealing with all the red tape and blasted bureaucracy one needs to go through at this time would try anyone's patience. Who knew taking care of a loved one entailed so many hard decisions?"

"I know. Your uncle looked after all that for Mani, and now I realized why he came home afterwards so exhausted and wrung out." Barb hung her head, her eyes tearing once again. "Poor man. I was such a shitty wife to your uncle, Leni. Not like he deserved. Now it's too late."

"Stop it. You were there for him at the end. I'd never seen him happier. He loved you so much."

"Yes..." Her aunt nodded, her sad face smiling slightly from Arlene's comment. "He loved me, and he loved you too. I guess we were lucky to have him. I'm going to retire now, dear. Don't stay up too late."

"Before you go, Barbara, is there any problem if I go away for a while tomorrow? I'm sure Faith would be pleased to come and visit to keep you company if you'd like. And I shouldn't be too late."

"Oh, honey, you don't have to babysit me like I'm a child. Today, I admit, I needed your support.

On the other hand, if Faith and that gorgeous little Raoul want to come and see this old lady, I'd be thrilled. We could take him for a walk around the neighborhood, and I can show him off to all the old biddies that brag about their grandkids."

Chapter Seventeen

The drive seemed endless with Cassi pretending to sleep and Pete being annoying, driving like a maniac.

Fighting to stop from continuously revisiting the last wonderful night she'd spent with Trace, her will power faded, and she sunk into the memory.

Together on a blanket in the moonlight, Trace had been the gentle lover every woman dreams to meet but many never do. That night, while they'd made love, his sultry eyes had searched hers. She remembered how her adoration peaked when he'd spoken words she'd never forget.

Hell, baby, you're already so imbedded in my brain that your face is the last thing I see at night. And your image is waiting for me as soon as I regain consciousness. You're why I never hug the pillow anymore, trying to put off getting my ass outta bed. The sooner I get work over with, the sooner I get home to you. I swear, darlin', you're like those stars up there. You've sweetened my life in the same way they light up the night sky.

How could any woman hang on to her heart when a man romanced her so beautifully? And his actions, intense and thorough, had expressed more than his sweet words.

His kisses had been so intimate that she'd felt he'd drawn her core from her chest. In those sex-filled moments, she'd loved him more than she'd ever thought possible.

Wrapping her arms around his strong body, feeling the ripples of muscle on his back, the firm thighs that surrounded her legs and the warmth of his hands on her skin, she'd held on and reached heaven.

When her feelings became too intense to handle, she'd grabbed his thick hair and reached with her lips so she could tell him without words how much he meant to her. Not satisfied with speaking through actions, he'd voiced his adoration.

"Love me, baby. Yes." He'd forced her to meet his gaze and the concentration of his feelings seared her deeply. "Love me, Cassidy Santino." His gruff whisper mesmerized. "Like only you can, baby. Only you..."

Then he'd stroked her body, licked her breasts and kissed her everywhere until she'd shivered and burned at the same time. Drawn into her fantasy, she felt again how he'd manipulated her orgasm, powering his response to her pleasure by withdrawing time and again before he was ready to let passion reach the pinnacle.

Wet now, fidgeting in her seat, she experienced again his penetration, how deeply he'd scored her body with seductive hunger and brought her to the brink, titillating, teasing until even he couldn't take it any longer. With a last savage plunge, pounding into her so she'd hummed with pleasure; intense pleasure, he'd lifted them both from earth to hover among the stars.

As if Pete sensed her torment, he growled and brought her back to the reality of her predicament. "We're getting close to the city."

Cassi clenched her legs to stop the stimulation caused by her vivid imagination and rubbed her shackled hands over her knees.

"You've driven here many times, I imagine." *Keep him talking so he doesn't figure out where your thoughts have been.* Not sure if men like him could sense her earlier emotion or catch the scent of her body's reaction, she didn't want to take any chances.

"Yeah, I grew up here. Shit place. Shit life. What more can I say?"

Hopefully nothing! Directly following his gruff voice, those words came back at her and she knew them to be true. She didn't want him to talk after all.

Instead she watched their approach to the city. The number of lanes on I-5 were confusing and mostly empty of traffic other than the transport trucks one passed all the time. Seeing as it was close to sunrise, Cassi wondered how much longer it would take them to get to where they were headed.

According to what Pete had confirmed earlier, about taking her to Dani, Cassi couldn't decide if it was a good thing or not. All she knew was that she needed to find Trace. And if meeting Dani would make that happen, then fine. She'd deal.

Finally, he took a ramp off the highway and they headed into an area full of buildings and warehouses. From then on, she watched every turn Pete took, wanting to remember where they were going but she was lost. Los Angeles wasn't a familiar city and the street names meant nothing to her.

Not speaking much during the long ride, he now sat beside her, burping and farting, fiddling with the radio controls and switching every station she might have enjoyed. Aching, still sore in every part of her body including her soul, she waited.

Finally, they were driving on a dark street, past rundown shacks that might have been decent homes in the 30s. Pete appeared lost until he spied his bike parked in the yard of an old house, and he let out a cuss of pleasure.

What a loser! Sounding like a frantic mother who'd spied her lost child after being separated, his moan of pleasure gave her the creeps. Of course, Cassi kept her opinions to herself.

He stopped at the curb, pulled out the key and turned to her. "Dani's inside. Let's go."

Cass hesitated until she saw him reach for his gun. "Fine. But I can't open the door. In case you forgot, my hands are bound. And in case you care, they're numb because you tied them too tight." Hoping her ploy for some sympathy might work, she waited.

"You're lucky I didn't duct tape your mouth and throw you in the trunk."

Shrugging at his uncaring response, she fanned the building flames of anger. *No sympathy. Okay, asshole, let's play it your way.*

Pete came around to her side, leaned in and grabbed her arm to haul her from the passenger seat. Playing for the right moment, she pretended to flinch away, forcing him to bend further into the front seat for a better grip.

The sicko aimed his hands in such a way so they'd skim over her chest, he even pushed down on her breast and lingered. Once the moment was perfect, she aimed her booted foot just so and drove it upward, right into the family jewels between his open legs.

"Shit!" His scream engulfed her with pure satisfaction. In seconds, his knees gave out, he whimpered and he dropped his hold. When his head fell toward her lap, using every bit of power she had, she thrust her knee bone into his face and enjoyed the crunch as he took the punishment.

She shoved him aside wanting to escape before he gained his senses. Knowing the animal would be out for blood, hers, she became frantic to get leverage to dump him so she could leave the truck. Exerting herself, she shoved, and he slid to the ground. And she followed. *The gun!* It had fallen out of his pants during the tussle; she'd heard it hit the gravel.

Desperate, she searched, knowing it would keep her safe. She needed to find it. And she'd have done it too if Dani hadn't been standing in the shadows enjoying the fun. Or so it looked that way from the shit-eating-grin she had plastered over her face.

"Are you looking for this?" She waved the weapon before sticking it in the waistband of her tight jeans. Coming forward cautiously, she spoke. "Let me help you."

Cassi stayed perfectly still. Her shock at the way the boss looked, sickly and unkempt, not even close to her usual style, made her hesitate. She hadn't known how she would feel when she saw Dani again. Hatred reawakened, but slowly – mixed with a strange kind of sympathy.

Remembering her bitterness from the night before, Cassi swallowed the curses and calmed her mind. Dani had taken Trace away from her and before too long, she would know why. Pray God, he still lived, and she'd find out where they held him. Then, if it was the last thing she ever did, she'd set him free and make this tramp pay... for Trace and Raoul.

"The asshole said he was bringing me to you, but I didn't believe him, Boss. Not after he kept putting his greasy hands on me." Cassi mixed a half lie with the truth to see whether Dani'd be sucked in or not.

"I told the bastard to keep his filthy paws to himself." Dani went to hover over the still writhing specimen of a sorry-assed loser and her actions made Cassi's blood run cold. Pulling out the gun she'd retrieved, she thrust it into Pete's painful groin. "You son of a bitch. I told you what would happen if you over-stepped."

Terror could be heard in his renewed scream of pain and it made Cassi's senses go ballistic. Her ears, sensitive to his terrified noises, buzzed painfully to where she had the urge to throw up her hands and cover them.

Trying to move quickly, her body, throbbing from the pain of kneeing him in the face and heaving him off of her, wouldn't follow her brain's instructions.

Hating the ugliness she never imagined witnessing, she wished she could close her eyes and block everything out. Only she didn't dare.

Even the smell of the early morning, rotting vegetation, uncovered garbage and her own sweat made her want to gag.

It all became too much, and she broke, yelling. "Stop!"

Dani froze and looked her way as did Pete.

"Just stop. I can't stand it anymore. Why did you make Pete bring me to you, Dani? Either tell me now so I can figure out if I want to stay. Shoot me so I can't leave. Or untie me and we'll talk."

Stillness settled. No one moved for a few seconds while Cassi's words echoed in the fading dusk. Then Pete swiped at the bloody mess on his face and began to carefully move away from the gun and crawl to the SUV, using the fender to stand upright. Or as straight as possible with knees wobbling and his groin being held in such a way that one might expect he needed to use the shitter.

Dani hesitated and then stepped down. "You're right. We need to talk. Okay, Pete, thank Cass for saving your sorry ass. Go make contact with Drew and you'd better come back with good news – that he wants to meet, or we'll be having this talk again."

Pete nodded and headed toward his bike.

"Oh, no, you don't. Use the SUV. I know you'll come back for your precious baby if we keep it here."

Pete's ugly mug sneered, and he wiped the spittle from his chin. His tattooed face exposed his hatred as plain as if it were written in words across his forehead.

Then Dani showed why she'd become the boss of the gang and played the card that she knew would gain back his loyalty. "Pete, you do this for me, and I'll see you get a huge bonus. You good with that?"

He stopped and stared at the ground. As if he needed to switch gears, his head moved up and down, he yanked at his greasy beard and then he growled. "Yeah. I'm good."

"Okay, then. Follow the plan." Dani held out a hand to Cassi. "Come inside with me." When Cassi hesitated, she spoke only one word that made up her mind. "Please."

Chapter Eighteen

"Welcome to the pigsty I called home until I broke out at sixteen." Dani remembered the night like it had happened an hour earlier. Her mother dragging her from her room, forcing her to submit to yet another jerk screwing them both so they could earn enough for the booze and drugs the old lady needed.

Only this animal beat on her mother, and then turned on Dani. Hurt her bad enough that he'd driven her into retaliating. She'd left him with sore nuts, and in the ensuing scuffle to escape, she'd wrenched out of her mother's hold, which made the furious woman fall backwards and break her arm.

Mother! No one would honor that old bitch with the coveted mom title. As many times as Dani strived to get a small sign of approval, never mind affection, she'd been slapped, called names and pushed aside.

The next day when Dani had tried to return, if for no other reason but to get her things, the door had been locked and her mother had ignored her pleas. It was the last time she'd seen or heard from the wicked bitch until she'd been contacted by the courts that her mother had overdosed and she'd inherited the dump left by her grandmother.

Being it was the only home she'd ever known, Dani claimed it and kept the taxes paid. And whenever she spent time in this city, which was seldom after the move to Las Vegas, she remembered why she not only hated her early years, but why she hated most men.

These horrendous rooms were a shrine, a fuck-you to the woman who rejected her at the worst moment of her life. She'd left everything the same: dirty curtains, scuffed linoleum, disgusting toilets and filthy walls. It was her reminder, her tortuous reminder of who she really was.

Every time she allowed her mind to flip to the past, she heard the last words her mother had screamed before she'd threatened to call the cops. *"Get lost, kid. You're like the sad son of a bitch who fathered you, no good for nothing. And you'll end up in a jail cell, same as he did."*

"Dani?"

"Huh?"

"I asked if you'd cut me loose?"

"Sorry." Dani shook off the rage that always

attacked whenever she allowed herself to sink into early memories and pulled a knife from her back pocket. Careful not to cut Cass, she soon had her free. "The bastard left marks." Dani rubbed at the welts, revealing her disgust until Cassi stepped back.

"It's better now." Cassi wriggled her wrists. "Why'd you leave town, Boss?"

Dani raked her hands through her flattened hair and walked into the living room with her fingers interlocked behind her neck. She hoped Cass would follow her, and she did. "I needed to talk to a man about resuming our shipments. If I don't get our supply chain set up again, we'll be forced to come back and deal with the shit market here. You wouldn't believe some of the slimeballs in this city, Cassi. Men who'd bleed us like hanging pig carcasses until every drop is theirs, and we own nothing."

Dani glanced around trying to visualize the place like Cass saw it and the reality saddened her in a surprising way. It dawned on her that what the other woman thought mattered. Fuck, it mattered too much. She cared about Cass Santino more than any person alive. Why it happened, she had no idea. Never before had anyone wormed their way into her heart to make a difference.

Why this testy chick with her baggage, her gorgeous blue stunners and her shit attitude? God only knew. But she couldn't shake her worship, she'd tried. Hell, it was like taking the next breath. And that sorry fact described her world right now. Cass made a difference.

As proof, at this moment, Dani felt more alive than she had for ages. If she had a choice in the matter – could stop her pitiful heart from setting off fireworks whenever she saw the other girl – would she end this crush, this adoration? Yes, goddammit! But there you go... she'd always known her luck would run out.

Cass, restless and pacing, finally lost patience with her silence and words broke loose. "In case you've wondered why I let Pete hogtie me and haul me here. I came for one reason only, Dani. I need to know. What about Trace?"

Faced with the truth, her heart dropped to the floor and lay there sobbing. It's always Trace. "What about him?"

"Look, I'll beg if I have to. I'll do anything you want if you'll tell me where you're holding him."

Dani saw the instant that Cassi figured it out.

"My God, is he dead?"

Not able to stand Cass's pain any longer, watching the one woman she'd ever cared about beg for a man, Dani exploded. "What the fuck do I care? Look, darling, he's gone. I need you. Doesn't that count for anything?" Shocked at the teary pleading she'd just revealed, Dani wrapped her arms around her body to hold in the pain.

No one loves me. No one ever has. I'll die and there

won't be anyone to grieve. How fucking sad is that?

***

Cassi's irritation over Dani's wretchedness appalled her until remorse replaced her anger. The shock of her first glimpse of Dani had faded somewhat, but hadn't totally disintegrated. Other than the last few days when she'd been stoned, the red-head always appeared perfectly made-up.

Face creams slathered thick to cover her bad complexion. Clothed in her customary tight jeans, fancy heels and her signature white, see-through blouses, eyes highlighted with deep blues or greens depending on what she wore and lips coated red, she'd been the queen. A strutting, hard-ass of a boss who'd held every one of her men's respect if not fear.

Now in her sloppy shorts with her powder worn off and mascara smeared, she just appeared pathetic... until one gazed deep and saw the threat. Cassi knew the woman who ruled *Las Armas* hadn't left the body. The eyes never lie.

The question hung between them, waiting to be answered. *Is he dead?* Her breath stuck in her lungs, choking her, while she silently begged... *Please, God, no.*

"Christ, Cass stop looking at me that way. How the hell should I know if he's dead? I didn't even know he was missing." Dani dropped onto the rickety, blanket-covered couch, her hands covering her throat. "In case you haven't figured things out,

I've had a war on my hands, a bunch of greasers who have no idea what the hell they're doing, the old boss has turned up and is making it known he plans to take over, preferably because I'm dead and my supply has been cut off so my customers are turning tail and going to the competition." Dani coughed throughout the wild speech, and at the end the spasms didn't let up until exhausted, she dropped her head into her hands.

Appalled at the guttural screech, Cass moved closer as if to help and had no idea why she did so.

"Take it easy, Dani. Where's the kitchen. I'll get you a drink."

"Get me a beer and one for you, too." Pointing to a doorway at the back of the room, Dani slumped back against the shabby sofa cushion, exhaustion clearly evident.

Cass rushed to the room where Dani had gestured and saw the same destructive mess as the rest of the house. The stench here was worse than what she'd smelled when she'd stepped through the front door and that was eye-watering. Fit only for a torch came to mind, but she shrugged the thought aside and rushed back to the other woman.

"Here, this will help clear your throat."

"Nothing will clear it, Cass. At least that's what the doc told me last week when I saw him. According to the biopsy he took, it's full of cancer – Stage 3."

"Oh my God, Dani, I'm so sorry." Cassi reached for Dani's hand and held it between her own. She noticed that the other girl clung tightly and the small flame of regard she'd sometimes experienced for this complicated individual burst into real caring. "When is your operation?"

"Never!" Dani glared at her, opposition to the comment revealed in her marble black eyes. "No one's cutting me open, sticking me with radiation and chemo until I'm worse than I am now. When living gets too hard, I'll take care of myself."

Shocked to silence, Cass thought over what Dani had said and realized she had no comeback. The decision had been made.

Dani's bleary eyes searched hers, and Cassi waited. There was more. "I don't want to die, man. Who does? But... when the time comes, I don't want to go out a loser who let down her boys. That's why it's so important that I make this deal, give our guys back some dignity and product for their customers. If I can do just one good thing before the end, Cass, one fucking thing I can be proud of, then it'll be okay. Do you understand?"

Cassi touched her knee. "What can I do?"

Dani's probing stare searched hers obviously seeking sincerity and found it. Her face disintegrated into a cry for help, and Cass wrapped her arms around the other woman, cradling her and held on tight.

Dani cried for a long time. Tears flooded both

their faces and Cass's chest. While she hung on, Cassi tried to visualize what Dani's earlier life had been like, living in this hellhole and knew without being told that she must have suffered as a child. Without thinking, one human trying to sooth another, she kissed Dani's head time and again, caressed her arms and back and spoke gently, "I'm so sorry, darling. I'm so sorry."

Chapter Nineteen

Trace rushed up the stairs and found that Sergio had blocked the door to give him and his bud enough time to skedaddle before Trace broke through.

A few good kicks, and he was free. Sitting on an old bench by a broken window, Trace found the keys to his handcuffs, a cheap burner phone and a Ford focus waiting outside with the ignition wires hanging loose. Not caring if he drove a stolen vehicle or not, Trace sparked it to start and once it turned over, he hit the numbers for his partner's phone. Driving away from the dilapidated old house where they'd kept him prisoner, he pounded the wheel impatient for Michael to answer.

"Detective Kowalski here, what's up now?"

"Shitty phone attitude. That what they teach you back where they found you?"

"Nah! I'm just busting my butt, pulling a second

all-nighter trying to find a missing partner. You have any information on the prick and where he might be?"

"He's heading into the station as we speak. Is he gonna find you there?"

"Fucking rights, man – with fresh coffee, stale donuts and a big hug. Boy, will I be glad to see you."

"Set up the tape from Cassi. See you soon!" Trace hung up so he could maneuver the car better through the early morning traffic. The city never slept, never shut down, but the vehicles on the road at this time of the day were the early-bird drivers, half-asleep working dudes with places to go.

He squealed into his parking stall and nabbed one of the rookies. "Found a stolen car, Officer. You might want to return it to the owner. Thanks."

He rushed up the stairs to his department and found a huge number of expectant co-workers milling around with eyes bright and smiles wide.

"Hey! No one doing any work around this place anymore?"

Insults came flying back to him from most of the smiling throng, along with backslaps, hand punches mixed in with a few hugs. Even his cranky boss, Chief Hank Lester, haggard-looking, hair on end, trying to hide his beaming grin, stuck his head out of his office and acknowledged Trace's return. He also held up his thumb and pointed it to his office. When Trace acknowledged with a five-minute signal, he nodded and disappeared.

Michael had held back until the others had their turn at saying hello but he soon stepped up and grasped Trace's held out hand, grinning as if he knew Trace was sidestepping a hug.

"Partner, you keeping your promise of fresh coffee?"

"Right here, hot and strong, just as you like it. Got the Pepto handy for your chaser too." He passed Trace a steaming mug. While he sipped, grimacing and gesturing for a phone, Michael knew exactly which one he wanted.

"How'd you know about Cassi's recording?"

"It's a long story and can keep. Is this it?"

"Yeah, this is the one."

Trace listened to the speaker, his face turning hard and dangerous when he heard Cassi warn the sick pervert about his wandering hands. Disgust appeared when Bradford continued to babble his bullshit. Finally, he slammed his fist on the desk when he heard the bastard talk about Dani – so much for gang loyalty. What the hell had Cassi gotten herself into?

"The stupid bitch made me trade with one of the others. Didn't want them to know where we'd be going, and she figures I'll be des-creet." He snorted. "Des-creet, bullshit! She's scared shitless and doesn't trust her own men to protect her. She needs me 'cause I'm her link to the big guy in L.A."

"You had to give up your bike? Man, that's gotta be a

piss off."

"What's the piss off is that I had no choice, and it's all your fault."

By the end of the harangue, Trace's fear pounded in his stomach and the pain almost put him to his knees. To stay upright, he had to lean his hip on the nearest desk. "Where'd you find it?"

"In the back yard. She must have gone out there for some reason. I'm betting it was after seeing the front door had been damaged, maybe left open."

"You figure he waited for her there? Any video footage from the neighbors or street cams?"

"Yeah. The guy to her left had surveillance and was more than happy to share. It clearly showed that Pete had been parked in the back lane. He left the SUV, we figured when he saw her lights come on, and ten minutes later, he reappeared with Cassi, her hands tied in front. Or so it looked like on screen."

"Was he forcing her?"

"No. You heard the tape; she didn't put up any fight at all. I'm positive she went with him solely because she was so sure Dani had you. Hell, that lady would do anything it took to find you, man. You gotta know that."

"It works both ways. Look, Lester wants me in his office, and I can't keep him waiting any longer. Last thing I need is to waste time chatting with him, but it is what it is. I want you to get us a helicopter. I don't care if I pay for it out of my own pocket, but I'm going after her."

"Already in place. So you know, Arlene Montgomery worked in Los Angeles with the gang back in the day. She feels she can help us find where Dani might be holed up. Seems she had to deliver a few packages to her house."

"Get the address, we'll stop there first."

"No can do. She has no address, only her memory of how to get there. She's willing to tag along and show us, but she needs to organize her home situation. Her uncle died and her aunt's having a rough time of it. Rather than leave the woman alone, Arlene figures she can get a friend to go and babysit. I'll call her and see when she'll be ready."

"Tell her we have no time to fuck around. I need to get there yesterday."

Michael grinned and added. "Take it easy on Lester, man. He was pretty shook up when you disappeared. We had a confab the other night, and he let it out that you were one of the men he most depended on. Just play it cool."

Shock had him spinning back to face Michael to see if he'd been messing around or had spoken truth. According to this silly grin, all doubt fled. Well, for fuck's sake. Maybe the old man liked him after all.

Chapter
Twenty

Arlene answered Michael's call from her old bedroom and made the date for an hour later.

Surrounded by her mother's memories, frivolous things that young girls hang on to if they're in any way sentimental, she took her time. After finding the box at the bottom of the heap in the garage last night, but too tired to deal with it, she'd carried it upstairs, left it on the floor and dropped into bed with her clothes on and her face unwashed.

Waking early, angry at her lack of discipline, she showered, exercised and checked on her still sleeping aunt. Grabbing a coffee and muffin, she returned to her room and placed a call to Faith who promised to drop by later in the morning and spend the day.

Having some time to waste, Arlene began rifling through the items stacked haphazardly. That's when she found a young girl's pink diary still locked and looking mighty grubby. The name *Judy* inscribed with pink rhinestones showed at the bottom.

My mother held this.

The thought sparked her imagination and she tried to visualize her mother back when she'd been young, had just given birth, only to flee from the fallout.

Her uncle had kept an album of pictures of his little sister, younger by ten years, and had shown them to her many times. He'd even framed the best one for her and she'd kept it on her night table until she'd moved to L.A. and left it behind.

Rising, going to the dresser, she opened the drawer and found the same photo under some old pajamas she'd also discarded. Fancy that her aunt had left her room the way she'd abandoned it so many years earlier. Her uncle's influence seldom shocked her, but she knew while growing up in his care, he could get mighty stubborn about certain things and no doubt, he'd laid down the law about keeping Leni's room for when she wanted to come home.

Affection swelled for the old man and the pain she'd been experiencing at low ebb swelled and swamped her once again. Sniffing, but refusing to give in to the weakness, she redirected her attention.

Over the years, she'd spent hours searching for a

likeness in the photo she held of a gorgeous young woman with a sparkle in her eye and a killer figure. Till now, she'd never seen it clearly. There, in her mother's face, she saw herself, the forehead, chin and even the smile.

Her father... Her thoughts spiralled to where they'd spent so much time as a youngster. Ignoring the visceral pull to wanting answers, she did as she had always done. Shrugged her shoulders and quit letting it matter.

She checked her watch and saw there was still twenty minutes before the car would come to pick her up, and so she took a pair of scissors and mangled the latch on her mother's diary until it finally gave way.

Going directly to the last page, interested in when she'd made the final entry, she saw that the date would have been only a few days before Arlene's birth. Her mother had been eighteen when she was born.

It shocked her to think that her mom would still be writing in a diary at that age. But then again, her uncle had told her that in her earlier years, the girl had been sheltered by his domineering father who'd held incredible restraint over both his wife and daughter.

Uncle Phil had explained what had happened. How he'd felt terrible, seeing Judy changing, becoming wild, but with a new wife himself and a baby to bring up, he'd ignored the signs of his sister

Judy's dissatisfaction.

Even after his mother had begged him to step in and help them, he'd made light of their concerns and looked the other way. Late nights, drinking and drugs, disappearances for days, her wild ways became uncontrollable until his parents had finally kicked her out. The last time he'd seen her was when she'd dropped Arlene off, begged for his help and waved good-bye, never to be heard from again.

According to what he'd admitted, at first, he hadn't bothered to search for her and by the time he'd begun to worry, the trail had grown cold and no one knew where she'd disappeared to.

Arlene flipped back the pages until she found the section close to the end where she believed Judy had begun to rebel.

Her mother had written about being jeered at by the other girls in school for being such a goodie-goodie, and the boys coming on to her but only wanting one thing.

Skipping pages, scanning, she suddenly found the page that had something to say.

I found him, not a kid. He's a MAN, the man for me. He tells me he's too old, but I don't care. He's so handsome and strong and can't keep his hands off me. We're in love. A boxer, he's on the top of the world and he's taking me with him. Promised to leave his wife and twins after this next fight – I can't wait. Then he'll be mine... all mine. He says we'll run away and have the baby, our baby.

And soon after, this note...

He's a lying, cheating asshole. I believed every word out of his mouth, but he didn't mean any of it. He lost his last fight and he's drunk, mean and stupid. And I don't want to be near him anymore. I'm leaving so he can't find me. And I'm ditching everything that has anything to do with him, even his kid. Can't look at her without seeing the mess I've made of my life. José Santino, divorcé and liar, could have married me months ago instead of hiding me away, watching me suffer alone through the pregnancy nightmare and the gossip. That man can go straight to hell and take his Middleweight Championship belt with him.

Before she could unread the truth of her heritage, Arlene heard the roaring from the emotional tsunami heading straight for her. The ringing in her ears was superseded by the painful tension in her gut, the clawing, grinding disbelief that held her in its grip.

Hatred began to build until she recognized the utter stupidity to spend so much energy on a dead man. Better to shift her anger to his next of kin. *Her sister! Fuck!* Cassidy Santino was her half-sister. The same girl she'd promised the cops she'd help save from the likes of Pete Bradford, card-carrying misogynist, an animal with mean tendencies and a gun to help him see them through.

Then it hit her like someone had slammed her face against a brick wall. She'd held the gun that had killed her own half-brother. And Cassi had sworn to find this woman, no matter how long it took. And make her pay.

Shit, Shit... SHIT!

Chapter
Twenty-one

Trace couldn't sit still, fidgeting, fisting his hands and then swinging them to get rid of the numb-like soreness. He sat at the front of the helicopter beside the pilot while Michael and Arlene shared an uncomfortable silence in the back.

Tuning the headphones to one frequency, they drowned out the motor noise and that of the rotor blades. He decided that talking would help pass the time because his thoughts were too scary to linger with.

Turning, he saw Michael lift his hands in a gesture that clearly said *What?* and Arlene shrugged before giving him the cold shoulder. *Hmmm*, something was going on between those two. He knew the boxer chick had a piss-poor attitude about most things, but he'd sensed that her behavior this morning had put his partner in a spin.

"Mike, did you organize a car to be waiting at the airport? I want to leave right away and not waste any time on administrative bullshit."

"All done. One of the cops I know cut through the red tape and will be waiting for us. She's a real trooper."

Trace picked up on Arlene's quick glare before her focus returned to the side window. He doubted if Michael saw it since he had his attention on his phone.

Guessing she wasn't immune to his bald-headed, green-eyed, good-natured partner after all, he spoke directly to her. "Arlene, I want to thank you again for assisting us this way. I understand you recently lost your uncle and left your aunt today to come to Los Angeles. He appeared to be a good, decent man. I'm sorry for your loss."

Arlene's stony look faded a bit, and she shed her attitude long enough that he saw her pain. "Same to you, Detective McGuire. I heard about your mother."

"Hell, the whole country's heard about my mother and the way she died." He made light of an uncomfortable subject.

Arlene continued, "They're holding Mary Devin's trial next week; it's in all the papers and social media. There's a huge controversy about the woman. I wouldn't want to be on her jury."

"Why? Because of the harassment those folks will be facing?" Michael popped in on their conversation, his question, without malice, came from a man wanting clarity.

Shooting back her answer, Trace knew she didn't have time to construct a politically correct reply, just a response from her gut. "No. Because I'd have a hell of a hard time convicting the woman even though she caused so many deaths. It's one thing to kill innocent people with the rest of their lives in front of them. It's another to help victims with a terminal illness, in horrible pain, leave their crippled bodies behind and find peace."

"You read that in one of the pro-Mary editorials?" Michael fired back at her.

"Maybe I did, doesn't mean it isn't a valid point of view."

Trace piped in to stop the discussion from getting out of hand. "Guess we'll be finding out whose side will win soon enough. I'm thinking it might come down to the debating eloquence of the lawyers."

The flushed appearance of the girl sitting next to Michael, her braided hair leaving her whole face on display, spoke volumes. Something was wrong. Trace sensed she'd had a shock recently, and he'd bet his next paycheck it had nothing to do with her uncle's death.

Michael, not being as insensitive as one might think, nudged her shoulder gently before changing the subject. He aimed his question at Trace. "The boss fill you in on a gift parcel we received earlier?"

Trace grinned and replied. "Imagine someone sending Vince Chrome, notorious hit man for the wealthy and over-privileged, after me, a lowly Las Vegas detective."

Suddenly, Trace noticed Michael picking up on Arlene's body language. Had the name meant something to her?

"Arlene, do you know Vince Chrome?"

"Not personally. I just remember that Billy Duran defended him a few years ago – got him off, too."

The news shocked Trace until he remembered the relationship Cassi and Billy shared in the past. *Son of a bitch!*

"Did the boss tell you how shook up he was by the news of your kidnapping? I figure he saw his retirement being jerked out from under him."

Trace had no idea what Michael was blathering on about. Mind you, the chief had seemed uncharacteristically cheerful when he'd been debriefed.

Rather than go into it, Trace changed the subject. "At this moment, all I care about is finding Cassi and making sure she's safe."

Stunned, he noticed Arlene flinch when he spoke Cassi's name. According to Michael, Arlene had offered to come and help them today.

So, what the hell was that all about?

Chapter
Twenty-two

Cassi and Dani, emotionally spent, had fallen asleep embracing, covered with the blanket Cass had managed to reach and throw over them both. Out cold, neither was aware the sun shone until the front door shattered and two men appeared with guns and full intentions to use them. One stood by the doorway while the other rushed to stand in front of them, his legs spread, and his gun steady.

At first, disoriented and still half asleep, Cassi had no idea who they were, not until the one nearest to her and Dani spoke.

"Hi, baby. I bet you were expecting me to find you soon or later, right?"

Dani had stiffened. "Hey, asshole. I had no doubt you'd catch up eventually, even though you were always kinda slow on the uptake." Her bravado came through clearly and her attitude left no one in doubt she was willing to battle.

Appalled, Cassi let the blanket slide away from her face to be sure she'd identified the right person from his voice. Sure enough it was him.

Billy!

The man's expression switched from that of a killer's expression to pure shock. "Cassi? What the *fuck* are you doing here?"

Billy's anger spurring on her protective instincts, Dani surged to her feet, reaching behind her waist and finding nothing. She'd left her weapon on the far table out of reach.

Billy used his Ruger 9mm to stop her advance. "Uh huh, bitch. Stay where you are." He turned to Cass and questions were hurled at her in rapid succession, like a butt stock on a rifle firing continuous shots.

"Are you hurt? Did she force you? Shit, girl, just tell me she took advantage of you, and she's a dead slut right now."

Cassi's sluggishness fled to be replaced with confusion. "No!" She looked to Dani and when the other girl ignored her bewilderment, she asked her own question. "Why are you here, Billy?" Something told her he hadn't come to her rescue – the thought had popped in and just as quickly disintegrated.

From his appearance, the lawyer's regulation suit replaced with black pants and sweatshirt with the hood still covering his head, she accepted it had nothing to do with her at all.

Thoughts lit up like a dimmer switch being pushed up high. Her brain filled, and she knew instantly that Billy Duran had been Dani's nemesis, her old partner, and man she'd recently been fretting over.

Her Billy! The druggie she'd saved from the streets. That same Billy – lawyer gone bad! A guy she'd always looked up to and accepted as a brother, welcomed into her home and into her life. She'd loved him.

Billy, the man with a silver tongue and a criminal's heart.

If she had a gun, at this moment of utter disillusionment, she'd shoot him herself. Various people had let her down throughout her life, but this hurt. This stunk.

Billy?

"Cassi, don't look at me that way. You don't understand. This treacherous slut used me. She played me for a fool, going behind my back and working my men against me. She schemed her way into taking over and left me like a slug in the dirt."

"You were a slug in the dirt, shithead. You don't remember, do you? The nights I begged you to stay clean, to concentrate on the operation, be a man." Dani's face contorted with fury. She leaned forward, her hands fisted and waving at him in disgust. "You slapped me around and told me to shut my mouth, remember that now?" Her cheeks reddening and eyes bulging, added to the appearance of a woman pushed beyond endurance.

Billy's expression changed for a few seconds, his face turning pale.

"Yeah, now you get it. Too late, you stupid prick. I warned you we'd lose our position in the game, and you let it all slip right through your drunken fingers. If I hadn't stepped in and taken over, we'd all be rotting away in a jail cell, thanks to you."

"Hold it. My memory's not that off, Dani. You fed me the booze and the drugs. You're the one who made sure I sunk as low as I did. You weren't the only woman in my life back then. They've all told me what happened. You gave me the shit that made sure I'd be out of your way for good. Lucky you didn't kill me while you were at it."

"Me kill you? Shit, I wished I would have instead of just leaving you rotting in a ditch, begging for money for your next hit."

Cassi rose and stepped closer to Dani, hoping to stop any foolish moves. Billy meant business. His gun hadn't wavered. It aimed at Dani's heart with intent.

Wanting to calm troubled waters, Cassi broke in. "How did you know Dani would be here?"

"Hell, once I knew she'd left Vegas it was easy to figure out. She always returned to this dump whenever she had nowhere else to go."

Dani sneered. "And let me guess who informed you I'd left Vegas – your sweetheart, Maria. I saw you two at the sports center the other night. The snooty sister of our old connection's back in your life once again. You pretentious prick. You rose from the mud pretty high, Billy-kins, but then you always were able to get the chicks to fall for your bullshit."

"It got you."

"Yeah. So. I'm not proud of the fact that I forgot my principles and let a man get close."

"Hell, Billy, we got visitors." The lookout, who'd been checking the street periodically, appeared shocked.

Before Billy could reply, Trace suddenly appeared in the room from the back of the house, his gun ready and determination lighting his features.

Reflexively, Billy turned to fire his gun at the stranger who'd caught him unaware, and without a second's hesitation, Cassi flung herself to cover Trace.

Dani seeing that Cass would be the one killed, flew in front of Billy and took the bullet herself.

Trace, who'd caught Cassi and whisked her behind his back for protection, his gun still aimed at Billy, pulled the trigger and shot him in the head.

Chapter Twenty-thre e

Trace! Oh, my God, Trace. It's really you.

Time stopped, hung there suspended, while Cassi's brain took a few seconds to absorb the shock and see the threat to her lover. Instincts had kicked in and she'd flung herself in front of him. Afterwards, she couldn't have said if she meant to shield him or shove him. Danger threatened and protecting him mattered more than anything else.

His cop's trained reflexes snapped into action. Before she knew his intentions, he'd forced her behind him and had her shielded. Shocked reaction, created by the distinct blast of his gun, had her falling to the ground, reliving the previous time she'd heard death up close and personal.

Visions of Raoul's last few minutes swamped her until she cowered in a ball, crawling into the corner. Considering all hell had broken loose, it took some seconds before she sorted the real from the memories.

Wait, Trace was here. Alive! Her eyes searched the room until she found him bending over a female form.

Dani! No, please. God...

She scurried over to Dani's body and laid her head close to the woman's chest to see if she still breathed. Blood streamed from the bullet hole in her stomach and had to be stopped. Cassi used her hands to put pressure on the gaping wound while she begged, "Dani? Stay with me! Dani, please. Sweet Jesus answer me."

Trace bent closer and held his finger on the pulse in her throat. He spoke in a soothing way. "She's alive, Cassi. Don't cry baby, she's breathing. I've called for an ambulance."

Suddenly, Dani's eyes popped open, and she moaned, "Ca-ass."

"I'm here, Dani. I have you. Hang on. Help is coming."

Dani lifted her trembling hand to caress Cassi's cheek and try to wipe away her deluge of tears. Her words were muffled, low and almost indistinct. "It's. . .all good, baby. See, I got m-my wish. I won't die for nothing." She turned her glance to Trace, her expression hardening slightly. "Be good to h-her."

Trace nodded, lifted her other hand off the floor

and squeezed. He said nothing.

As Dani's eyes glazed over, all signs of life dimmed. She moaned softly one last time, her head lolled to the side, and she stopped breathing.

A scream built up inside Cassi but only a small whimper broke loose. Enough to have Trace's arms gather her close while he said her name over and over. He held her so tight, she could barely breathe.

It felt good.

Michael stepped close and Trace turned away. She hated to let him go but she had no choice.

Suddenly, not in the real world, she saw her hands covered in blood and like a small red key of liquid slime, it unlocked the self-loathing buried in her heart. Anger – rolled into a ball of hate – ripped at her conscience. The force caught her and swept her away. As if she time-travelled, she found herself hiding behind a warehouse while another murder took place. Once again, she felt the crushing fear and inability to move.

My God! They're killing Raoul. I can't help him. Coward! I'm a fucking coward. The ugliness reared and crescendoed, leaving her weak and pitiful. Before she could wallow in the horror, reality slammed into her like a fist in the face – a truth she saw now that she never could before.

It had been Raoul's wish that she be protected from the dark side. He'd never have wanted her to be in danger; he'd have chosen to die before letting that happen.

A spiritual message came to her – a gift if she'd accept it.

It was his time.

Oh God!

The truth slammed into her like a fist in the face. Her self-destructive emotions began to dissipate. It *was* meant to be. She did nothing, because at that time, she couldn't.

Exhausted, she touched Dani's face gently, leaving a streak of red.

Her mind whispered the words she needed to say – to hear. I forgive you.

Now I have to forgive myself.

***

Michael led Trace a few feet away. "The ambulance is on the way. I've called for backup, man. We need to secure the scene, and you need to be prepared to hand over your weapon." Michael's respectful tone cut through Trace's fog of fear and thankfulness.

He pulled away from Cassi slightly and gestured with his head at Billy's body. When Michael shook his head, Trace wasn't surprised. He'd aimed to kill rather than take a chance the man might pull the trigger a second time. "Yeah, right." He leaned over to speak directly to Michael, his voice in a near whisper. "Cover him so Cassi doesn't have to see him."

"You got it."

"Thanks."

Trace, seeing Cassi was in shock, murmured gently. "Honey, we have to vacate the room. It's a crime scene now, and the technicians will be all over here in a few minutes. They'll be needing to talk with me, but you can go with Mike and Arlene, and I'll meet up with you later."

Cassi heard his words, he saw her take them in. The one name that sparked any response was Arlene, so he called the white-faced girl over. Noting her distress, he hesitated to pass his love into her charge, but he had little choice. Cassi had an obvious wish to go to her.

"Arlene, she wants you. Take care of her. There're going to separate us and question each one so be prepared. Just watch over Cassi for me, small wonder, she's pretty traumatized."

As if she'd taken in his words and even understood them, Arlene reached to take Cassi from him. When she would have fought to stay close to him, Arlene wrapped her arms around Cassi's shoulders and hugged her hard. "It's okay, Cass. I've got you. I'll take care of you. I'll always take care of you. Come on now, brat. We'll wait. It'll be fine. We're good."

Trying to shield her from the sight, Arlene led her past another body, now covered. Cassi stopped. She remembered. "Billy?"

"I'm sorry, Cass. He didn't make it."

"He wanted to shoot Trace. I saw his face."

"Yes. He did."

"I'm glad he's the one who died."

"Me, too, Cass. Me, too."

Chapter
Twenty-four

Arlene led Cassi from the grungy room to the rented SUV outside. The stench of death mixed with the musty, nose-curling smell of poverty, couldn't be tolerated one second longer. Dani's callous indifference to her surroundings still shocked Arlene.

From the moment they'd reached the house earlier, and Trace had chosen to go through the back door, she'd remembered the previous times she'd been made to bring Dani deliveries, and the disgust she'd felt to see the boss in her childhood setting. The rundown building should have been condemned years ago. It was a blight on a street where others had upgraded and made small efforts to live decently.

They passed the body of a man, lying on the grass, handcuffed and unconscious. Thinking back to moments before, Arlene had to admit that

Detective Michael had impressed the hell outta her.

Waiting for Trace to give the all-clear before he'd enter, Michael obviously intended to go through the front. When he saw that she'd ignored his request and had followed him to the house rather than wait in the car, fear galvanized his behavior. He'd shocked the shit out of her when he'd turned all cop-like with orders.

"You get your ass back to the car, and while you're at it, stay low."

"No."

"It's not safe here. I want you out of this mess. And that wasn't a request, sweetheart."

"I can handle myself."

"Jesus, woman, either you listen to me or I'll throw you over my shoulder and lock you in the trunk." But before he could enforce his threat, which she had no doubt he would do, an armed assailant barrelled out of the building, coming close before he saw Michael, who'd stepped forward. Realizing his pathway was blocked, the thug brought up his gun to take aim.

Without hesitation, Michael chopped at the hand holding the weapon so it dropped harmlessly to the ground. With the whites of his eyes enlarged to madness, the attacker growled and pounced. He battled for freedom, throwing wild punches which Michael countered.

While they were busy, she'd run closer to the

house and watched the action through the open door. The theatrics in the front room kept her spellbound. All hell had broken loose. Two shots were fired in rapid succession. The devil had paid a visit to collect his own.

Scared shitless, her knees gave out, and she dropped to the ground. A gun, lying in the grass a few feet away caught her eye. Suddenly, she knew what she had to do. At a crouch, she fetched the weapon, making it a certainty that no shots would be fired outside the house, too.

The ongoing battle caught her attention. Thrilled at seeing how well the sexy, green-eyed detective handled himself, she stayed mesmerized. For her, boxing was a sport. But this shit portrayed a gruesome reality where men fought for their lives.

Within a few more well-aimed blows, Michael overpowered the other dude. While he cuffed him, if the fool would have refrained from struggling and trying to bite, his face wouldn't have suffered the last fist that put him unconscious.

Still working the scene, Michael pulled her out of harm's way and relieved her of the weapon hanging limply from her shaking hand. "Go back to the car and wait there. Lock the doors."

He dug his phone out of his pocket and spoke, his voice curt, official and blunt. "This is Officer Michael Kowalski, LVPD. Shots have been fired, two people down at 76 Smith Road. I need some backup and an ambulance." As he spoke, he headed inside to cover his partner.

"Where're we going?" Cassi interrupted Arlene's reminiscing and put on her brakes, refusing to take another step.

"It's okay, Cass. We're only going to the car out front. We won't leave, I promise. Trace just wanted us to get out of that dump."

Screaming sirens, distinguishable in the stillness of the early morning, warned they'd soon be surrounded with police and their subsequent horde.

"How come you're here?" Cassi, elbows on the car's hood, her head gripped in her hands, seemed to be working her way through what just happened. "And Trace?" She whipped around and searched Arlene's face. Eyes clouded with tears, shock trapped in her features, she questioned, "How..."

Still reeling herself, Arlene, aware of Cassi's distress, thought carefully before answering. Earlier that day, after realizing they were half-sisters, blame and hate had soaked her heart with self-pity and anger.

Her father, José Santino, big-shot boxer and low-level human, had never cared about her or her mom. She had his blood running through her veins and it sickened her. But it also gave substance to the rotten choices she'd made years before. They say the apple doesn't fall far from the tree.

Ashamed to own up to her small-minded behavior, she acknowledged some time had passed while she'd battled inside as to whether she'd take Michael and Trace to the right place. She could have pretended confusion, bad memory, any number of reasons for forgetting.

In her wicked vacillation, she'd actually thought that since her father had abandoned her, what the fuck did she owe to a sister she never knew.

Thankfully, it only lasted as long as it took for her conscience to wake up and remind her that she had a soul. Mani and her uncle had seen to that. Those disgusting notions faded completely when she admitted that she might not owe anything to a bogus sister, but to her new friend, Cassi Santino, she was indebted. And chances were good that Cassi had no idea her father was such a skunk.

Besides, didn't she have a horrible confession of her own that wouldn't be allowing her any haloes either?

Now, seeing how close Cassi had actually come to being a victim, a corpse, Arlene's attitude shifted completely. She'd never forget how Trace had appeared in time to protect Cassi after Billy had yelled at her. And when Billy had aimed the gun at Trace, Cass had literally flown to shield him with her own body. There'd been no hesitation. Her expression showed only fear for Trace... and love.

Neither had there been any hesitation for Dani

to use her own body to receive Cass's ill-fated consequence, a bullet that killed her. That Trace's return fire had been straight and true, she'd been relieved. It had ended the murderous sequence.

They now had to accept that Dani had cared about Cass, but then who didn't? Not able to completely overcome the shakes in her own body, Arlene wrapped her arm around Cass, the girl who let tears flow freely and who wasn't afraid to share her emotions. A person who hadn't built such a thick wall that she feared to let the world see her insecurities and feminine weaknesses.

"I'm sorry, Cass. What did you say? My head's full a-and I'm not concentrating."

Cass sniffled and swiped at her nose with the back of her hand. Tears cascaded but were ignored. Finally, she used both hands to wipe away her vulnerability. "I asked how you got here, how Trace... h-how did he get loose? From where?"

"He never said, neither did Michael. All I've heard was he'd shown up at the office after finding out that Pete had taken you to Dani. He arranged for Michael and me to come in the helicopter with him."

"I can see why Michael, but you..."

"I knew where Dani's house was, but I couldn't give them directions. I just knew how to get here by car. We never talked about this, but I used to belong to the *Las Armas* gang."

"I know."

Shocked, Arlene searched Cassi's features for rejection and found nothing but acceptance. Now it was her turn to question. "How? I never told anyone."

"You have their tattoo. I saw it at the gym."

"I had it redone, it's been changed."

"Not perfectly. I recognized the letters."

"Why didn't you ever ask me about it?"

"None of my business."

"But I was a complete bitch to you, many times. You could have squealed to Rusty. He'd have—"

"Done nothing. He isn't like that, and neither am I." Cassi's expression hardened with warning. Rusty was hers to protect.

Stunned speechless, Arlene absorbed this shock and wondered at Cass's ability not to condemn or judge. She smiled, and her lips wobbled threateningly. She held nothing back, an open invitation she'd only ever shared with two other people. "Thanks, Cass. I'm really glad I could help. That I remembered the way to this house."

Mollified, Cass put her arm around Arlene's waist and leaned her head for a second on the other's shoulder. "So am I, Arlene," Cass whispered. "I met the devil tonight. But I also found a guardian angel and now a best friend. How lucky can a girl get?"

And now you have a sister who loves you. I'd say you hit the jackpot.

Chapter
Twenty-five

In a L.A. hotel room, Cass propped herself against the abundant white pillows on the king-sized bed, wrapped a fluffy throw around her and waited for Trace. He'd promised to join her here as soon as possible.

Michael had arranged a meeting with an FBI agent for them and Trace, although reluctant, had agreed. "Honey, I have to go, I'm sorry. Look, I'm bushed, and you've had enough for today, so I got Arlene to reserve us a room. We need time together now that everything has died down. Wait for me?"

"However long it takes."

He'd kissed her with such yearning; she'd clung to the warmth and satisfaction of being held in his arms. Forced to pull away, he made his escape. Now she waited, reliving everything that led to her being here.

Going back in time, the drive with Pete became a blur. Being with Dani supplanted it completely.

Dani! How could she ever think of that woman again without fondness and thankfulness or was it pity? She searched her heart and felt relieved at the deep glow of affection that burned brightly.

Brought up by a dysfunctional mother, in an environment that would have twisted any sane person into a psycho, she'd striven to be a – a somebody. Sadly, she'd chosen a career in crime.

They'd shared a lot during the hours after Dani had confessed her illness. She'd rambled on about her mom, her wretched childhood, and her many regrets. Once her babbling had slowed, Cass asked about Raoul but Dani became somewhat cagey, even uncommunicative.

"Worst decision I ever made – that one. I swear to you, no one needed to die. Not by my orders." Then she'd admitted to putting Juan in the hospital for having ignored her instructions and letting Raoul be killed. But when Cass had asked about the rumored woman, Dani's lips had closed, and she'd been overcome by a coughing spell that had lasted a long time.

Once Cassi had helped her clear away the blood and mucus, she'd gathered the weak woman close, and they'd nodded off. In the end, Dani had proven her love to be true and strong. Cassi would never forget her and if she ever had a little girl, she already knew her name. And *her* Dani would know only love and tender mothering. Be taught how a strong woman should live.

Moving forward, the rest of the evening passed in a blur. Billy's shocking arrival and Trace's entrance happened so fast, she still hadn't computed everything. The scenes that followed fought to appear but she shoved them back into the black void of purposeful forgetfulness.

Next, she dwelled on Arlene's gentle assistance and wondered at the difference of the girl from tonight to that sullen, mean-spirited stranger who'd taken such a dislike to her at their first encounter. Dammit, it was hard to see them as the same person.

Earlier, as her warrior protector, Arlene had forced the cops to be quick and professional. Her concise and honest answers had helped the men with their badges and little notebooks to see everything clearly, step by step.

They'd kept the women together, segregating them with a younger male officer while others worked through their investigation routines.

The coroner's vehicle had arrived as did other police vans, a flurry of activity followed, including the "Police – Do Not Cross" yellow and black crime scene tape they used to cordon off the area surrounding the house.

The handcuffed man, who'd recuperated enough to walk had been led away while his Miranda rights had echoed in the no-nonsense voice of a disgusted cop.

Other officers were photographing the scene, bagging and tagging the evidence, taking statements, everything they normally did at any shooting.

When the girls had been summoned downtown for further questioning, Arlene had insisted on staying with Cass and only let them be separated when Trace stepped in and said it would be okay.

Then, when the questions were over and they were told they could leave, it had been Arlene who'd organized their reservations at the hotel, a room for her and one for Cassi and Trace. Thank god for small mercies, she'd even known of a small strip-mall close by where they could get the bare necessities for the coming night.

Now, alone, Cassi waited. Too alive with emotions to sleep, too excited to finally be with Trace again and too thankful for the people in her life that truly mattered.

***

Trace arrived late afternoon exhausted but thankful to find Cassi sleeping peacefully against the pillows she'd banked behind her. The girl appeared to be having a nice dream if the quirky little grin shaping her gorgeous mouth was any indication.

Being as quiet as a large man can possibly be, he slipped off his light jacket and removed his weapon, setting it close by in the top drawer of the night table.

Next he removed his shoes and very carefully he nestled as close as possible to his sleeping beauty. As long as his body touched hers, he was happy.

Her face, skin smooth and make-up free, appeared young and silky, her attractive eyebrows had been shaped to highlight those slanted blue heart-stoppers that never failed to dazzle him.

He took his time memorizing every little dimple, lips that had the wonderfully natural upwards slant, the small ear he could see from the side of her head where her hair had begun to grow back.

God, he couldn't get enough of having her safely next to him in a hotel room, the two of them together. After the nightmare of his imprisonment – not knowing if he'd ever be with her again – he started to choke up. Tears gathered and only by swallowing repeatedly could he put a stop to letting them fall. This time they were happy tears at least, not like the kind he'd shed in the darkness of his prison cell when he'd believed she was lost to him.

Still shocked by the happenings of the last few hours, he let his mind wander back to the day before and his delight when he'd broken his chains. He shuddered at the memory – his certainty that he could overcome one man until a second jailer appeared holding a gun, and he'd faced a certain death. The gut-wrenching knowledge he'd never see Cassi again had rendered him weak and so fucking sad.

Imagine his delight when instead of killing him, hoodlum and gang boss, Sergio Mandala, gave him enough information to know where to start his search for Cassi. He'd protected his ass from a serial killer who he'd sent "special delivery" to his office. And... had become his best fucking ally in the world, the same man on every official justice department's most-wanted list.

It was strange and bloody scary how the world had a way of shaking a guy up and giving him a swift kick in the ass every once in a while. Pre-conceived ideals weren't always black and freakin' white, not when humans were one of the ingredients in the bullshit agenda of life.

Suddenly, he felt eyes on him and slowly turned to see Cassi beaming her sweet smile that had won his heart. The same one he'd seen her aim at a camera lens to smack him in the gut in his hospital room.

Right! The one she'd sent him just before she'd crawled into the ring with a maniac who liked to hurt people. That smile!

"*Cas-si-dy!*"

Chapter Twenty-six

How could a man change so fast? One minute, the soft grin on his face had mesmerized her and the next, thoughts of escape flooded into her head. If he hadn't grabbed her and hauled her back on the bed, she'd have made it to the bathroom and a locked door.

"You lied to me. You were the fighter against Swift in the ring."

"No. I didn't. You took for granted that Arlene would be fighting. I just didn't mention that she'd gotten an infection in her hand, and I had to take her place."

"It's a lie by omission, don't play games, woman."

"How can you yell lying down? And so loud—"

"I'm mad at you. And stop looking at me like that."

"Like how? I'm happy to see you. Even if you

are glaring. I missed that adorable angry look you get—"

"Oh no, uh huh. You don't get to sweet-talk me. How the hell did you get roped into facing that crazy-assed featherweight dippy bitch? And I want the truth, young lady."

"Don't you want to know if I won?"

"Quit changing the sub—. Did you?"

"Nope. But she got what she deserved." Cassi snorted. "Will you stop holding me away, if I tell you what happened?" Her sparklers shone with loving glee as if she adored him and was enjoying his almost authentic anger. Bloody female had his number.

He allowed her to sneak closer. "Trust me, baby. I have a lot more things I want to say to you, but this needs to be cleared away first."

"Okay. Here's the truth. I took the fight for two reasons. Ariana refused to give Arlene another shot at the title unless I took Arlene's place. And... the dishonest bastard of a promoter had forced a huge buy-in from Rusty and threatened to keep every penny. That would be after he smeared his name and the gym throughout the boxing world."

Trace saw instantly that Cassi had no intentions of apologizing for making the choice she had made in her untenable situation, though her entreating expression spoke for her.

If he went back and put himself in her place, he most likely would have done the same. *Be honest you ass, you so would have done exactly as she had.*

Added to the rest of her anxieties, the man she loved had been shot and was in a hospital bed recuperating. Would it have been smart to upset him further? Hell, he had no doubt she'd known he'd have evaded the doctors and nurses to be there, no matter the repercussions.

Shit! She was right.

She'd had no choice but to keep the fight to herself. Too bad she hadn't known they'd have the event on national TV, splashed on the sports network, his favorite station.

Without his realization, sometime while he mentally worked his way through the quagmire of questions and answers, he'd shifted her closer.

Now nuzzling his neck, her kisses inflamed his senses. He groaned. "You're right, Cassidy. I didn't know the story. I'm sorry you were in such a pickle, damned if you did and damned if you didn't." He slid his hands up her shoulders and gently held her face. He needed to look into her eyes so she could see the devotion and understanding in his. "I'm sorry, baby. You must have suffered for being forced to lie to me again."

When her eyes filled with tears of relief, first it frightened the shit outta him. *Oh God, he'd made her cry.* He talked fast, trying to intercept her reaction. "I forgive you."

As soon as she groaned his name and flung herself close, her face pressed against his neck and her body shuddering, he added words with conviction. "And I'm a horse's ass." His final entreaty, "Please, please don't cry."

"I can't tell you how sorry I am. I hated lying to you again. I'd promised myself – no more – and then I had no choice."

"Shush, honey. Even if I'm an obstinate idiot who wants the world to make sense, I do understand that shit happens."

When she started to giggle, he breathed a sigh of relief. He'd been in a panic to get back to her all day, to hold her and tell her he loved her. How he'd ended up acting like a pig-headed tyrant, letting his misguided feeling of being let down interfere with what should have been a purely happy and sex-filled time, he'd never know.

His male genes, plus his fogged-up stupidity, thought the truth important and being a stubborn cop with a one-track mind, he'd reacted. Yet, now that they'd cleared the air, it felt right to let the reawakened love and lust fill every corner of his heart and mind.

***

Cassi sensed the change in Trace. His whole demeanor softened, and his body became pliant and welcoming. She'd answered his questions and he'd forgiven her. No... he'd actually understood, and that meant a lot more than unnecessary forgiveness. She'd done nothing wrong. Well... Not too wrong anyway.

When he scooped her close and began removing her T-shirt, she helped by lifting her arms and torso. While his hands were busy, she used her lips to good effect by scattering kisses all around his neck and working on releasing the buttons on his shirt.

Once she could lay her cheek against his naked chest, she spoke softly, "I'm so happy, Trace. You're here with me, safe and all in one piece." As if her words reminded her of the reason he'd recently been in a hospital, she checked his wound and placed another kiss near the scabbed-over skin.

"It's healed. I've been exercising my arm. Don't worry. Come here." He rolled her on top of him and could feel her swollen breasts, soft in their nakedness, pressed against his.

"You sure like to give orders, Detective."

"It's 'cause I have a badge, ma'am. You better do as I say, or I can arrest you for assaulting an officer." His cheeky grin turned her on and love overwhelmed her already heated body.

Chapter Twenty-seven

Softly, she caressed the growth on his cheeks, the dark stubble of a virile man who often had to shave more than once a day.

He arched up and rubbed this face against hers teasingly. "Does my beard bother you?"

"Not even a little. You look like many of the movie stars nowadays."

"Pffft. Trust me, baby. I'm no star." He lifted his face and rubbed it gently against hers. "Are you sure it doesn't hurt? If it does, you tell me."

"Trace, after me worrying you were dead and I might never see you again, a few scrapes will only make me relieved you're with me."

He rolled her over again so he could lie on top, his gaze studying her intently. "Cassi, all the time I was locked away, I thought about you – your lips and eyes." He kissed each gently. "Your wonderful body, so full and soft that when a man touches you he feels like he's the luckiest son of a bitch in the world." His hands caressed both of her breasts and then his lips followed. He nibbled at the skin all around the nipple until she called out, and then he sucked in the fullness.

She sifted through his soft hair, her fingers caressing his scalp, massaging, adoring... gentle. Words emerged; she couldn't have stopped them if she tried. "I was scared, Trace. How could I have gone on without you?" She shuddered. "Where were you all that time?"

"Locked up in the basement of an old house outside of town." He didn't want to go into too many details. "Let's just say they didn't hurt me and in the end, they freed me so I could go after you. One day, I'll tell you all about it. Not now. I have other things on my mind at this minute that seem a hell of a lot more important." He watched her and appeared mesmerized. "I was willing to do anything to get out alive, get back to you. Baby, you were my talisman, my reason to keep hoping."

A soft smile lit her face. "And I couldn't give up the thought that you'd be coming home, and we'd be together again. If my thoughts even wandered a little into the unthinkable, I had to stop or go crazy."

This time she kissed him and all the pent-up fear she'd controlled came through in her kiss. Her lips were hard and the kiss desperate. Without words, she let him feel her fear, share her distress, and she knew he understood.

Becoming charged, their kisses shrouded them in a world of magic where nothing else mattered. She couldn't get enough of her man, his arms, his body. The hardness thrust against her stomach proclaimed his adoration, his lust, his need.

Never before had desperation been a part of their lovemaking, but this time, it seethed all around them. She had to have him inside her.

"God, Trace. Please. I need you inside me now."

He swivelled to the edge of the bed and undressed with the speed of a man intent on getting it done quickly.

In the meantime, she also shed the rest of her clothes, and within a few seconds, he was back in place, only this time, he entered her soaking body with a groan of gratitude. "You're wet, baby. It's amazing."

"I love you, Trace." She reached to hold his face above hers so she could spear him with her announcement. "I adore you."

"Oh, Cassi. I love you too, baby. So much. Enough to fight off the world to get back to you."

Wrapping her arms around his back, she arched her hips and opened completely. Engorged, he plunged again into her receptive body – her hungry body. Their breathing became labored, and the sweat gathered. He rode her hard, and all the while she urged him on, happy with the madness of their coupling.

Gentleness had no room in her emotions now. Insatiable for his passion, pulsating, trembling, needing, she urged him on even more. "Oh yes. Trace. Make me yours. I love it. I love you." Her legs tightened, her breath caught. She reached and reached. Inside, shocks attacked, palpitations strengthened, her muscles tensed – clenched. And then...

"Cassi. Cassi? I'm... Oh, Lord, you're gorgeous, woman. I love you."

His thrusts, heated and hard, tore at her reserve. As she orgasmed, she panted like an animal. Wild, her release tormenting, she screamed and every inflamed cell in her body exploded. Shudders consumed her.

He gave the final plunge, pushing hard, harder, and shudders consumed him.

Then all was quiet. All was well.

They were together.

Chapter Twenty-eigh t

Arlene entered her hotel room, closed the door, and using it as a backdrop, she slid to the floor. Overwhelmed couldn't begin to describe her emotions. The last few hours had pushed her to the brink. Shocked stupid, heartbroken, saddened to the very depths of her core – that might come closer.

She wrapped her arms around her body and rocked from side to side. Then she reiterated the prayer that had replayed like a broken record in her mind since earlier when they'd arrived at Dani's house.

"Thank you, Lord! Thank you for helping me choose what I knew to be right – not evil. For showing them where Dani lived. For not listening to the devil's voice trying to talk me into making the biggest mistake of my

life and pretending I got lost. For finally growing up and not making everything about me."

Had it been close? It was the question that ate at her. It was past time for her to quit screwing around – to come clean. Vicious hatred had attacked after she'd found out the truth of her heritage. It had suffocated her, made her rash and mean. She'd fanned those revolting, dehumanizing thoughts, feeling righteous.

The memory caused a mass of tears. Animal sounds escaped as she shed both her crippling rage and accepted the irrationality of the hideous low self-esteem that had shadowed her for as long as she could remember.

It was because of those feelings that she'd come close to making the biggest mistake in her life. All the crushing emotions weakened her usual ability to wall them off. Weakened her to the point that she lay on the floor and open the floodgates. Once exhausted, she ended her outburst with sniffles and whimpers.

When had she become so hateful? Sure, her aunt didn't shower her with affection as she grew up, but Mani and her uncle more than made up for that loss. Maybe too much! Trying to instill a sense of belonging to her, they'd made her feel as if only she mattered.

Her aunt had a point about Mani protecting her, getting involved in the gang because he'd recognized it to be the only way he could get her out. And once he'd found her, hadn't she slipped back into her old habits and taken it for granted that he'd take care of everything?

Shame on her!

Hell, she couldn't even remember what had driven her to run away, to join with the *Armas*. Oh, right. She'd overheard her aunt giving her husband hell because he spoiled his Leni too damn much. Now she remembered.

Funny thing, her aunt was right. The more Mani and Uncle Phil gave in to her, the more she expected. After hearing her aunt's angry tirade, she'd become pissed and decided she didn't need them anymore.

Two days of fanning her indignation, she'd up and left. Hitchhiked to L.A., got involved with Juan and the next thing she knew, there was a tattoo on her back. Often drunk, high and playing a role, she became a drug runner and a go-between from the street sellers to Dani.

Of course, that was after Billy had finally sunk so low that it was easy for his lady to step in and take over. She remembered him in the early days, before he'd gotten hooked on his own shit. His elite law office had become the place to go for the high-flyers in the business. Mainly because they could afford his prices, and they knew he'd get them off with misdemeanors and petty charges.

While lawyering, he'd gotten involved in the game, or had he always clawed at the outer rim?

She suspected he'd wanted in on the big money, so he'd organized the *Armas Jóvenes* to become one of the larger, more unified gangs out there. Young people flocked to join because of his magnetism, the smooth way he had of making a person feel they couldn't go wrong. *This choice will change your life, make you matter – A Somebody! Stick with me and you'll never be alone or broke again.*

Yeah! Right... such bullshit. And she'd fallen for it. Charisma – he had buckets of the stuff, and with his glib tongue, he'd instilled in all of them that they were the best. Now wasn't that just the perfect message to pull her in?

Later, when he'd hit the skids, Dani stepped up and decided they needed to get him away from the many temptations in Los Angeles. From his so-called friends who egged him on to join them in their never-ending quest for wild parties.

They moved to Vegas, and that's when he really flipped out. Went missing for days at a time until they'd find him in some alley, stoned out of his tree, robbed and beaten.

It was the beginning of the end. He made one too many disgusting scenes before Dani dumped him, hooked up with Rodrigo at the Lipstick Club and took over as boss.

Not long after, Mani found her, negotiated his way in and saved her life.

Only to lose his...

Oh, God!

No wonder her aunt hated her. Okay, not actually hate her, but was disgusted about the circumstances. How could Arlene blame her? From now on, she'd do anything she could to make Barbara's life easier and happier. If it meant staying with her at the house, she would do so. If it meant working in her real estate business as she'd hinted a few days earlier, she'd do that too.

Hold it, chickie! What about your boxing career?

Panicking, her chest muscles were being squeezed until only short panting breaths stopped her from passing out. The pressure finally eased. She sniffled. Tears returned to burn her face.

God, please, don't ask me to stop doing the one thing that makes me feel alive.

Boxing had to be non-negotiable, it had to be. Being in the ring let her breathe... be herself, strive to be the best. The rules kept her from going wild yet still enabled her to release a lot of the pent-up fury she'd carried all her life.

The challenge made sense in her otherwise empty existence.

Empty?

Suddenly, the image of a green-eyed, bald-headed law officer, comfortable in his role as protector, appeared and she couldn't shake him loose.

His parting shot at her earlier returned. "Are you sure you're all right?" If truth mattered, and tonight it did, his soul-searching eyes full of concern for her – just her – had boosted her morale.

Still curled on the floor, her head cushioned by her folded arms, she panicked when a knock sounded at her door. First, she wiped her face, using her sleeves to dry her cheeks. Stiff, exhausted, she rose and checked the peephole.

Chapter Twenty-nine

"Hi."

"Hi." Arlene didn't open the door completely. She stood, half hiding.

"Are you okay?" Michael paused, watching.

"Yes." She waited for him to say more while his all-seeing eyes were busy searching her face. His appraisal frightened her. Her earlier emotions curled up and slunk back into hidden areas in her heart from where, just minutes earlier, they'd escaped. Reclaiming her usual I-don't-give-a-shit attitude, she slouched against the door frame and folded her arms. "Why?"

"Because you have tear tracks on your face and you look like a soul who spent time in purgatory."

She flung away from him. Before she could slam the door in his face, he forced his way into the room. "I thought we'd gotten passed this bullshit. That we were friends."

"I don't need more friends. And I don't know what the shittin' hell you're talking about. Look, Michael, it's been a nasty day. I need to hit the sack." She gave him her back in a sarcastic dismissal and waited to hear the door close behind him. Still on the brink, she couldn't take much more.

Instead, she felt his big, gentle arms wrap around her, gathering her submissive body in close. His head snuggled beside hers as he crooned, "It's okay, baby. You don't have to be strong with me. Any woman alive would have reacted to what happened earlier, and honey, you're all woman."

The soft tone of his masculine voice, whispering to her, cajoling her, giving her permission to be human, worked the magic better than anything else could have done.

She slumped, and he caught her. The wail she couldn't stop started low and built until he cradled her in his arms like a baby, holding her as close as possible and all the while he rocked her back and forth. "Have at it, girl. Mikey's here to take care of you. You're safe with me."

***

"I'm sorry." Arlene forced him to release her so she could use the facilities to wash her face and try and make herself look less like a victim. Cold water and hot towels helped, as did the brush she'd bought earlier.

In the mirror, her long hair, dark and curling

from being braided, fell to her shoulders and clouded around her pale face. She peered into eyes still red-rimmed and slightly swollen. They looked better, kind of like she felt. Clearer, softer – untainted.

Shy now, she returned to the bedroom where he waited. "I'm sorry, Detective. I didn't know the trauma from earlier would hit me so hard."

"Detective? I call bullshit. My name is Michael, Mike or Mikey as my mom loves to use. I kinda think there was more involved than what occurred at Dani Andino's place, *Miss Montgomery*. But I won't intrude, digging isn't my style. Just know that one day you'll share your secrets with me. And it'll be because you'll want me to know as much about you as I hope you'll want to know about me.

"But... I can wait. In the meantime, I'm going to take you for dinner, hold your hand and get my goodnight kiss before we part. It'll be considered our first date. And... no matter how hard you try and lure me in to your room afterwards, it won't work. Smooching is where I stop until our next date."

Understanding she was being played, but kind of enjoying the light-hearted joker's way of teasing, she asked. "So... what happens then?"

"Oh, no, you don't! You'll have to come with me to find out."

Chapter
Thirty

Still on top of the world, Cassi headed to Rusty's after the four of them landed in Vegas. Even though she'd called him the day before from the hotel room to let him know she'd been away but was fine, she knew he wouldn't relax until he saw her in person.

Then she'd made an appointment to stop by later and see Maria. No doubt, the woman knew about Billy's death. But Cassi felt it imperative that she be the one to fill in the details. Right from the beginning, she'd gotten the impression that Maria had deep feelings for Billy. That their relationship hadn't just started after Billy's return to Las Vegas. Now that she'd discovered he'd been the founder of the *Armas* gang – the original brains – maybe she'd learn the truth about other things. Like who killed her brother.

She'd also called Sam. Since he hadn't answered,

she'd left a message. She'd have worried except Trace reassured her the night before that they'd been in communication with Sam and he was fine, back working at the club.

On their return trip, it became noticeable that the relationship between Arlene and Michael had changed. He treated her more like a girlfriend, kind of like the way Trace behaved with her. And Arlene, blushing slightly, allowed this familiarity and even seemed pleased from the attention.

At the airport, the girls had a few minutes to share when the men were about their business. Cassi had opened the conversation. "Arlene, I want to thank you for everything you did for me yesterday. I don't think I could have made it through the day without your help. The way you put those cops in their place and made them back off from grilling me, particularly those grueling moments after the shooting, well... I won't forget."

"You thanked me already. I'll tell you now what I told you then. You'd have done the same for me."

Arlene's eyes were kind and different – soft. Cass liked this new Arlene, trusted her.

"Cass, we need to talk soon. There're things I need to share. About my life and... well, secrets. It's important, but not here." Arlene held up her hand to stop Cassi from saying exactly what she had been about to say. "Soon, okay?"

"Sure. Once we're home, just let me know when and where."

Remembering the way Arlene had reached out for her hand and then clung, stunned Cass. Other than after a battle in the ring when emotions were high and crazy with excitement, or when they were in shock from events that would devastate anyone, Arlene had never voluntarily touched her.

Now, entering the gym, her thoughts turned to Rusty and the cross-examination she'd soon be getting from the man who meant more to her than her dad ever had. If the truth were told, she'd adored him all her life.

Glancing at one of the well-used benches against the wall he'd kept around after he'd had the place renovated, she recalled the day he'd told her and Raoul about their father's death. He'd led them to that same spot and made them sit.

Ever since she could remember, he'd been careful to show his respect for José, hadn't dwelled on his rotten behavior or focused on his many faults. In fact, Rusty had always stood up for the man, always made excuses, always tried to instill some sense of pride in them for their dad.

Protecting them as much as he could, he'd downplayed the circumstances of their father's demise. If she hadn't read the truth in one of the newspapers lying around the library one day, she might not have known that José had died in a bar fight. He'd broken a guy's arm only to have his friends jump into the brawl and one kick too many in the head had ended her father's life.

It was on that bench where she'd cried heartbrokenly in the arms of the two men who loved her most. Raoul's promise that he'd take care of her still rang in her head. Her brave twin, whose eyes, so like her own, had begged her to trust him. Not to worry.

And Rusty's gentle hand, patting her shoulder while he hugged them both and told them they still had him to come to anytime – for any reason. He'd taken care of it all. To this day, the funeral arrangements, the ceremony packed full of respectful mourners, in fact everything to do with her father's passing seemed unreal – dreamlike.

Except for the bench. It reminded her of how lucky they'd always been to have such a wonderful man in their lives. Supportive, loving and... as crusty as a giant, mooshy heart wrapped in a gruff exterior could be.

"Hey, brat! You daydreaming about sumpthin?"

"Just about how fortunate I am to have you in my life."

"Oh no – no, no, no. That's not gonna get you off the hot seat, little girl. No, ho. Not with me. And don't be blinking them globby blue persuaders at me either. You've got some explaining to do with ole Rusty."

Cassi laughed at the twinkle he couldn't hide from his one good eye and reached to hug him. Since he allowed the cuddle, she knew she'd slipped past yet one more crisis.

Now for the next one – *God, don't let him have a heart attack when she explained what happened yesterday.* Responsibility kicked in, and she accepted he needed to know about Billy – from her.

It took some time to get through her story, explain about Billy's involvement and skim over what actually happened. The reason for it taking so long was because Rusty didn't let her get away with the nonsense. He drilled her on everything she said.

"He shot at Trace? Billy Duran? He had a gun and shot at a cop."

"Yes. But Trace had entered the house from the back and startled Billy."

"So, he drew out his gun and tried to shoot him. Doesn't make any sense."

"He didn't actually draw the gun. He already had it aimed at Dani Andino, the person he'd come to threaten."

"The same person who was holding you hostage."

Cassi saw the cliff and rather than letting him maneuver her over it, she sidetracked. "Not quite. I – I never felt like I was in any danger, Rusty. Seriously. The only reason I went to her place was because, as you know, Detective McGuire had gone missing, and I thought Dani might be able to help with some information."

"Did she?"

"Did she what?"

"Know what had happened to McGuire?"

"No. He wouldn't tell me who kidnapped him. He escaped and came to find me. Arlene—"

"Arlene? Hold it! Our Arlene? Are you telling me she was involved too?"

Shit! Being truthful just seemed to get her into more trouble. Now what could she say?

"Ahhh... yes. Her brother Mani worked for Dani Andino. He was her second-in-command, and through him, Arlene happened to know where Dani lived. Problem was – she didn't know the actual address, so they brought her along to show them her house."

"Who're they?"

"Oh, Detective McGuire and his new partner, Detective Kowalski."

"Right. So, Billy had his gun on Dani and your Trace startled him and so Billy shot at him."

"Right."

"Then why isn't he wounded or dead?"

Oh,oh! Now things were getting squirrely. *Keep it short.* "Because Dani jumped in front to save him and took the bullet."

"Why in God's name would she have cared whether a cop she must have hated got shot?"

Aw, fuck!

She knew the minute it hit him by the stiffening in his frame and the cuss word he let loose under his breath. Hiding her eyes, looking everywhere but at him, she searched desperately for the answer that would detour him and satisfy his keen questioning.

"It all happened so fast."

"I'm calling bullshit, Cassidy Santino. She didn't jump in front of him. You did. Didn't you? And don't lie."

"I only wanted to push him out of the way."

"So, she actually saved you."

"I guess you could say that."

"Why?"

"In the end, we were friends." *Now she could open up.* Hopefully, if she kept talking, maybe he'd stop flaying her with a look that would have sent her running to hide when she was little. "Turns out, Dani had throat cancer and didn't have long to live. We talked before Billy and his sidekick surprised us. She was a sad, lonely, frightened woman, Rusty. Her story broke my heart."

"Looky here, brat, she was a gang-boss lesbian killer with the morals of an alley cat and a hunger for the crap they sell to the sorriest of the losers on the street. You think the boys around here don't talk? But she's dead and you're not, so for that I'll bless her every day."

Still raw from what had happened, Cassi hated to let him get away with that inadequate portrayal of the character called Dani Andino. There were numerous layers to the woman, and after listening to her story, Cassi had a pretty good idea of what had driven Dani to the life she'd chosen. One day, when her old friend wasn't so riled, she'd try to explain.

Unfortunately, like a runt in a litter, Rusty wouldn't give up that bone clamped in his jaws. "Okay, so Billy shoots at Detective McGuire, right?"

"Yes."

"What happened then?"

"In self-defence, the detective returned fire and Billy was killed."

"Good. Stupid bastard! Putting you in jeopardy like that."

"Rusty, you – of all people – are shocking me. Weren't you the one who taught me never to judge others? What was that old saying? Until you walk a mile in their moccasins... wasn't that it?"

Still scrunching the tuke he'd pulled off his head earlier, Rusty gave her the evil eye and snorted. "Billy has been playing different roles most of his life, young lady. I tried to tell your old man he wasn't worth the effort, but José wouldn't listen, wanted to give the kid a chance."

"He wasn't all bad, Rusty. You know that."

"Listen to me, monkey. Anyone who shoots at my girl, ain't gonna get a kind word from me." Before she could retaliate, his hand jabbed the air near her chest. "And don't try pulling any baloney on me about you not being in danger from the little jerk. He was always about number one. So, I won't hear it."

"Fine. We won't talk about him anymore." Breathing a sigh of relief, Cassi was glad to be off the hot seat. She'd confessed to herself the night before at the hotel that the disappointment called Billy Duran would always haunt her. What a waste! Why he'd turned from making a living legally as an upstanding attorney – and there was no question about his qualifications – to choosing the illegal life of a criminal, she didn't even want to explore.

"With him gone, who's going to take on the Angel of Death case the papers and TV are so full of?"

Oh, God! She'd forgotten about poor Mary. Without the silver tongue of Billy Duran, the woman's best defensive ploy was gone.

Chapter
Thirty-one

Once she left the gym, Cassi's relief at having settled things with Rusty filled her to bursting. The man hadn't let her get away with anything.

She chuckled, then stopped her car in the parking lot near the lawyer's office. Since she was a bit early, she sat in the Mustang and checked her e-mails.

A text had arrived from Trace, which she read first. His loving message and goofy countdown timer showing how many hours and minutes they had before he'd be arriving at her place made her smile first and then grimace. She'd intended to go into work tonight and by his count, that wasn't happening.

Figuring if she played her cards right, maybe she could still use the blackmail she'd hoped to get off her hidden camera. That's if Rodrigo even had the name of the woman who'd been there the night they'd killed Raoul.

She realized Trace believed that she'd stop her quest now that Dani had died, but she'd believed Dani when she'd said she hadn't been there. Which meant it was another female. Whether Dani knew her name and refused to reveal it was a totally different matter.

Scrolling through the rest of her various e-mails, she didn't see the man approach her car until he tapped at the window on the passenger side, demanding entrance.

"Sergio. Am I glad to see you."

He seemed taken aback by her enthusiastic greeting. "Why're you so surprised?"

"I overheard Detective McGuire and his partner discussing some of the action that took place in the city over the last few days. Seems they made a lot of arrests, took a number of the boys to the hospital and shut down some of the hot spots in town."

"That's what you heard, and you figured I'd be involved."

"Worried would be more correct."

"You'd worry about me? Sergio Mandala, a street bum and criminal?"

"Stop, Sergio. Stop trying to put words in my mouth. I was concerned for a friend."

"I get it. Your blabber-mouthed boyfriend told you."

Innocent, yet highly intrigued, she shrugged and held her hands up. "*Oye, mi amigo*, I swear your name never came up. What is it you're not telling me?"

"*Nada.* I have nothing to say. I'm here to get the real truth about Andino and who shot her."

"Billy Duran did."

"Yeah! True? He shot the bitch? I knew there'd be a showdown."

Cassi stared at him and waited for him to see she intended to get his attention. "There was no bitch at the party, Sergio, just a woman with throat cancer facing a miserable future who died while saving my life. So, you can't talk shit about her – not around me anyway."

"S'truth?"

"Honest to God!"

"Whoa! Who plugged Billy?"

"Detective McGuire."

"That's it? That's all you gotta say?"

"No, I want to add that if Trace hadn't arrived when he did, I don't know what would have happened. Billy had come to even some old score with Dani. It was obvious he meant to harm her. He just hadn't counted on me being there."

"I'd liked to have seen his face."

"It was a nightmare, Sergio. Billy had a grudge against Dani, and he meant to take back control of the *Armas.*"

"Then there would have been a real war. What passed the last few days was a small skirmish, honey. Believe me." He started to open his door and Cassi stopped him. "Sergio, I have no idea why I need to say this, but it feels right to thank you."

"Yeah, whatever. Stay safe, girlfriend." He jerked away from her hand and opened the door, then before he slid completely out of the seat, he stopped, his face still turned away. Whispered words were cut off. "If only—" He swore softly, then slammed his way out of the car.

The Hummer pulled alongside and a couple of blinks later it peeled away. She leaned back against the headrest and took a few seconds to go over their conversation.

Stirred, emotional, her heart still beating fast, she knew Sergio cared for her and not like a brother. No woman could have failed to notice his behavior for anything but a man who had feelings that he'd suppressed.

Her respect for her brother's old friend rose to new heights. She had no idea how often she'd be able to see him in the future, but she knew one thing for sure. His number would get used from time to time no matter what Trace might say.

Shaking off her melancholy, she stepped into the law office where Gladys, dyed-blonde hair puffed and sprayed not to move, arranged around a face full of misery, greeted her.

"Mr. Duran is dead. The office is closed."

"The door was open."

"Miss Delgado must have forgotten to lock it when she arrived. She's not seeing anyone today."

"Look, Gladys. I'm really sorry about Billy's death; you must know we were friends. But I do have an appointment with Maria. May I go straight in?"

Begrudgingly, Gladys stared at Cassi over her glasses, her eyes drilled holes in Cassi's composure. Before she could refuse, and Cassi had no doubt she was tempted, Maria yelled out. "Quit being so bitchy, Gladys. Let her in here. I have a few choice words I want to say to Cassi Santino."

Chapter
Thirty-two

Trace felt good returning to the office he'd wondered if he'd ever see again. With affection, he gazed at the squeaky chair, chuckled at the desk drawer that wouldn't stay closed and felt a ridiculous sense of nostalgia for the pile of papers he needed to file.

His mood lighter than it had been in a long while, he went for coffee and winked at Mike as he passed his desk.

Though he hadn't actually brought up the point of Cassi's future when at the hotel, he'd taken for granted that she would finally let go of her quest and they could move on. He actually whistled until he heard his name bellowed in Hank Lester's rough voice.

"McGuire, I need you."

Dammit! I knew this was too good to be true. He saw Mike's shrug, but he also saw a strange grin the other man didn't bother to hide. Then he looked around and noticed not one other person in the office would meet his eye. *What the hell?*

He stepped into the room he most detested in the building, the office that had a big hot seat smack dab in front of the large desk near the window. The same place where he'd been reprimanded more times than he wanted to think about. He hovered in the doorway, muscles contracting, an acid explosion in his stomach.

"Yeah, boss?"

"Sit."

Christ! How had a man of so few words made it as far as Chief of Detectives? He sat. Put his coffee on the desk in front of him, crossed his arms and waited. He wasn't gonna give this prick the satisfaction of seeing him nervous.

"You okay?" Lester looked at him from under his bushy gray eyebrows, his expression serious.

What? "Yeah, I'm good."

"I heard you rented a helicopter to get to L.A."

"I did. My choice, my charge."

"Don't be a bigger dick than necessary. You submit the requisition, got it?"

"Yes, sir."

"The chopper delivered you in time to stop Duran from succeeding in his revenge, right?"

"Except, we didn't stop him. He shot Andino."

"I know, and you retaliated."

Stiffly, Trace pointed out. "Had no choice."

"Don't go getting all hot-headed and defensive. I read the police reports and Internal Affairs will come up with the same conclusions. It was a righteous kill, never had any doubt."

Unwinding, Trace slouched back in his chair, crossed one leg over the other and relaxed his arms. He took a sip of the hot coffee and the tar-like-shit slid down his tight throat to join with the other explosives being detonated.

Lester picked up his pen, and, as was his habit, started tapping it on the desk in front of him. "You know my plans to step down in the next few weeks, right?"

"Yes, sir."

"I've been asked to name my predecessor and after discussing my choice with the rest of the staff, I've come up with a name."

"Okay." Trace wished he'd get this over with. He had so many things to take care of and the dithering going on tended to drive him into imagining his hands placing duct tape over his boss's mouth. While this vision played out, he missed whatever Lester said next.

"So, what do you think?"

Forced to admit he hadn't heard, knowing the other man expected a reply, he said, "Excuse me?"

"Aha! I thought you'd be shocked, but I hope you're pleased too. Look, Trace. You're a good cop. Okay, my best. You work your ass off for this department, put in a lot of hours, and don't think it hasn't been noticed. Over the years, you've been my most reliable detective and you and your partners have closed more files than anyone else. You're a natural to take on this position. I've groomed you without you even being aware."

Stunned, his mouth dry, shock rioted through Trace's system. A million questions blared in his head and yet not one seemed adequate. Even though Michael had hinted at this happening a while back, he'd never expected to be the chosen one.

After all, there were others with more experience who'd been there longer. Finally, he asked what he most needed to know. "Why me, boss? I'm not the highest in seniority. There're at least two I can think of and maybe more."

"Yeah, we know. And we discussed this appointment with them. But we're all in agreement. Since you have more knowledge of today's technology than any of the others and are comfortable with all aspects of the computer age each department has to deal with, you'll slide into the slot with very little training needed.

"Trust me; those old dogs know it, too. And they're comfortable working out their time till they get pensioned off without the stress I've been under the last few years. It's all gotten above me, McGuire. I'm a good cop; know my men and I give a shit. But between the harping of the mayor and the media riding my ass, my last day can't come fast enough."

Trace couldn't believe this talkative guy could be the same jerk who'd seemed to find fault and had expected better of him for years. The softening in Hank's eyes allowed him to see the man behind the title.

Looking closer, he noticed the tired lines grooved in the other man's face and the age spots decorating his hands. Overweight, gray haired, grumpy, and just a little burned out, Hank Lester had covered his ass many times since he'd started working for him. After he'd reamed him out, of course. Affection for the boss crept out from where it lay buried for years.

"Not sure I can do the job as well as you, sir. And I mean that sincerely. If you think I'm your man, then I guess I'm your man. So's you know – it won't be the same without you."

Lester leaned back in his chair, relaxed now that Trace had all but accepted the position. "That's what I've been trying to tell you, Trace. It can't be the same. Times have changed. Everything is moving so fast, an old fart like me hasn't a chance to keep up – hell, truthfully, I never got past the first few levels and a man can only fake it so far. But you – this is your world. You understand the technology, how all that freakin' Wi-Fi, internet and Bluetooth crap works."

"Not all..."

"A hell of a lot more than I do. And you can take

advantage of those classes they offer to keep you up to date. Me and the wife, we're heading to Florida where we'll buy us a nice little bungalow near her sisters'. She can play cards and do her yoga shit and I'm going to read all the books I've collected and never had the time to enjoy."

Chapter
Thirty-three

A tide of misgivings washed over Cassi as she stepped into Billy's office. The room looked like the aftermath of a wild tornado. Files exploding onto the floor, tables full of open books stacked on top of each other, yellow and white tablets everywhere while individual sheets, torn from the pads had been scrunched, thrown and missed the wastebaskets.

"Oh my God!"

She'd seen this office looking as if a windstorm had blasted through before, but today, the emptiness made her feel sad and abandoned as if it took the presence of the man to stir the energy.

Maria came to the connecting doorway from her office in time to see Cassi's shock. "Yeah, I know. This is how the genius, otherwise known as Billy Duran, worked. I almost walked out when I arrived this morning."

Cassi switched her gaze to the other woman. She looked pale – terribly pale.

And shaky.

And unapproachable.

Cassi sensed a distance between them that hadn't been there before. Contempt radiated in waves from the woman opposite her. Standing with her arms crossed and her brown eyes hard, full of fury, she stared at Cassi. No... she sneered at Cassi.

Oh, oh!

Searching for just the right words to describe her jumbled emotions, nothing came except the bare, unvarnished truth. "I'm so sorry, Maria. I know you cared for Billy, too."

"And he only cared for you."

Stunned, Cassi stiffened. "That's not true." Even as she said the words, she remembered one of their last times together as they'd walked to the restaurant down the street. She shrugged the uncomfortable moment away. "Not on my part. He was like a brother to me."

"Blind little Cassi, I get it. Whenever you were near, the man's heart glowed in those big green bedroom eyes he used as weapons to suck in every woman around him. Yet, you blew him off like his feelings didn't matter. I'm not a complete idiot."

"Okay, then what do you want me to say? That I'm sorry he's dead? Can't do that! He came looking for trouble, shot a friend of mine and was aiming for the man I love." Cassi lowered her voice from yelling to less strong.

She watched as the shock Maria couldn't hide, wore down her defenses. "Am I glad he's gone? Of course not! I'm just so fucking sorry he came looking for trouble in the first place. If he had waited just a few weeks, Dani Andino would have died from natural causes – she had throat cancer and only a few weeks to live."

"What?" Maria's face crumpled. She looked as if her inner circuits had gotten a surge of electricity and overloaded. Turning, her shoulders slumped, she took tiny, shuffling steps into her neater office, heading for her office chair. Cassi followed.

Weakened from the outpouring of her reaction, Cassi dropped down where visitors sat by the desk and rubbed her thighs. She breathed in a lungful of air and finally added, "You can blame me if it makes you feel better, but I wasn't the one who filled him with vengeance and told him to bring a gun to Dani's with killing her on his mind. That freak was a complete stranger to me – a scary, horrifying man with no soul."

"No. That would be me."

Silence reigned. A silence full of screamed questions Cassi didn't voice. Instead, she waited.

"I told him where he could find Dani. He'd gone looking for her at the Lipstick Club and found the place deserted. He became incensed, wanting to end the war, take his rightful place as the boss. A friend of mine knew she'd returned to Los Angeles so I passed on the information."

"A friend. You mean Sergio Mandala."

Maria finally allowed a reaction to break through her monotone. She scrunched the material of her navy suit skirt. Her eyes flashed with horror. "How did you know?"

"I saw his number on your phone. He'd given me that same number after Raoul died. They were friends from when they were younger, before all the gang stuff."

"Why didn't you question me about it?"

"None of my business."

Maria seemed to be weighing her next words, and finally, with a shake of her head, she voiced them. "What else do you know?"

"That you and Sergio have a business relationship that includes your brother."

Maria interlocked her fingers and leaned forward to rest them on her desk. "Unknown to Billy, my brother dealt with Sergio for years. When Drew knew I was moving to Vegas, he told Sergio he was to call me periodically to see if I needed anything. It wasn't business."

"Okay, I accept that. Yet you said nothing to Billy about this, or did you?"

"Keep in mind that I didn't want Billy to get involved in the *Armas* shit again, so no, I never told him I was in contact with Sergio. I hated that whole side of Billy, the mob, all of it."

"I feel the same. That shit has nothing to do with me either. All I want to find out is who killed my brother, Raoul."

Maria searched Cassi's features, her eyes like a drill boring through concrete. Convinced, she relaxed and added, "Billy tried to find that out too. Yet with all his connections, he never did learn the truth. Drove him crazy."

Emptied of the earlier irritation, Cassi only felt curiosity. "Do you mind me asking how you and Billy came to know each other?"

Maria stared at Cassi and seemed to relax after their eyes met. Cassi didn't flinch or turn away – a woman with no guilt, only concern.

"We met at law school, years ago. I fell for him so hard that he upended my whole life. It was because of Billy that I became aware of my older brother's real occupation, not as the entrepreneur businessman I'd always believed him to be, but a billionaire shipping magnate who had ties with the mafia and organized crime."

"How did Billy know?"

"He never revealed his sources, but he knew. And he played me like a harp, soft and sweet, to get close to my brother, Drew."

"Was that how he came to set up the *Armas*? With your brother's help and a steady shipment of drugs to depend on?"

"In the beginning, probably. Billy had a gift – the ability to negotiate and get people to trust him.

Truthfully, they kept me out of it. From conversations I overheard, I gleaned some information but kept it to myself."

"Were you still with Billy when he moved back to Las Vegas?"

"No. He'd dumped me after his operation became big. He still worked as a lawyer, but his clients had become even too sleazy for me to accept. Then I found out about Dani, that he was carrying on with her. I was horrified that he could want someone like her over me. We had a fight and I accused him of using me because of my brother."

"That must have hurt." Cass sat forward, her eyes full of sympathy.

"He didn't deny it." Maria wiped away fresh tears and then leaned her head against the high-back, black leather chair. "He said he'd fallen for Dani because with her, he never had to play a role. Then he walked out. I didn't see him for some time."

"Until he called you from the rehab clinic."

Maria's gaze swiveled to where Cassi watched her. "How did you know?"

"I paid the bills. They sent me a breakdown of his purchases, everything had been monitored. Since patients weren't allowed cell phones, they'd added copies of his telephone call list and the charges."

"Ah! So, you were aware we'd been in contact."

"I knew. They recorded his visitors, too."

Maria nodded. "We talked – a lot. He'd cleaned up, became sincere in his regrets, or so he told me, begging me to believe him. Even offered to leave L.A. behind and start small in his home town. Promised we'd set up a law office together and work like we used to dream about."

"In Las Vegas."

"My consent was based on one condition; we'd keep it platonic until I felt ready to get back into a relationship with him."

"He agreed?"

"Of course, he needed me. I can see that now. So, I went ahead and found the position for us with Sampson and Little. They were thrilled to hire two good lawyers at the same time and it helped that they owed my brother a favor he'd done for Mr. Sampson years earlier."

"When did you realize Dani had moved the gang here, too?"

"Not until I saw her at your boxing match with Ariana Swift. Then Billy came clean and told me he needed revenge and why. That she'd killed your brother, a man he cared about deeply. He shared the story about how he'd stayed with you many nights as a younger man and how you treated him like one of the family. I believed him. In fact, of all his many lies, both in the past and recently, I knew he was honest about those sentiments. His love for y-your family was probably the only decent thing about him."

Nervous to cross over that particular line again, yet knowing the truth had to be revealed, Cassi quickly added, "It's true that he spent a lot of time with Raoul, going to the pubs – hanging with the guys. Ray bragged about Billy, about his smarts and his ambitions, to anyone who'd listen."

"Billy told me, said he'd never appreciated how much it meant to him. It wasn't until he'd hit the skids and climbed his way out that he saw those occasions more clearly. He cared about Raoul a lot."

"So, you believe his revenge on Dani – his plan to kill her in cold blood – was because of Raoul?"

"No doubt, that was a part of why he did what he did. Don't you believe it?"

"Not even a little. He wanted to kill the bitch – his words, not mine – because he believed she'd facilitated his decent into hell by feeding him powerful drugs to get him hooked. Then she stole his position and left him lying in the gutter."

Cassi watched to see how the truth, as she knew it, affected Maria. If she'd kick her out so she could retain her rose-colored dreams about the multi-faceted personality of the strange creature they both knew called Billy Duran.

While Maria took her time, her expressionless face solid in its refusal to hint at her feelings, Cassi skimmed quickly over the conversation she'd heard after Billy had broken into Dani's house. The bizarre moment when she'd met the real Billy and learned the truth of how low he'd sunk.

She believed Dani when she'd admitted to her love for him and that she'd tried to help him get clean only to have gotten ridiculed for her efforts. She remembered her last sight of him, hate written all over his features and his intentions to kill clear.

Maria's voice had lost its usual vigor. She spoke low, almost in a whisper. "What do you want from me now, Cassi?"

Phew! This was a good sign. "First, I came to say I'm sorry. I knew Billy meant a lot to you. I'm also here because of Mary Devin. She needs you now, and I hoped you'd see your way to continue with her case."

Before Maria answered her request, Cassi's phone rang, and she saw Arlene's name showing on her call display.

"Arlene, can you hold for a few seconds. I'm just leaving the law office." Without waiting for an answer, she lowered the phone and stood.

"Maria? Will you take over Mary's case? I know Billy put in a lot of time on her behalf. I truly believe he cared about the outcome."

"Or the challenge..."

"Whatever. I care about the woman."

"Me, too. Yeah, I'll continue if you're sure it's what she'd want."

"Thank you. I'll call you later. And remember, I'm here to help if you need me."

Maria's face crumpled. Tears slid free and she

caught her breath. "Just give me a few days. Then come back, and we'll brainstorm. Right now, I need to collect and organize those endless pieces of paper with Billy's notes so I can follow where that devious mind of his meant to take this."

Cassi held her hand over her heart. "Thank you." Then she left the office, nodded to Gladys, whose lip quivered before she turned away, and finally answered the call.

"Hey, Arlene."

"Cassi, can you come to my aunt's place as soon as possible? We have a problem."

Sensing she needed to move and not take time for questions, she replied, "I'm on my way to the car. Message me the address, and I'll be there as soon as I can get through traffic."

Once she added the info to her GPS, turns out the older white home surrounded by lovely gardens was close by. Not ten minutes later, she rang the bell, only to have the glass-paneled door flung open and Arlene push her back so she could join her on the outside steps.

"What's up?" Cassi watched Arlene's expression change from feigned politeness to downright mean. Her beautiful, deep-set brown eyes, oddly familiar, were full of scorn. "That bastard has to pay."

"Oh...kay. Lemme at him." Cassi grinned her joke but sensed immediately that Arlene found no humor in the situation. Weirded out, Cassi became serious. "What's going on?"

"Faith was working for that father whose baby had no mom. You know, as a nanny."

"Sure. She was ecstatic."

"He fired her."

"Seriously? Aw, fuck!"

"That's what I said. Hell, even my aunt said it. But not Faith – oh no, not our Sunshine. She's taking it like she deserves to be shit on. Like he had every right to break her heart and then trample it until she can hardly breathe. The bastard!"

"It's about her earlier career."

"That's what she said. Someone recognized her when she went to meet him at the casino and approached with an offer to party for the night. Steven overheard and punched the guy, had him thrown from the Mirage. Then he questioned her."

"And she admitted everything."

"Of course." Arlene threw her hands in the air. "You should have been here earlier when she arrived. It was pitiful." Arlene grabbed her hips as if she needed to keep from hitting something. "You knew Faith and the baby hung with my aunt while I went to L.A. with the guys. You did, didn't you? Yeah, I told you. Whatever..." Jabbering, pacing in circles, she continued, "When we decided to stay the night, I phoned and begged her not to leave my aunt alone. Barbara's done so well keeping away from the wine bottle, and I was scared for her to be left by herself in the empty house full of ghosts and temptation."

"She agreed."

"What do you think? You know Faith. Anyway, she called Steven and asked if it was okay to keep the baby with her. I guess he gave her permission and all was well. When I got home earlier, they were happily headed to meet him at the casino for lunch."

"Where she got approached."

"That part's kind of vague. She said she went to his office." Arlene's forehead wrinkled, her eyes held questions and she bit her lip, looking the picture of a woman who was totally confused. "I'm not really sure of the sequence of events at this point. She left with him to go to the restaurant, but I don't think she had Raoul. Except I have no idea what she did with the baby."

"Ar-lene." The message was clear – get on with it.

Flapping her hands irritably, Arlene continued. "Anyway, when Steven turned his back for a few seconds to answer his phone, the asshole waylaid her, and you know the rest."

"Thank goodness she came back here."

"I know. I thought the same thing. From what I understand, when they first set her up as Raoul's nanny, he'd talked her into moving from her old place and giving it up. So, most of her things were at the new apartment. Guess she had nowhere else to go."

Cassi leaned against the pillar by the front door and crossed her arms, her heart breaking for the friend whose last image had been a woman with stars in her eyes and a smile so wide, one couldn't help but feel their hearts lift and smile back.

"God, Arlene. This can't be allowed. She'll fall apart. I mean, she was devastated after Raoul died. We both know she turned to drugs with full intentions of never surfacing again. To lose the second Raoul, the little baby who loves her so much, that will surely kill her."

Arlene's pity turned to anger. "I want to slug that guy so bad, I'm shaking."

Cassi checked, and sure enough, Arlene's whole body shook. "We can't stand by and let him get away with it. At least, I can't. I'm going to find out his schedule, what time he gets home or when he'd be likely to return to the baby's place, and I'll be waiting for him. That prick's going to get a piece of my mind."

"Count me in," Arlene said.

"Only if you promise not to punch his lights out."

"Can't do that."

"Arlene?"

"Fine, I promise – as long as he doesn't push too many buttons."

Chapter Thirty-four

Michael and Trace took care that no one would see them enter the trailer park. They'd even parked their vehicle a few blocks from the place and divested themselves of their suit jackets and ties, changing into the golf shirts Trace had in his golf bag in the back.

"Hey, how come you get the pretty blue one?"

"'Cause it matches my pretty eyes. And... because it's mine."

"So! I hate red."

"I can see why. It kind of clashes with your bloodshot eyes."

"Prick. You got to sleep in the hotel bed with your girl last night, and I got to do all the paperwork, take a cold shower at the L.A. precinct and try to sleep on the office bench using my jacket for a pillow."

"Don't talk smack, whiny. It doesn't become a

macho man to act like a cranky baby."

"So, now I'm macho?"

"I called you a whiny baby, too. Okay, it's this way." Trace strutted along the lane and turned in at the third trailer where he banged on the door and waited.

As soon as it opened, he and Michael slipped inside. "Hey, man, I need an update."

Sam strode into the tidy kitchen area and returned with three beer bottles and handed them out. When he saw the others hesitate, he added, "They're non-alcoholic but they're cold and better than nothing. Mine's regular." The devil grinned, straddled the tall barstool, twisted the top off his and took a long slug. "What's up?"

"The conference call didn't exactly describe the steps your boys were taking to get Drew Delgado behind bars. I expected to see breaking news on CNN and headlines in the L.A. Times."

"Yeah, well after Andino got shot and Billy too, someone tipped him off and Drew got cold feet. He slipped away in his private jet – we figure heading to China. According to the coded files I lifted from Dani's computer, he's got a lot of contacts there who'll offer him protection while we're left sitting here, whistling Dixie."

"That's a bummer. Did you at least close down his operation?"

"Sure, took out most of the bigger gangs around California. The smaller groups like Mandala's *Los*

Soldados are safe for now. We can control them; in fact, they work with us. We all know the drugs will find their way to the streets, but it's better to have dealers willing to operate with law enforcement to a certain extent than those crazy vigilantes who believe they're all-powerful and can do whatever the hell they want."

Trace had to ask. "What about the Lipstick Club?"

"Turns out, the business is listed under Rodrigo Muñoz. He's the legal owner and has no intentions of shutting it down."

"You mean he's going to run the gang himself, take over from where Dani left off?"

"Beats me." Sam shook his head and took another drink from his half-empty bottle. "My belief is that he's scared of Pete and taking orders as if Dani were still around."

"Shit! I'd hoped that with all the recent violence, someone had taken out that mean bastard and the gang disbanded."

"Rumor has it that a lot of the guys did take off, but Pete's got pull with the more hardened pricks. I'll find out more tonight at work."

Trace stiffened. "You're still working? Has Cassi mentioned anything to you about whether she intended to go back there?"

Sam stopped dead and then scratched his scruffy beard. "I guess you still don't know about what she did in the basement of the club on the night you were shot? Remember when she caught me telling tales at the hospital? I didn't get to share everything."

Trace's heart dropped, and his recently calm stomach flared up. "I can't take much more of this shit, man. I gotta tell you." He rubbed the painful area and put down the beer.

Michael, who'd been quiet till now, spoke up. "How about we shut the place down? That'll be the end of her job."

Trace answered, "Wish it was that simple. She won't give up until she knows what happened to her brother."

Sam interrupted, "And that's what I need to tell you about. Our girl hasn't been waiting for the cops to yank the rabbit out of the hat. She's pulled another trick of her own." Sam proceeded to detail the events of the night she hid the camera, taking care to leave out the battle with the two losers.

At the end, he added. "She might just have enough evidence to make things happen with Muñoz. He's the typical kind of slug who'll sing like a canary if it benefits him. We'll even go as far as offering him witness protection if he'll finger Pete for anything we can jail him on, and most importantly – if he reveals the person who killed Raoul."

"When will you retrieve the camera?"

"I'm hoping the boys will be partying tonight. Remember at the last warehouse takedown, Pete drove off with one of the trucks? It held a shipment for the streets and they've distributed most of it. I'm thinking they should have a good deal of money to count, and hopefully, there'll be flapping lips along with busy fingers."

"And Cassi?"

"She didn't tell you? She's scheduled to come in at nine."

Chapter Thirty-five

"Hi, Faith." After calming Arlene down, Cassi entered the house and slowly approached the disheveled young woman nestled into the corner of the couch. The sadness in her expression tore at Cassi's soft side, ripping her heart to shreds. If lying beside her and crying with her would do any good, Cassi would have done so in an instant. Except, she was smart enough to understand that it really wouldn't help.

Faith's blonde hair, usually worn down over her shoulders, thick waves framing her lovely face, had been scraped into a ponytail so tight that one wondered if the maker hadn't wanted to inflict pain.

Free of the surrounding golden halo and makeup-less, her face appeared young... so freakin' young. Like that of a teenager.

Freckles decorated her small nose, and her lips

without their customary bright red covering made one see the vulnerability of this small person. Instantly, Cassi's sympathy took over, making it hard for her to meet the other girl's heartbroken gaze.

Arlene's aunt Barbara sat beside the distraught girl, patting and rubbing her covered feet as if just by touching her, she could ease her obvious pain.

"Hi, Cassi. Arlene told you that I've lost baby Raoul, didn't she?" Faith's face began to crumple, and she used the wad of tissues in her fist to swipe at her reddened, swollen eyes. "See, you were right. I should have told him before I took the job."

"You were scared. It's understandable."

"Not to him. He called me a liar."

"You didn't lie."

"Maybe not in so many words. What I hate myself for – what makes me cringe – is that I was too much of a miserable coward to tell the truth. How disgusting is that?"

"Aww, sugar, I've done the same thing many times, especially lately."

"No!" Faith would have none of that. "You'd have told him and then dared him to use it against you." She switched her glance to Arlene. "You, too. But me, scared-stupid whore that I am, didn't have the guts. Really, I have no right to be in charge of such a beautiful little spirit like Raoul's. God knew better, and he's made his wishes clear."

Cassi slid onto the floor beside her, reaching to

caress her cheeks and lean her forehead against the other girl's. Arlene nestled as near as she could on the arm of the sofa. She took Faith's hand in hers and held tightly.

Barbara still rubbed Faith's leg. When she spoke, her tone made one aware that she would tolerate no argument. "Honey, you're a lovely person, soft-hearted and kind. You told me about how you started on the streets, because of your mother – to protect her. And look how you came to take care of a silly old lady when a friend asked. Please, don't talk foolish."

Arlene spoke up next. "You saved me from getting raped by a monster and used your body to do that. You took the bruises and lived the nightmare for me. Do you think I'd ever forget?"

Next, Cassi gently but firmly took Faith's chin so she couldn't look away. "My brother loved you, Faith. He saw the real you and gave you his heart. This isn't God's plan, Faith. He'd never be this cruel."

Faith's tears flowed, pouring from her pale blue eyes. "He is to me. That's what I've been trying to tell you all. He's taken away everyone I've ever loved. He wants me to suffer." She closed her eyes, laid her head down and begged, "Can I sleep now?"

***

"You sure he's here?"

Cassi parked near the building where she knew Faith had been staying with her charge. She turned off the ignition and paid attention to the fidgeter in the passenger seat. "Hell, that's what his assistant at the Mirage said. *He's not at the hotel at the moment. You will need to contact him at his office in the morning.*"

"I guess it kind of makes sense he'd take Raoul home where all the baby shit is, right?"

"That's what I figured too. Let's go."

They both stepped out of Cassi's Mustang and headed for the front door. A pad of buttons faced them, and they had no idea which one would take them to Steven Corella. Soon as they began checking, Cassi pointed to a neatly printed tag showing *F. Whitely,* and they had their apartment.

Before Cassi could push the right one, Arlene grabbed her arm. "We're not going to hit him, right? Just talk."

"Right."

"You do the talking then, 'cause I want to pound the living shit out of the idiot so bad, I only hope I can keep my cool."

"Arlene, think of Faith. We're not here to make things worse for her. We just want to tell him some truths he needs to know. Then the decision has to be his."

"Right! His. Shit, shit, SHIT!" Arlene cradled her fist in her other palm.

Before Cassi could react, the front entry of the apartment building opened and a disgruntled couple appeared, the angry man wearing a frown and the woman trying to placate. "Babies cry, John. It's what they do."

"Not for three hours. That kid is either sick or hungry. Hell, I don't know."

"Well, you didn't need to go and bang on the guy's door and make such a fuss. The poor father promised he'd tried giving the baby milk. You saw he had the bottle in his hand, right?"

Faith and Cassi stood back and listened until the others were too far away for them to hear their argument.

Arlene wore a nasty grin. "Looks like Raoul misses his Sunshine."

Droll, her heart uplifted somewhat, Cassi answered, "Looks like."

They'd grabbed the handle of the slow-closing entrance door just in time before the lock clicked and headed to the second floor. As they reached the landing, they heard the wails of a very cranky baby.

Cassi knocked, and they waited.

The door flung open to reveal a distraught, good-looking Latino male wearing spit-up and rage. The screaming baby on his shoulder wore only a diaper slipping precariously, and his tiny arms flailed in every direction like a puppet whose strings were being pulled randomly without rhyme or reason.

Steven's flattened black hair and undone shirt told its own story, as did the bare feet and slumped shoulders. "I'm sorry he's annoying you, but the kid won't stop crying. I've done everything I know." The door started to shut, and Cassi moved quickly to use her foot as a doorstop.

"We're not here to complain. We're friends of Faith's."

Steven's disgruntlement turned into total rejection. Again, he tried to shut the door.

Arlene, her anger apparent, shouted over Raoul's roar, "He wouldn't be so friggin' pissed off at you if she was here right now where she belongs, looking after him."

Steven gave up on the door and reached for the bottle sticking out of his pocket. When he held it against the baby's mouth to tempt, the volume turned up even more.

"Oh, for heaven's sake! Give him to me." Cassi reached for the baby and very gently she held him against her chest, rocking and making the shushing, loving noises that come to most women instinctively.

Exhausted, being tricked by the feminine sounds, Raoul's screaming lessened to wails and then simply to occasional bursts where he seemed to remember he had a legitimate complaint but couldn't quite dig up the same effort to let everyone hear about it.

"God, thank you." Holding his head in his hands, his daddy dropped to the sofa and then leaned back. The man's patience had been drained and every second of the marathon showed in his beaten expression. "He wouldn't stop crying. No matter what I did. He should be hungry, but he refuses his bottle. Faith fed him and had him sleeping before we went for lunch, but he hasn't closed his eyes since then."

"Because you kicked her out." Arlene couldn't stand tippy-toeing around the elephant in the room.

Steven shot to his feet, his hands on his hips and his face mirroring his feeling of shock. "Easy for you to say. How can a father who cares about his son accept not only a liar but a lying sex worker as a nanny?"

"You bastard!" Arlene stepped into his space, shooting him flares of hate.

"Arlene!" Cassi's tone brooked no nonsense. "Stand down." She lowered the now sleeping Raoul into his cradle and wheeled it to sit around the corner in the hallway.

Sauntering back toward the other two, she spoke. "Look at it this way, Mr. Corella. Raoul will have to face the fact one day that his prick of a father put his mean, small-minded principles ahead of his son's happiness and wellbeing." Cassi tipped her head, her hair falling back leaving her expressive eyes now visible. "We all know your son loves Faith and he needs her. What you maybe don't know is how much she needs him."

Steven, a man who controlled hundreds of

employees, was nobody's fool, nor could he be intimidated easily. "Look! Faith seemed too good to be true when I first met her. I should have known that with my luck in women, it would turn out to be that way. She's lived in a world, done things I-I can't accept."

"But then it's not about you, is it? It's about your tiny son who appears heartbroken that you've taken away from him the one person he's bonded with, the woman he senses who loves him so much that she soothes whatever pain he feels that makes him cry so heartbrokenly. Can you live with yourself if you do this to him?"

Arlene, seeming cooler now, added her own words, and the calm way she voiced them left no one in doubt as to their sincerity. "Sunshine has the most beautiful spirit of anyone I know. She's gentle and caring. She saved my life once, and she's given so much to help others, you have no idea. It's your son's loss if you walk away from her, man. Your baby's fucking loss."

Her finger had poked his chest twice before Cassi gently pulled her back and added, "Faith didn't choose to do that kind of work, circumstances forced her into it. Get her to tell you about her mother sometime before you judge her."

Steven's trembling fingers rubbed his eyes so hard the skin around them turned bright red. He stood alone, a picture of a stubborn man now indecisive... hurting.

Cassi took Arlene's arm and led her to the door. She stopped to leave her parting remark. "You have her number."

Then they left.

Chapter Thirty-six

Arlene sat quietly next to Cassi while they headed back to her aunt's place. The creep boss at Arlene's cleaning job had fired her when she'd injured her hand, so she was in no hurry to be anywhere.

After her uncle passed on, she'd agreed to move back into her old room and stay with Barbara for a short time and her living there now had become a blessing. With all that had happened lately, her uncle dying and Barbara's breakdown, her aunt needed her, and now Faith had a place to be.

Days ago, she'd called Rusty and explained her hand still had some swelling, and he'd given her a few days respite from training as long as she'd promised to exercise her body and keep up as best she could without the actual gym equipment.

Deep in her head, her thoughts spun in circles around the inevitable confession that rode her back constantly.

It's now, Arlene. You have to tell her about her dad and your mom.

Realizing she couldn't put off the obligatory discussion with Cassi any longer, she broke the silence.

"Cass, we need to talk. Can we go somewhere?" Arlene didn't want her aunt or Faith any more upset than they were now, and so she'd decided earlier that it would be best to take this discussion to a different location. Preferably one where they sold alcohol to give her liquid courage.

Not having any idea how Cass would take the news of their relationship, she prayed it wouldn't come as too big a shock.

That after she had time to acknowledge the truth, Cass would accept her as a half-sister and a part of her family.

That they could have a bit of a relationship.

That she wouldn't hate her.

Hell, she'd be willing to work things out if Cass would meet her halfway.

Yeah, you're taking that stance because you shot her brother – your brother – though, it wasn't your fault. And you're terrified of what will happen when or if she ever finds out the truth.

"I'm sorry, Arlene. It can't be tonight. I'm working at nine and just have enough time to drop you off and get home to change."

Reprieve! You sick puppy... you're relieved, yet you know this can't be put off.

"Are you still working at that fucking club, Cass? What are you, a total maniac? Don't answer, we'll meet tomorrow."

"I'm there just for one reason—"

Arlene cut her off. "Tell me when and where."

"I promised Rusty I'd work with you at the gym tomorrow, you still on for that?"

Yes! Rusty will be there and he can intervene. Why didn't I think of that myself? "I forgot we'd booked the first practice for tomorrow. Okay, at the gym. We'll talk. Good idea."

"Are you all right, Arlene? You seem weirded out about something."

"I am. Faith did save my life and it's killing me to see her so unhappy. The rest of the shit can wait until tomorrow. We're near my place. Drop me off and I'll run the rest of the way. Listen, you be careful at that crazy club."

"Will do, my friend. I hope things aren't too difficult for you tonight either. Try to get Faith to eat and maybe give her something to help her sleep."

***

Getting ready for work later, Cassi thought over the day, and eventually, her mind turned to Arlene. She'd wanted to talk, and Cassi had felt bad having to put her off until tomorrow. But damned if she didn't get the strongest feeling that Arlene seemed relieved.

What in the world she needed to discuss, Cassi

couldn't imagine, unless it was about her ongoing battle with Ariana Swift. Maybe she had some ideas how they could organize a title fight for her, and she needed Cassi to intervene.

When she arrived home, Cassi flung her clothes everywhere, ignoring her yappy guilt demon. In the car, she'd plotted the text she would send to Trace so typing it didn't take long. He'd be upset, but in her mind, she had no choice.

That barely left her with enough time to shower and change into her bartending persona – eating was out of the question. This time before she left, she set the alarm, a custom she'd stopped after Juan was no longer in the picture. If she'd kept it up, maybe when Dani had paid a visit, the alarm would have made her think twice before breaking in. She hurried to her car. Though the day had flown by, a promise to Sam that she'd be there at nine had to be kept.

During the drive, munching on a health bar, she again replayed Arlene's earlier request. In fact, she couldn't seem to let it go. *"Cass, we need to talk. Can we go somewhere?"*

She'd hated to turn Arlene down. It was the only time the other girl had issued an invitation in a voice full of soft entreaty. Yet, once they'd decided on the time and place, Arlene had reverted to her usual self.

"Are you still working at that fucking club, Cass? What are you, a total maniac?"

Cassi had chuckled, knowing that Arlene had made an Arlene joke. "I'm there just for one reason." Before she could go on, Arlene had cut her off. Strange! Most people were all too happy to discuss Raoul's death, get the real lowdown on what happened. Yet, Arlene consistently shied away from the topic.

And Faith... She remembered them being in the ladies' washroom at the club when she'd questioned her about Raoul. But before she could answer, Maddy and her sidekick had busted in, and the moment had been lost.

Of course, with everything happening in Faith's life at the moment, it wouldn't be proper to tackle that subject. But she wondered if Trace had ever approached the blonde. Especially once Cassi had told him about their relationship. She must ask him.

Minutes later, walking to the entrance, she spied a Harley rigged up with all the bells and whistles one could put on a motorcycle. Seeing it parked in Dani's old spot in front of the joint sent shivers up her spine.

Her old friend, Pete Bradford, was back.

She almost turned around and walked away.

Almost.

Chapter
Thirty-seven

As soon as Cassi stepped into the club, she sensed a difference in the atmosphere. First, there were half the customers. Probably because a lot of the gang, who were loyal to Dani and disliked, or more importantly, didn't trust Pete, had taken off.

Considering the change-over, those members would have made judgment calls. Cassi recognized that now would be a good time for them to break away from their gang affiliations without any repercussions. Dani had kept their loyalty after Billy by having been one of them – living the violence and reaping the rewards. Pete, on the other hand, couldn't give a shit.

Her mind floating to Billy, Cassi had overheard many stories about how the old boss had stood up to giants and overcame their resistance. That he'd kept the boys in line and could be cruel when necessary. How he'd silver-tongued his way into contracts with various dealers – and had even begun to worm his way into buying straight from the L.A. source.

Knowing now who they'd been referring to when using the title *old boss*, she had no doubt he'd had the guts and enough bullshit to make that happen.

But Pete, being a newcomer and a vicious brute, had already challenged the status quo. His multiple run-ins with a few of the older, well-liked guys hadn't gone unnoticed. Now, he'd have to earn their trust and respect, which wouldn't be easy considering he had the personality of a wounded grizzly with a branch shoved up its ass.

Music turned low, the ever-existing cloud of stinky shit drifting and fogging up the lights near the bar and the slots, Cassi wrestled to shut off the little voice in her head telling her to turn and run.

Sam, in his place behind the bar, caught her eye and his welcoming grin relieved the tightness in her chest. She slid in next to him and dumped her belongings in their usual place. Then she moved close, leaning near him against the counter, crossing her arms in the same way he had of relaxing.

"It's quiet tonight." Cassi broke the silence.

"Not for long. The idiots downstairs are counting a big haul, using what little brains they have. No doubt, they'll be here soon, clamoring for booze and then upstairs for their nose candy and women time."

"You sound peeved. Something happen?"

"No. I'm just so sick of this scene. Look at that bunch over in the corner. Most can't be more than eighteen years old. Probably heard the *Armas* were looking to bring in new members. And like other arrogant kids on the prowl, they want to belong, join a gang and be somebody. Stupid young bastards!"

Cassi checked out the noisy bunch in the corner and sure enough, most didn't look old enough to drink, never mind puffing on the crap they were passing around. "We can refuse to serve them."

Sam laughed, a sound without humor. "You go for it, girl. But before taking that step, check out the bulges under their shirts in the back. Then refuse to accept the fake IDs every single son-of-a-bitchin' one of them is carrying. Hell, if that doesn't make you think twice, look at the strutting bastard who figures he's the new boss."

Cassi did as he suggested and saw Pete holding court at Dani's old table. Surrounded by some of the meanest of the gang, both men and women, he appeared to be in his element. She shrugged. "Not me, man. I'm gonna be the sweetest little barmaid you ever did see. Keep my mouth shut and wait for you to retrieve that camera I planted downstairs. I'm only here as backup for you when the time is right."

Sam glanced sideways at her and grinned.

"Figured that's why you agreed to come back."

"Couldn't let you stick your neck out alone, and I kinda knew you would."

"Funny thing, princess. I thought the same fucking thing." He held his hand out to the side in her direction, and she slapped it as he expected her to do.

What she didn't expect was him to grab it and hang on hard. "I need your word you won't do anything stupid, lady." Sam growled the words and his tone meant business. "We work together on this Cass, or I'll tan your backside. You hear me?"

She squeezed and nodded. "You got it. I'm serious about being nervous, Sam." Flipping her hair to the back, she showed him her expression and didn't try to hide her sincerity, her anxiety.

"Okay, then. We're glued at the hip. No doing anything – and I mean anything – on your own."

"Right. Oh shit, here come the boys."

The door opened, and a noisy pack headed for the bar. The quiet time had ended. Both Sam and Cassi worked their buns off for the next couple hours. It seemed like the whole underground neighborhood decided to show up at the Lipstick Club that night.

During the next lull, Cassi spotted Rodrigo coming from the room behind the bar, Pete right behind him. Rodrigo looked exhausted and sickly, like he wished he could be anywhere but where he was.

Pete glared in her direction but passed by the bar. He strutted to a chair at his now special table and joined the raucous group waiting for him.

Rodrigo did stop though, perched halfway on an open barstool. Tonight, the fancy dresser seemed disheveled, almost grubby and his hands appeared grimy.

"Hey, boss. You okay?" Cassi passed him his favorite margarita, shaken with ice chips and a rim of salt.

"Hmm." He took a sip, relishing the taste. Then he reached for the dish of peanuts she'd placed near him, only to notice the disgusting filth from counting stacks of money on his hands. He stopped. "Not okay. Never be okay again. But thanks for asking, Cass."

Cassi passed him a soapy wet paper towel and watched as he scrubbed at the mess. "I'm sorry, Rodrigo. About Dani and Billy and what happened."

"Yeah, whatever. Shit happens in our world all the time. But damn, I never expected to get a double hit in one night. I'd hoped that when they met up, and it was bound to happen, one of them would still exist. Now we're left with that miserable devil incarnate." His head tilted for a second in the direction that Pete had taken. There was no doubt who he meant.

"Will the boys accept him as their new boss?"

"Hell! Do they have a choice? He'll shoot anyone

who stands up to him. Not for the first time, either." As if he realized he'd said too much, he lifted his drink toward her as a thank you and headed for the staircase – a sad, solitary man.

Floss, Cassi's favorite barmaid, approached at the end of the bar with her empty tray. Appearing exhausted from the last rush, she stopped to chat. "Rod looks down tonight. In fact, he looks like I feel."

"I know what you mean."

"Most of us girls are talking about leaving, quitting now that Dani's gone and the place is literally uncontrolled. Can't you sense the violence, Cassi?"

"Sure, it's like a thin layer stretched over the top of the normal dysfunction."

"Only reason we're still here is we need the wages and because of you and Sam. Why have you stuck it out?"

"Truthfully?"

Floss nodded.

"Because I need to find out what happened the night they killed my brother."

Floss's face dropped, her big eyes commiserating. "I can't tell you much about that night, just what I told the cops. Dani was upstairs. Around ten, she and Mani left with a few of the others. Whatever happened, she was pissed. We could tell by her language that something had upset her.

"When she returned, she had blood on her clothes and later I heard she'd given Juan Acedo a terrible beating for disobeying her orders. It put him in the hospital for weeks. I remember, she ranted for days that no one listened or did what the fuck they were told to do."

Cassi added, "I know that Juan was there, besides AK and Miguel. What I need to find out is who the female was."

"Hmm. Okay, that rumor spread a few days later. What I heard was she didn't belong to the gang and only showed up to try and stop any violence against Raoul."

Stunned, Cassi stared at Floss and found her expression completely believable. "Excuse me? She didn't shoot Raoul?"

Floss held both hands out in front. "Hey, I don't know who actually shot him. But as far as I know, this chick arrived to help just before the cops appeared, and she ran away like the others. No one has ever named her."

Cassi put her arm around Floss's shoulder and side-hugged her. "You've made things better, Floss. There's still a mystery about the shooter but knowing this, I can handle it if I never find out. Thank you."

"Hey, Cass. Anytime."

"What're you two female yappers on about? I've been trying to get a drink, and won't nobody pay any attention." Pete glowered at them from behind

Floss where he'd approached unnoticed.

Cassi's first instinct – to tell him to mind his own business – never came out. She stomped down her attitude and started to move behind the bar and get him his favorite beer.

Before she knew what happened, he'd shoved Floss aside and grabbed her arm. "Don't you walk away from me when I'm talking to ya, bitch."

In seconds, Sam appeared, his gun held by his side. "Hey, boss. Maybe you don't wanna grab at her. She's got a real short fuse."

Pete never even glanced Sam's way, but he did answer. "Fuck off, Sam. Go do the job you're getting paid to do."

"My job entails that I stop fights from breaking out. And you know Cass's reputation? She's put more men on their asses for acting like complete dicks than anyone else I know. Come on, Cass. Get back behind the bar."

Cass made eye contact with Pete and shivers began to build. His beady wicked windows, full of venom, speared her with hate. Violent, a sick-minded man, he dared her to step out of line.

Dared her...

God! How could she hesitate?

Everyone nearby went quiet.

The world around her stopped as Cassi sunk into the morass of disgust and filth in his expression. He'd kill her. He wanted to. She had no doubt. But if she didn't take a stand now, every minute he didn't get revenge, she'd worry that next time she'd be alone, without backup.

Fuck!

"What do you want from me, Pete? You need a beer; I'll get it for you. You really want to fight a girl who weighs half of what you do, bring it on. You need an apology for some unknown slight that's pissing you off, I'll say I'm sorry." She watched to see how he liked her so far. His expression didn't change but his face began to smile. "So, big boy, what is it you need me to do?"

He squeezed her arm tighter, making sure it hurt. Then he dared her to retaliate by shoving his face closer, so they were almost touching.

Still, Cassi didn't move. Neither did she back down. But those watching saw her eyes grow cold as ice and her mouth tighten.

Oh, no. The pig isn't satisfied. He wants me to grovel at his feet. The violent prick has no intention of backing off.

As if she said the words aloud, he took offense at her unspoken loathing. While he held her in place, quick as a rattler, his empty arm raised to slap her. But it never connected. Giving no mercy, she drove her fist into his throat and watched the shock the prick couldn't hide. Then, she went for his eyes, her fingers gouging.

Finally, he shoved her away, and when his hand reached behind for his weapon, Sam stepped up and pulled it from his belt. "Sorry, Pete. You don't get to play dirty."

That's when Pete's new loyalists forced Sam aside, blocking him.

Having no other choice, standing down not an option, Pete rushed her, enclosing her into the small area in the corner of the bar. He picked her up with intentions to slam her into the counter. Only he hadn't banked on her ability to wriggle away, duck, and on the way down, plow her elbow in the small of his back.

Furious, he turned in time to see her flip to her feet. When she slugged him in his fat stomach, spittle flew from his mouth and his face turned red while sweat beaded the tats on his forehead. Grabbing his scraggly beard, she slammed his head into the edge of the bar.

Groggy, but not finished, Pete reached over, and before she knew his intentions, he grabbed her hair. He drew back his fist but hers connected first. She went for the throat again and watched as he gagged. Unfortunately, it still didn't stop the crazed idiot who had a lot to prove.

In a move she hadn't anticipated, he grabbed the beer bottle that Sam had brought out. He smashed the end off against the bar and swung the broken edge directly toward her. If he'd connected, her face would be horribly slashed. The reason it didn't was because of Trace. Having just arrived, he'd roared his way between them and was now punching Pete's lights out.

***

The furious cop didn't let up until Pete lay prone on the floor. Blood poured from the cut on his face where first the counter, and then Trace's fist, did the most damage.

"Pete Bradford, you're under arrest for kidnapping, murderous assault, drug trafficking and... in case you thought you'd get away with it, I'm still digging into the murder of Harry Cruder." Trace's expression changed from official to a man at the end of his rope. "Plus, for being an ugly son of a bitch and a host of other shit I can think to throw at you."

Sam, wrestling away from his jailors, drove one in the face and pushed the other over so hard, he landed against the booth and took a header. Then he handed Pete's gun to Trace. "Here's his weapon."

Trace motioned to one of the cops nearby who pulled out a plastic bag to store it. Trace watched as Michael handcuffed the groggy prick and then passed him to the waiting officers.

Cassi had stood back during the battle, but now she stepped forward. Earnest, shaky, she spoke in a tone that rang with truthfulness. "I promise I didn't start this, Trace. In fact, I did everything I could not to play his game. I even apologized."

Sam nodded. "She did, Trace. The bastard wouldn't let her go. Sorry, man."

Trace refused to make eye connect with her. The

fury he was in the process of burying would frighten her. Instead, he flexed his battered hand, the abraded skin sending out messages that he'd hit damn hard. He stayed strong until he heard her sobbing breath, then he lifted his arm so she could bury in close.

"Sam, Cassi wants to quit."

Sam waited. The silence grew louder. Everyone in the place was now watching the serial.

Sam finally spoke. "Cass? Is this right?"

She didn't look up, but she did raise her voice. "Yes, Sam. I quit. My last day will be tomorrow."

Sam's voice smiled. "Good. About time."

Trace roared, "Not tomorrow. Now! God dammit!"

Cass hugged him harder but her muffled voice still came through loud and clear. "Tomorrow."

Trace made sure that Cassi didn't see the glaring order he sent to Sam, but the agent got it.

Trace had had enough.

There would be no tomorrow.

Chapter Thirty-eight

"Quit pouting. I told you I didn't start the fight." Cassi tried to get Trace to discuss the issue, but his chilly silence spoke for itself. He was still fuming at her refusal to instantly stop working there.

After she'd insisted she'd return the next day, he'd coldly informed Sam that for tonight, her shift was done. Then he'd made a spectacle of both of them by throwing her over his shoulder and carrying her to the car. "And stop driving so fast. You're a danger on the road."

"Look who's pouting now," he added. But he slowed down. "You just had to argue the point of when you'd quit that fucking place, didn't you? My bloody stomach can't take much more of this stress, baby. I'm just sayin'."

Instantly contrite, Cassi reached for his hand and had to pry if off his thigh. But once he gave way, his fingers tightened in such a way to let her know how much this mattered.

"God, I'm sorry, Trace. I really didn't want the showdown. Trust me, please. I did try to stop it from happening."

"I know you did, sugar. I know. I arrived in time to see you attempting to talk him down. I was so proud of you, I thought it would work. Then before I knew what happened, he'd gone berserk and you were beating the shit out of the maniac. You'll never know how hard it was for me to wait for my chance to help." He squeezed her hand harder.

She clung, a feeling of overwhelming love for the man flooded her. His respect for her brought tears, and she sniffled. "I couldn't have been happier when you stepped in. I was terrified of the bastard."

"You could have fooled me. In fact, from the look on your face, you kinda scared everyone in the joint. I'm thinking, I'll be a good little boy from now on."

Unexpected, Cassi's laugh broke free and a lightness of spirit followed. "That remark alone will bring its own reward, just get me home so I can show you how good a little girl I can be."

The car sped up noticeably before slowing again. Trace's laugh rang out. Then he became serious. "I'm just thankful I was there intending to arrest the disgusting slug anyway. We do believe he killed Harry Cruder and we'll prove it too. Plus, he kidnapped you; we have the tape where you're saying as much.

"The FBI also wants him for trafficking. They found a lot of information on the Delgado files they were able to get from L.A., besides a video of him approaching the big dealer himself before he escaped. The reason we've held off until now – the District Attorney wouldn't let us move on him until everything had been verified and the case was foolproof."

Trace stopped in front of Cassi's house. When he went around to her door, she'd already stepped out, and they met in an embrace that lasted for a long time. Unable to wait and prove how vital they were to each other, they kissed and held on tight and then kissed again.

When they stumbled in a clinch against the car, it broke them apart. With a growl, Trace lifted her so her legs wound around his hips, and he carried her up the stairs.

Once inside, they stripped down, leaving a trail of clothes to the bedroom. Landing on the mattress, first her and him following, they slowed their assault and stared into each other's eyes.

"I never want to live through that kind of nightmare again, watching you fighting off a psycho and not being able to intervene." Trace's fervent words came from his earlier fear.

"You did intervene, exactly when I needed you. You're always there when I need you."

"Baby, can I ask one promise?" He watched her

reaction.

"Anything." The glowing blue highlights were so sincere that it left no doubt in his heart that she'd give him everything she could, whatever he wanted... within reason.

"Will you promise to marry me, be the mother of my kids, and try to behave yourself as the wife of the new Chief of Detectives for Las Vegas?"

"What!" Delight rang in her voice as she squirmed to lie over the top of him and cover his face with kisses. "I'm so happy for you, baby. So freakin' happy, I could shout."

He laughed. "You are shouting."

"I don't care. I want to tell the world."

"How about you just telling me your answer is yes?"

Pretending confusion, she asked, "What was the question again?"

Tickling her, he rolled over on top and kissed her hard. Then he stopped and held away from her searching lips. "Uh huh. Not until you say yes."

"Yes. YES! Now come here and make me glad I've agreed." She lifted her arms around his neck and tugged.

His lips found hers in a kiss that scorched. Hot and steamy, his tongue searched, insisting she respond. He left her in no confusion as to how much he wanted her, how much his body wanted her.

Hard steel, his member nudged her stomach and

slipped lower, so she opened to him. Wet, her body soaking, needing, she welcomed him home. His groan of appreciation delighted her, and she made a similar noise.

Her fingers scored his back gently but soon rose to sift through his hair and guide his head to her chest. His mouth now on the same path as his hands, he caressed and squeezed the swollen mounds that tingled from the tips of the nipples to the very center of her groin, sending signals to her brain that she was being adored.

He kissed each nipple, laving them with his burning tongue and then sucked them into his mouth so he could drive her even crazier.

"Oh, Trace. Only you can make me feel this way – this good." She lifted herself and felt him plunge into her body, wriggling his hips to go deeper still.

"Only me, baby. Forever. Only me."

"Oh, Trace. Only you. I love you so much." She whispered her promise and kissed him wherever her lips could reach – his head, his neck, his shoulders.

Her hands now on his butt, rubbing and squeezing in her frenzy to get him fully entrenched. Her legs rose around his waist, allowing him access to sink even farther into the moist tightness he loved so much.

Suddenly, his demeanor changed, as if her hint had worked its magic. Aroused to where his breath came in pants and his body trembled with passion, he pushed, faster, grinding, moaning – plundering her with hot wildness.

Shuddering, muscles clenching and pulsating, she felt the building fury and her groan of satisfaction rang before he joined with his own. Quivering, both caught in their own worlds of sexual ecstasy, they shared one last tender kiss full of promises before they hugged and cuddled.

Chapter Thirty-nine

Arlene headed to the gym earlier than the planned time so she could get Rusty alone before Cass appeared. She carried her mother's pink diary in her backpack, thankful now that she hadn't followed her first instinct of ripping it to shreds.

Earlier, contemplating how she could approach the subject, her anger had rekindled. Like a flame in the pit of her stomach, it seared and hurt like hell. The secret, burned into her conscience, had haunted her all night. Shit, maybe she should just let it go, forget she ever read the stinkin' diary.

Then common sense prevailed. Slumping in a pile of misery, she laid on her bed and scenarios filtered through her head.

Cassi, a woman anyone would be proud to call a sister, had always shown true loyalty to those she cared about. And Arlene didn't have anyone of her own, not really. Sure, she was building a sweet relationship with her aunt, but years of resentment and jealousy had left its mark, left her with a distrust one couldn't overcome in a few weeks.

And Michael, who knows what he'd think when he realized what a baby she really was on one hand and a killer on the other? A person scared to make a commitment or live up to their truth. Would he still want to create a relationship with her after she confessed?

If I confess!

With Cass, who knew her at her worst, they could start fresh. Arlene recognized that the girl loved deeply; look at the way she'd dealt with Raoul's death and how much he'd meant to her. And her devotion to the old man they both worked with had brought its own kind of sick resentment for Arlene early on. Now, she only knew envy and gladness that Cass would always be there for the old rascal they both loved.

The desire to have a connection where you absolutely knew you could depend on the other – exactly like the link that bound her and Mani before she'd fucked it up – that dream was what drove her to see this through.

Mani! Oh, God, she'd never overcome the sorrow she felt at his dying so senselessly and because of her stupid choices. Though her aunt and uncle forgave her, and her aunt had even pointed out that Mani was a man who'd ultimately made his own decisions, chose his own path, in her heart she knew the real blame would always belong to her.

These thoughts had her hesitating. Would this decision be something else to regret? Could she bear having a bigger load of shit for her conscience to carry?

Still indecisive, she entered the gym and stood in the shadows. The old man, his tuke sideways on his head, white softness like a halo around the edge, had taken one of the younger guys over to the press bench and had helped him lift weights.

She watched as Rusty praised the younger man, leaving him feeling good and she knew her old trainer had a gift for knowing when he needed to be tough and when a listening ear or a soft shoulder would benefit his fighters more.

Feeling better, knowing he'd guide her well, she approached him. "Hey, Rus, you got a minute."

"Sure, brat. You're early today, couldn't stay away, huh?" He winked with his one good eye and turned toward his office.

She loved it when he called her brat. Had no idea why it meant so much. Maybe because it was a sign of endearment and respect he saved for Cass, and that's why it mattered. Walking behind him, she noticed that his back was slightly more bent and his stride not quite so stable.

The sight of his aging and the thought of him getting old broke her. *I can't lose him, too.*

Again... it's all about you.

Shit girl, it's time for you to grow up and be accountable. Stop living a lie. Face at least one hurdle rather taking the easy way out.

They entered his office and one look at her face had him closing the door. She shook off her despondency, swallowed her hesitation and began rifling through her backpack. Glad as hell he said nothing, only waited for her to explain, she knew she couldn't back out. Finding the diary where she'd left it, her hands shaking, she opened to the pertinent pages where he could read the same words she'd read before her trip to L.A. and a thousand times since.

First, he looked at her and then he took the book, sat at the edge of the small sofa and patted the seat beside him. "Sit, kid. You're making me nervous with your hovering. Christ, you're shaking. Okay. I'll read whatever this is, but trust old Rusty when he says nothing's too bad that we can't fix it." He patted the seat until she followed his orders.

***

"Holy shit! That sleaze. Not your mother, kid. Stand down."

Arlene had shot to her feet, her hands clenched. Carefully, gently, he guided her to reoccupy her seat. "I'm sorry, Arlene. I'm really sorry. I don't know what else to say. I feel guilty because I knew José always had a skirt on the side."

Rusty, restless now, paced the small space

himself. "Even after he got married to the twins' mother, he never changed his behavior. When his wife left, I'd hoped he'd grow up and take on the responsibilities of being a single dad, but Raoul and Cassi pretty well raised themselves. It's the reason they were joined at the hip from the time they were kids."

"I knew Cassi and her brother were close. She's proven it by the dedicated way she's determined to find his killer." Arlene almost choked on the word.

"Yeah, yeah. It drives me crazy, this vengeance she's been living for. Raoul's dead. He made bad choices, got mixed up with the wrong crowd, and they killed him. Her problem isn't that she needs to find out who did the dirty deed. She needs to forgive herself that she didn't stop it, or at least try."

Oh, God. I know exactly how that feels. Yet, I did try to stop it and look what happened.

A sick feeling swarmed, forcing her to bend over her knees. *I'm going to throw up.*

"Oh, no, you don't. Breathe! Breathe deep. That's it." Her trainer knew the signs well.

Finally, her rioting emotions and the juices in her tummy settled enough so she could speak. "What should I do, Rusty? You know her better than anyone. Tell me, and I'll listen to you. I don't want to make things more difficult in her life."

"Difficult? Are you crazy, girl? You think this will be a downer for Cass? Shit me, you don't know our

Cassidy Santino if you think that. Of course, you must tell her. She'll be over the moon when she reads this."

Cheered, feeling lighter than any time since she'd first read her mother's revealing words, hope began to lift her spirits. "You truly think she'll be happy to know we're half-sisters?"

Rusty reached down with his gnarled fingers and caressed her cheek, a move she'd never have expected from the rough old man, and yet it seemed fitting somehow.

"I'll stay with you. We'll face her together. You trust old Rusty, don'tcha?"

Nodding, knowing she'd trust him with her life, and was going to, she whispered, "Yes. I do."

"Good. Because I think she's here now."

The knock on the door signaled a visitor and Cassi stepped in after Rusty gave his permission.

"Hi, Rus. Oh, hi Arlene." Cass waved. "They said you were in your office. Oh, sorry. Am I interrupting? I'll come back."

"No, Cass. Stay. There's something here you need to read."

Chapter Forty

Cassi's thundering heart almost choked her. Her eyes filled, making it difficult to read the words. She took the tissue Rusty held out and continued.

The silence from the other two was telling – they were waiting for her reaction. She looked at their faces, Rusty's grinning, expecting, knowing.

Totally different from Rusty's, Arlene's expression held despair, fear and... and were her tears covering hope? Was she happy? Did she want Cassi in her life? Oh, my good Lord, could it be true? She still had family after all? A person to love, to protect and cherish? She reread the words, and they hadn't change.

She had a sister.

Dropping the diary, she stood. Arlene slowly came to her feet and they faced each other. Cassi reached first, and they were hugging. Joy filled her, love followed, and she pushed Arlene away so she could look into her eyes. "Hi, sis."

Arlene, unable to speak easily, choked out, "Hi."

Cassi hugged her again but lifted one hand for Rusty to take. "Did you hear this, old man? Arlene's my sister. No wonder she always seemed so familiar." Suddenly, Cassi stopped her excited ranting and asked a pointed question. "Now that we're related, can I call you Leni?"

Arlene stared at Cass to see if this was a dig of some sort. Finding her expression totally open, filled with affection and with a need to get this important detail covered, she asked, "Why?"

"Because you blew up at me last time I used it, and I figured you only let people you cared about call you that."

"Okay. Of course, you can, you too, Rusty."

Full of emotion, his lips quivering, Rusty wrapped his arms around both girls for a few seconds and then tenderly pounded their backs, his hands not hurting. "The Santino sisters! What a billboard!"

Cassi laughed. "Ain't gonna happen, Rus, you old reprobate. But you could start calling attention to the newest Santino daughter – Arlene Montgomery Santino, soon to be the US Featherweight champion."

Arlene spoke up, her voice soft. "Make it Leni Santino, boss. I'll be using my real name from now on."

Chapter Forty-one

Cassi walked on clouds, her satisfaction so complete that she wanted to shout it to the world. She had family, a sister.

Alone in her car with Leni now, she decided to clear the air and apologize for her father's, no, their father's cruelty to Leni's mother, Judy. As a young girl who gave her heart to the wrong man, she needed to be understood, if not forgiven.

"Do you hate our dad, Leni? You have every right, and I'll understand if you do."

"Oh, trust me, I did at first. When I read her words, I hated them both. Had it in for you, too, until I smartened up and realized how stupid that would be." Leni appeared shocked for admitting what came next. "I was so angry, I almost tore up the diary and turned my back on the whole situation."

"I'm glad you didn't."

"Me, too."

"One day, I'll show you the photo albums so you'll get to know José better. You'll see his career in the ring, and I'll share my stories, too. He wasn't a good man by some standards, not like Rusty, who was always there for us. But he did love me and Raoul. He just loved himself a hell of a lot more."

"And I'll tell you about my childhood with my aunt and uncle. He treated me like a daughter, and Mani babied me as long as I can remember. Things could have been a hell of a lot worse. If my mother would have taken me with her, who knows what kind of a life we would have lived or where I'd have ended up. Truth is, I had it good compared to so many others. If only I'd recognized it as a teen. Instead, I rebelled and caused such heartache – like mother, like daughter." Shaking off the moodiness she was all too well acquainted with, she asked, "Where are we going?"

"I'm thinking your aunt and Faith could use some cheering up. I'm heading there so we can tell them the good news."

"I'm not sure this is the right time to tell Faith." Leni's voice sounded loud, which seemed to annoy her.

Surprised that Leni balked at the idea of sharing their news with Faith, Cassi chose to overcome her argument. "Faith doesn't strike me as the kind of person who'd refuse to be happy for others just because of the sadness in her own world. Neither is your aunt. It's the opposite effect I'm hoping for, to give them a reason to celebrate and cheer them both up a little."

Approaching the house, they saw a black Lexus sedan in the drive. Parking instead on the road, they walked past, and Cassi spied a baby seat in the back. She pointed it out to Leni who grinned her acknowledgment that she'd seen it too.

"He's here." Cassi spoke the obvious.

"Uh huh. I wonder if he brought Raoul?"

"Should we intrude?"

"Bloody right. What if the jerk hasn't come to make up, but to do more damage?"

"Oh, Leni. Have faith in your fellow man." Cassi chuckled at Leni's sour expression. They moved forward only to have the door open before they could grab the knob.

Steven, still disheveled – very much as he'd looked the evening before – appeared first. Faith, glowing with thankfulness and motherly love, followed with a bedraggled Raoul clutched in her arms.

The baby's face showed signs of tears, his hair was sweaty, and his diaper hung revealingly. But at this moment, he chatted rather than screamed, his arms waving in all directions and his loud baby sounds came through as delighted rather than annoyed or angry.

Cass and Leni backed away, leaving center stage to the other two. Steven didn't acknowledge them at all, neither did Faith.

Instead he talked to her, demanding answers. "You'll go home and look after him like before. You promise."

"Yes, of course. I missed him dreadfully."

"Not as much as w-he missed you. You'll be there when I get home?"

"Yes. Cassi will drive us."

"We need to talk. I need to forgive you."

"Me, too."

Cassi wondered exactly what that meant. He needed to forgive her for what – her earlier life – her not being there for the kid when he was forced to take care of him alone? What? Then when she heard Faith's reply, again she wondered.

Did she refer to needing to forgive him for the horrible hours of torture he'd just put her through. Or forgive herself for the earlier choices she'd made in her life? Maybe one day she'd get up the nerve to ask about how their conversation went. Right now, she made sure Leni didn't intrude until the car pulled away.

Then they watched as the happiest woman in the world kissed the child, swung in circles, and laughed out loud, her smile making the sun pale in comparison.

***

"Leni, you mean to tell me that José Santino, Cassi's father, the famous boxer, is your father also? My goodness, it boggles the mind." Aunt

Barbara had just finished reading the diary. Getting the affirmative nod from Cassi, she passed it to Faith.

Cassi answered, "We're so thrilled, we wanted to share it with her family. I hope this is happy news for you, too."

"Of course, it is. I'm delighted to welcome another woman into our lives. Trust me; it can be very lonely when you face the world on your own. I've been doing it for too many years, so I know what the hell I'm talking about."

Cuddling a sleepy baby, his bottle almost empty, Faith took the book, but her gaze searched Leni's face before she started to read. The muffled sound of misery couldn't be concealed nor could the look she flashed Leni, her face full of sympathy and understanding.

What the hell? Why would their news rattle the other girl so deeply? Questions teemed, but Cassi recognised this wasn't the time.

Aunt Barbara proceeded to congratulate the two sisters, but now, Cassi, sensing something was wrong, watched Faith grab for Leni's hand before she spoke to all of them.

"I'm really happy for you both, terribly happy. And I know Raoul would have been delighted. After Leni's kindness to me, he'd talked about meeting her away from the club, and getting to know her. It just never happened. We never had time. And for that and other things, I'm so terribly sorry."

The words echoed as she dropped Leni's hand, lifted the baby and fled the room, tears spilling.

"Poor thing, she still hasn't gotten over Raoul's death." Aunt Barbara filled the silence. "Okay, enough sadness. Let's celebrate. I'm taking you both out for lunch after we drop Faith and the baby off at their place. And I won't put up with any arguments. It's time we all got to know each other better."

Chapter
Forty-two

Later, as they drove away after dropping Barbara off, Cassi waved and then turned to Leni. "You were quiet at lunch. Is there something wrong?"

"No. I guess I'm still overwhelmed with everything that's happened. Do you think Rusty was serious when he said he'd be getting on to Ariana Swift's manager to start working out plans for a title fight?"

"Sure. Rusty never jokes about stuff like that. He's like a kid with a candy cane. He'll slurp on that sucker until he has what he wants. Once you get your name legally changed, and he can bill you as a Santino, he'll be in his glory. It's always been his dream to train another winner in our family for a championship fight. Who would have guessed it would happen, just not in quite the way he'd envisioned?"

"Do you mind?"

"Of course not. I'm tickled pink, and I'll be helping you train as promised – you're welcome very much."

Leni laughed. "Tickled pink! I couldn't imagine you in pink."

"But then you don't really know me yet. Spoiler alert – it's my favorite color. In fact, my favorite dress is pink and with ruffles too." Cassi's tone dared her to laugh and was pleased when Leni did. Her good mood seemed to be restored, and so Cassi drove in the direction she'd craved to go all afternoon.

The recent text from Trace informing her he'd be in the office most of the day, kind of convinced her. After all, she couldn't think of anyone better than him and Michael to share their fabulous news with next.

"Are you taking me back to the gym to get my car?"

"Nope. I'm going to kidnap you for a little while longer."

Leni stared at her surroundings. Suddenly she caught on. "Are we heading for the police station?"

"Yep." Cassi pulled into a visitor's slot and turned with a laugh. "Why? Does the Cop Shop give you the willies? We're just ordinary citizens not criminals. We get to leave after we see Trace and tell him our great news. Come on."

Heading to the building, Cassi happened to catch a glimpse of Leni in another car's side mirror and the distraught look on the hesitant girl's face shook her.

Once there, Cassi purposely checked the tall glass windows to see if Leni still seemed upset. What she saw reflected were two girls, both slender, both dark and for the first time, she noticed their resemblance. They were the same height and even had a similar way of moving.

Only obvious difference, other than face structures, were their eye colors. While Cassi's flashed blue like a sunny summer sky, Leni's were brown with lights that shone golden when she laughed and sparks that glowed black when she was angry or upset.

Right now, sparks were building and as Cassi looked her way in the elevator, she knew something ate at her sister, something devastating. Should she mention it?

Shaking off her misgivings, Cassi stepped out on Trace's floor and headed toward his office. All around them, suited men were working; many had shed their jackets and loosened their ties. Uniformed police were prevalent also, and the desks piled high with papers, used coffee mugs and half-eaten donuts suggested that it was a place where people had a lot going on.

Banks of monitors in the background were muffled and flashing while technicians wearing headsets, operated a mouse with one hand and held files, pens or cell phones in the other. The smell of coffee, strong and black, permeated the place and had Cassi yearning for a hit.

"He's over there." Cassi pointed to the small area where Trace spent most of his days. Before they could angle past other desks, a voice stopped them.

"Hey, pretty ladies. You need a cop? If so, I'm your guy."

"Detective Michael." Leni faced him first and Cassi heard the gladness in her voice. *Oh yeah, she's interested!* He carried two steaming coffees in porcelain mugs and Cassi had to stop herself from thanking him and grabbing one.

"We stopped by to see Trace, but you can come with us if you want to hear some great news."

"You kidding? Working in this place? I'm always up for something to make me smile. And seeing you two pretty ladies has done the job."

Leni snorted while Cassi played along. "Sweet talker." She grinned and kept moving toward Trace. "Is he free for a few minutes?"

"Actually, he isn't right now, but if you want to come with me, I'll let him know you're here. Right this way."

Cassi leaned around Michael who'd tried blocking her vision and stopped dead.

"Why is Sam Smith and Rodrigo Muñoz here, Michael? What's going on?"

Michael stepped again to block her view.

"They're here to answer some questions, Cassi. Police business. No big deal."

She purposely moved around him. Then before he could stop her, she stomped forward. *What the hell's going on?* Her instincts screamed that she needed to protect her bar partner from whatever trouble he'd found himself in.

She knocked once and before Trace could answer, she entered the room to be greeted with astonished looks on the faces of all three men.

"Cassi! Sweetheart. What are you doing here?" Trace half rose, and she noticed him looking toward Sam. She turned in time to see Sam shrug, and then she saw something that boggled her mind. The man wore an FBI badge in a holder around his neck. A big gold badge that signified how he'd played her for a fool.

"Agent Smith?" She crossed her arms and stood with her feet spread, her posture rigid. She glared at him with all the animosity raging through her disbelief.

Sam stood also, towering over her as always. "Cass, sugar, don't look at me that way. I was undercover. No one knew."

Cassi swiveled toward Trace and saw the redness working its way into his cheeks. "Uh huh! No one. Got it."

"No civilian, I mean. Look, we got our man. Rodrigo is willing to plea bargain. *My* little clock video worked just the way I'd hoped." She picked up on his emphasizing the word "my" and understood it was a warning. Fine, she'd go along but wait until she got him alone.

By now, the other two had entered the small room and Michael passed coffees to Sam and Rodrigo while Leni moved closer to Cass. She sensed her presence as if the other girl was there to protect. It felt good.

Rodrigo crossed his leg over the other and took a sip from his steaming mug. "You might as well hear this, Cass. It's about the night your brother died."

Leni took Cass's arm and she resisted the tug from the other girl. No way she'd give up the chance to hear the truth. She took Leni's hand in hers and waited, holding the other girl by her side, wanting to share the news with her sister. It was her right to hear this as much as Cass's.

"What happened that night, Rodrigo?"

He looked at both girls and seemed startled to see Leni there also. Then he shrugged as if he didn't give a shit before continuing. "The boss, Dani, had told Juan to take a few of the boys to initiate Raoul as an *Armas* member.

"After she'd found out that your brother and Sergio had a history, and Raoul could get close to him, she wanted her biggest rival taken down. She'd issued an ultimatum and when she gave an order, she expected it to be followed. Juan claimed he knew Raoul and figured he might not agree. He asked what he should do if Raoul refused to carry out her instructions. All she'd said was for him to teach Santino a lesson – he needed to obey her commands.

"She never told him to shoot the kid. When the word came back that's exactly what happened, she freaked. Her and some of the others found Juan and beat the shit out of him for letting it happen. Only he refused to take the blame. Said he didn't pull the trigger. They tried to get him to reveal a name, but all he'd say was his girlfriend.

"When Dani questioned AK, he backed up Juan's story. Said it was dark, the cops had called out and his attention had been diverted. But a chick had appeared, her face hidden, and she came carrying. There was a slight struggle and the gun went off. They all ran after that, the girl included."

Leni let out a small cry.

Cassi felt faint. Sick to her soul, she sagged into Sam's vacated chair. Being the closest, he'd shot forward to help.

Oh, Lord! It was Faith...

Juan said – his girlfriend – Raoul's girlfriend. Picturing the scene, Cassi had no doubt Faith had come to stop the killing, and when Juan struggled with her, the gun must have gotten turned on Raoul. No wonder she'd taken all those drugs after his death. The poor, poor girl! What a horrible load on anyone's conscience, accidentally killing the man you loved. And then to find out she'd lost their baby... *My God!* Cassi's heart melted in pity.

Finally, returning to the moment, she looked around to see Leni's white face and the tears on her cheeks. She reached out and wondered at Leni's hesitation before she clasped Cassi's hand. "Poor, Faith."

"What?" Leni's shock appeared.

"Faith, his girlfriend. She must have tried to stop the initiation. I'll never be able to repay her for attempting to do what I couldn't. She loved him enough to brave the horror and put her life on the line."

Rodrigo nodded. "That's why Dani never hassled her about the night; why she told me to let her do whatever she wanted, give her whatever shit she asked for. We figured she'd suffered enough."

Sam stood. "You finished with us for now, Trace? I'm gonna take Rodrigo to the bureau and we'll start proceedings on his charges."

"And for the witness protection you offered me if I'd talk."

"Yeah. That too."

Sam crouched in front of Cassi. His hand reached to brush away some of the tears that had escaped. "We good?"

She reached her arms around his neck and squeezed. Her muffled voice came clear to everyone in the room. "Not even close, you shit. But if you give me another riding lesson, we might be able to work something out."

Laughing, Sam patted her back and stood. He winked. "You got it, princess. Anytime."

Holding the door, he waited for Rod, took his

arm and then the door closed behind them.

The four left in the room didn't move for a few minutes until Michael spoke. "That closes the case, right?"

Trace came slowly forward. "Cassi? You okay with his evidence?"

"Yes. It's done. I'm satisfied. I can finally let Raoul's spirit rest now." She wiped her cheeks and straightened.

Leni's cry startled the two men, but Cassi instantly understood. She quickly went to the other girl and put her arm around her shuddering shoulders. "It's over, Leni. He's finally at peace."

"But, Cass—"

"No. You didn't know him like I did. He would have wanted us to let go."

Trace interrupted. "My thought is he'd never have wanted you to go as far as you did in the first place. But now that the truth's finally out, if he is looking down, he'll be thinking what a lucky man he was to have a sister like you."

Cassi took in a deep breath to stop her lips from quivering and added, "*Two* sisters like us."

"Whaa?" Trace's stunned look brought a giggle. Cassi, lighter inside than she'd felt in many months, suddenly wanted to sing and laugh and share her happiness in their wonderful news.

"It's why we came to see you. To explain what we've found out. Leni's my sister." She explained about the diary and what they'd learned. By the time she was finished, both men were grinning and even Leni had loosened up and wore a small, shy smile.

Michael nudged Leni's arm to get her attention. His words were directed at her, but they were meant for everyone in the room. "I think we should help these ladies celebrate. What do you say, Trace?"

"Oh, yeah! Tonight, we take them for dinner and dancing. It's time we lived like normal people and had some fun without that big black cloud hanging over our heads. You girls up for a night on the town?"

Cassi saw Leni's indecision and decided to take the step for both of them. "Sure, we are. I'd love nothing more than having both my fiancé and my new sister together to celebrate the end of the worst period of my life. Yes, and yes, again. I can't think of anything I'd like better."

"Uh, ma'am, you forgot about poor little ole me?" Michael interjected, grousing in a mock whine.

"You're right. New friends are precious too." She patted his cheek. "We'll be ready..." Her face fell, and she turned to Trace. "I'm no longer working at the club, right?"

He winked. "You got it."

"No, you crafty jerk. You got your way after all, and I can't tell you how relieved I am. Pick us up at my house at eight." She leaned over and planted a huge kiss on his lips and started for the door.

Leni stopped her. "Hold it. There's something we didn't cover."

Cassi grinned, knowingly, her faith in her new sister shining. "There is?"

"You said *fiancé*? As of when?"

Chapter
Forty-three

Cassi answered the door to Leni's knock when the clock showed 7:45 p.m. Wearing her pink sundress, her hair pinned back with a shiny barrette and the makeup much less than she'd normally wear, she laughed at her sister's shock.

"You don't look like yourself at all."

"I know. It was exactly what I was thinking when I stood in front of the mirror earlier."

Leni, wearing a short-skirted, red dress and eye-catching jewelry stepped around her. "Your hair's growing out."

"Should I let it? Trace likes it longer."

"What does Cassi like?"

"Not playing a role."

"That makes sense. Me, too."

"You've never been anyone but who you are. It's something I've always respected about you."

Seeing her face fall, Cassi reiterated, "I mean in

the ring, you come on strong, fight hard, you give it your all. That's honesty. That's you."

Before Leni could reply, the doorbell rang, and Trace and Michael appeared. Both men looked scrumptious in their casual, dressy clothes that made their appearances unlike the cops they normally starred as.

Trace swept Cassi in a hug and stole a kiss before she twisted in his arms shyly. Not wanting to make the others uncomfortable, she added. "Behave. We have the rest of our lives for that smoochy stuff."

"Yes, ma'am." Trace rested his chin on the top of her head, snuggled his arms around her waist from behind and watched as Michael released Leni from the slow hug they'd shared. "So, partner. Where did you make the reservations? And it better not be your favorite strip joint or you're fired."

Michael laughed. "Nope. I went country instead. Hope you all like huge, succulent steaks, baked potatoes full of bacon and sour cream and more finger-lickin' good, buttery corn on the cob that you can eat... oh, and line dancing."

***

Michael led them to a reserved table on the outskirts of the dance floor, a perfect setting where they had privacy and yet didn't feel too secluded. A band playing a soothing country ballad filled the room with music and the background noises of people enjoying themselves gave the place a festive spirit.

The fact that the only smells in this room came from the delicious meals being prepared behind the open kitchen area, and the plates piled high on the tables they passed, made Cassi thankful. She didn't miss the ugly stench she'd been forced to suffer most nights.

After four beers were delivered, they scanned their menus for their food selections, Michael and Trace chose the dinner wine while the girls argued about what looked best for dessert.

Trace placed his hand over Cassi's on the table, and she thought the night couldn't be more perfect. The setting was elite compared to the dive she'd been stuck in for months, and the company wonderful.

Michael opened the conversation. "To sisters." He held up his bottle for them to join in. After they all drank, he asked, "When did you first read your mother's diary, Arlene?"

"Leni." Both girls jumped in at the same time.

"Sorry. Leni."

"It was the morning we flew to Los Angeles."

"Okay, that explains it. Why you looked so pissed that day."

"I wasn't... pissed."

"Yeah, you were. It came off you in waves. Look, you had every right to be."

"I was confused."

"You were angry."

"I was hurt." Her voice rose, and others glanced

over and quickly looked away.

"Ahhh. That makes sense. It must have been like a kick in the stomach to learn why your mother had left you."

Leni stared at him until she saw that his expression wore only concern and compassion. He asked because he wanted her to know he understood. She checked the others' expressions and saw the exact same looks. They didn't condemn. They cared.

"Yes. It took me a while to think straight."

"And then you led us to Dani's house in time, so we could save your sister. I'd say that was very brave of you."

"Yeah, well, I put myself in Cassi's place and just did what I knew she'd do. Turned out to be pretty fucking easy after that."

Cassi sent Leni a smile that said it all. How could one girl be so lucky? From then on, the jokes flew, and the merriment was catchy. They all laughed and enjoyed each other's company.

Later, after they'd eaten, with the lights lowered, the band played a slow and dreamy love song called *Amazed*. Trace had his arms around Cassi, holding her as close as was humanly possible without her slipping right through his skin.

Nuzzling her neck gently, he began to speak. "Every time I've heard this song, and it's been years, I wished I could feel this way about someone, meet a woman who suited the words. When you came into my life, I knew I'd found her. So, I requested they play this music for us tonight."

She kissed his cheek before nestling closer. "It's always been one of my favorites, too."

"Are you ready?" He breathed the words in her ear, making shivers float over her body like dust rising after a dry cloth makes a swipe.

"Always. But not here. When we get home."

He laughed. "I meant, for this." He searched in his pocket and came out with a gorgeous engagement ring. A cluster of diamonds surrounding a huge stone in the middle glowed in the dim light, catching fire when he slipped it on her finger. She held it in front of her and it glittered intensely through the tears on her lashes. "I had it made especially for you so I could add some of the stones from my mother's engagement ring."

"Oh, Trace, it's beautiful. I'll wear it proudly." She wrapped her arms around his neck and added, "When I look at it, it'll remind me of Kathleen and what a fantastic son she raised."

**

Michael leaned across to take Leni's hands in his and squeezed them hard to get her attention. The earnest look on his face made her stomach cramp and his words stunned. "Don't tell her."

Shocked to her core, Leni played dumb. "Tell who what?"

"Tell Cassi it was you there the night your brother died. You're the girlfriend. Juan's girlfriend."

Unwilling to give up the happiest hours of her life easily, Leni tried bluffing. "Why in the world would you say that?"

"Because I've read the notes on this case until my eyes bled. Because, early on, Juan had a girlfriend called Leni. That's you, right?"

Still hedging, she agreed, "Yes. But it still doesn't mean I was there that night." She hid her face so he couldn't force her to meet his eyes.

Not letting her hide, he gently drew her chin his way. "Baby, I saw your expression earlier in the office. I was probably the only one looking at you. In fact, your face draws me, amazes me." He listened to the song's words for a second and then sadly smiled, gentleness beaming from his soft green eyes. "It's you, Leni. I'm right, aren't I?"

"Yes." Oh God, she'd almost gotten away with her deceit. She'd told herself a million times, she had to come clean. Cass was her sister. They needed to start their relationship off honestly, without this horrible sham hanging between them. But what if Cass didn't believe the truth about how it all went down. What if she couldn't look Leni in the face without remembering it was her finger on the trigger?

Tears hovered as she tried to explain. "I didn't mean to kill anyone. Just stop them beating on Raoul. Juan grabbed the gun while it was in my hand. He tightened his finger over mine and swung it away from him and over to Raoul. He forced the gun to go off."

Aggravated, he said, "I never imagined you went there to shoot anyone, so don't be silly. Just tell me what happened."

"Faith had overheard them talking in Dani's office. She called me. When I showed up, she begged me to stop them from hurting Raoul."

"Why didn't she go herself?"

"She's really a softie, didn't believe she'd have the guts or that they'd listen. She gave me the weapon Raoul had given her for protection."

"Do you still have it?"

"No. Juan kept it and threatened to use it against me if I talked to anyone."

"And you believed him."

"Of course. What breaks my heart is Raoul died because I brought the weapon. Maybe they would have just beaten him like Dani ordered. Sure screwed that up good, didn't I?" Too numb to cry, she faced him with dry eyes, so filled with hopelessness that he crumbled.

"Would you believe me if I said you aren't to blame. That your heart was pure, your intentions honorable?"

"I'd want to. Man, you can't know how much I want to."

"Then believe it. And when the time is right, you'll tell her. And if the time never comes, then you'll suffer alone to save her more pain. You're one hell of a woman, Leni. I'm glad we met." He leaned in and kissed her gently. Soon, it changed and became heated, hungry... sweet.

"Hey, you two. Get a room." Trace and Cassi took their seats and began to gather their belongings. He pocketed his cell phone while she reached for her purse. "We're off. Thanks for joining us tonight you two. We'll call a cab, so you won't need to see us home, Mike."

Leni held out her hand for Cass's. "Lemme see."

"You noticed? I didn't want to brag."

"Sure. You always wave your fingers around like some dumb chick on a reality TV show. Come here. Oh, dude! It's gorgeous."

"Thanks." Both Cass and Trace answered, making the evening end with a laugh.

Chapter Forty-four

Rusty bellowed yet again. Cassi knew he meant to make them get serious, but they didn't have the same drive to push their limits.

"You two numbskulls get down here. Now." Mock anger filled his voice, yet he meant to be heard.

Cass and Leni stopped sparring and plopped side by side on the edge of the ring, facing their trainer. His black woollen tuke askew on his head, his one good eye spitting bullets, he raised his finger and let them have it.

"Quit messin' around up there. You two gonna get serious, or what?" He'd been after them for the last hour to work harder, train with another bout in mind. But neither girl could rouse their ambition.

"Hey, Rus. Call for you." Adam, their extra sparring partner, shouted over the noise.

"You two better decide when you're going to start working." He pointed at Leni. "I need a boxer who wants to win. Every friggin' bout I sign you up for. Got it?"

"Yeah, yeah. I got it." Leni used his favorite way of agreeing back on him, and while Cassi chuckled, he recognized the tease. Punching Leni's mitt playfully, faking anger, he roared. "Get serious or I'll drop your ass and get a girl who wants to work." He stomped off to his office, his hand pulling off his tuke so he could mangle the white curly mess over his head.

"You think he means it?" Leni took off her mask and wiped at the sweat with a nearby towel.

"Nah! He loves us too much."

"You maybe. Not sure he even likes me sometimes."

"I'd say just the opposite, especially since you told him who you really are."

"You mean he doesn't just love me for my freakin' sweet personality?"

Cassi laughed. "I had a wonderful time last night. It was fun to be like other people, enjoying an evening out with another couple. It felt normal and I haven't had much of normal lately."

"I know what you mean. The food was great. I loved the dancing and it was nice to help you celebrate your engagement."

Cassi nodded. "How did your evening end?" She watched the soft glow return to Leni's expression.

The same one she'd noticed this morning when they'd first arrived. "Aha! You two got it on, didn't you?"

"Some. He's a hard man to pin down. Old-fashioned. Takes his time."

"I like that. Hell, I like him."

"Me, too."

Rusty headed toward them and this time his gait had sped up and he bristled with excitement, energy pouring off him in mega doses. Finding the girls where he left them, he whistled to get their undivided attention.

Then he spoke. "Okay. Listen up, brats. I just talked with Swift's manager. They got my notice about Leni's name change, and they're interested. Very interested." He pointed to Cassi, his gnarled finger surprisingly steady. "I think Ariana's finally given up on getting you in the ring again, Cass, so now she wants a chance at the other Santino sister."

Leni's interest piqued. "She does?"

"Sure, the fool thinks you'll be an easy win. The papers weren't so complimentary on her bad performance in the last fight. They're still talking about the knockout. Her manager knows damn well that a fight like this will get top billing, every TV station around will be clamoring for the rights to film and the casino will make a killing. It's a bloody good step for her career, to take you down."

"No doubt." Cass could see it made total sense.

"Remember, when she was incensed after our match, she vowed not to fight you, only a Santino? Well, now, she can do so without going back on her word and looking foolish."

"Ya see." He pointed at Leni. "But there ain't gonna be a fight unless you can show me you're a Santino, that you have the guts to take her punishment. We all know firsthand the way she works – dirty and mean...and to win. So, brats, we got a lot of training to do in the next few weeks. You up for it, Arl-Leni? And I mean all the way? Else, I'm just gonna retire to some tacky senior's condo in Florida and be like the rest of the old farts – bored out of my gourd."

Both girls jumped to their feet, galvanized. Cassi talked while Leni nodded. "You tell us what to do, Rus. Make up a game plan and we'll follow whatever you say."

Leni piped in. "No way is the crazy bitch going to win, boss. No fucking way. She's going down. And I'll do it legitimately – by out-boxing her. And if it means I need to perform her way, then unlike Cass, I can be ruthless, too. She's not the only fighter who knows how to play dirty."

Chapter
Forty-five

Still sore from the practice before lunch, Cassi sat in her basement steam room and let the heat melt out the aching areas on her body. With a title match at stake, Leni had become a machine, a driving force to be reckoned with.

Determined to make her name in the Boxing World of Fame, she'd changed. Now she was all business. Closeted with Rusty in his office when Cassi'd arrived, they'd had their heads together, working out plans, and they were back at it after she left.

Since the truth had been revealed, Cassi saw the resemblance to her father in the determination and single-minded ambition that drove the other girl. It was awesome and very exciting. And Cassi couldn't have been happier for her – hell, for Rusty, too. They were zinging with purpose and it was delightful.

But she had another agenda. Poor Mary Devin needed attention, and with all that had happened lately, Cassi felt guilty not spending more time with the woman... and on her court case.

Glad to see the text message after her workout this morning, inviting her to the law office this afternoon to work with Maria on the approaching litigation, Cassi quickly showered and searched through her closet for decent clothes that she could now see herself wearing.

The earlier drab articles from her days as a librarian needed to be bagged and given to a charity. Yet the recent style she'd adopted proved to be too revealing for comfort in a day setting. Not having a lot to choose from, she pulled out a black skirt she'd bought online years earlier and had found it short and snug fitting, which would have brought frowns to her men's faces. So, it hung in the back of her closet.

Toned and more slender than those early days, she slipped it on to find it looked good. She liked the small swirl near her knees and teaming it with a silk blouse she'd modernized by undoing two buttons and adding a scarf, left her looking different but classy.

Standing at the mirror, the sheer white top brought memories of Dani. She stopped to let her thoughts range. Searching inside for any animosity toward the boss, she lowered her defenses. After finding out it was her orders that had been the ultimate reason for Raoul's death, she should hate her.

Closing her eyes, she waited for the rage but there was none. The idea that Dani had only ordered Raoul to be punished left her feeling a lot lighter than thinking the woman had commanded his execution.

Since that belief had troubled her, niggling at her whenever they were together, it was one of the reasons she'd had such distaste for even being near Dani. Yet, in the end, she'd been drawn in. Her soft heart had succumbed to the utter wretchedness of the other's world. Shaking off her melancholy, she gathered her belongings and headed for her car.

Soon, she opened the door to the law office and Gladys actually greeted her pleasantly. "Hi, Cassi. Maria's waiting for you in her office."

"Thanks, Gladys. Can I ask you a question before I go in?"

Appearing surprised, the receptionist nodded. "Sure. Glad to help."

"Truthfully, as a normal person—"

"Okay, stop if you're going to insult me..." Gladys laughed at the astonishment Cassi couldn't hide. "I'm kidding. Okay, I'm normal. So, what do you need to know?"

Steady again after the shock of finding that Gladys had a sense of humor, Cassi grinned and went on with her question. "If you were on the jury, how would you vote for Mary Devin? Do you believe she's a cold-hearted killer? Or an angel of mercy?"

"I'd put her away for the rest of her life. Sorry if that's not what you wanted to hear. But my mom's getting on, and there isn't a way in hell that I'd want someone like Mary making choices for her as to whether she should live or die." Waggling her plump hands in front of her as if to say, you asked for it, she went on. "Does that answer your question?"

Cassi took the hit and kept her expression blank. Forcing herself not to express her dismay, she said, "That's it. Thanks for being honest." She headed to Maria's office and saw that the other girl stood in her doorway listening, her face unreadable.

"No problem, honey. Anytime." The clicking of the computer keys followed her into the next room.

Maria closed the door behind them, led the way to her desk and slumped into her chair. "Just so you know, Gladys's mother is fairly young and healthy so it's easy for her to take that stance."

"She has the right to her opinions."

"Yes. Unfortunately, her sentiments are felt by the majority. We did a poll, and I'm sad to say Mary lost. More people showed they're against what she did than those who supported her." Maria straightened her back, needing to release the kinks. "Our country is stuck in the middle ages."

"No! Okay, yes. Kind of. Look, it's a personal question and not everyone is faced with the situation where a loved one is suffering." Cassi thought about her words before adding, "You know, I've never advocated that Mary go free. As much as I feel sorry for the woman, she's guilty and should be punished. I only hoped we could force the courts to be lenient."

"I know – me, too. But Billy had full intentions to win. I've read over all his notes I could find, and though he's listed a lot of the arguments, he hadn't come to any conclusion as to his closing remarks. He'd already warned me that this case would be tried on sentiment, not logic or laws. That we needed to get a jury of hearts rather than brains. He believed that if we could hook them in the end, make them cry, we'd win."

"In other words, no highly educated professionals."

"Yes. His theory was to get the housewives, teachers, maybe younger retirees and people who weren't stuck with the status quo. He knew we'd need to shift the religious belief that only God had the right to stop people's pain."

"And good luck with that route. They're so many fanatics staunch in their faith that I'd be terrified to shake them up. Do we even have the right to? I never realized before what a hell of a mess this might turn into."

"No wonder every lawyer in the district would

love to try this case, Billy wasn't kidding. I'm just afraid I won't be up to it or good enough to give her the defense she needs."

"Do you care about Mary?"

"Of course."

"Do you care about the notoriety the case will bring?"

"Hell, no."

"Then that's all I ask. That we give her a chance to be vindicated enough so she can live out the rest of her life appropriately, behind bars but in a minimum-security setting."

"You should have been a lawyer, Cassi. Your mind is sharp, and you have the gift of the gab and the art of making people care."

"Funny you should mention that. I hoped to use some of the time today to pick your brain about law school. I only have a Library Science degree. I'll need to look into how to upgrade and what courses I'd need."

"Seriously?" Maria brightened, and she appeared excited. "You'd be perfect. I'll help you if you want me to."

Cassi saw uncertainly in the other woman. "Why wouldn't I want you to? We're friends, right?"

"I hope so. I wasn't sure if you'd want to be involved with me now."

"Because of Billy?"

"Yes. Because I gave him the address in Los

Angeles. And he went there to get his revenge on Dani."

"And he got it, may they both rest in peace now that their struggle is over." Cassi purposely added a message and hoped Maria would be smart enough to get the meaning.

"Over. Yes. I see. Thank you, Cassi. You won't regret this."

"I know."

Maria appeared lighter, smiling without any hesitation. She showed trust and it brightened Cassi's spirit. "Maybe you could work here while you go through your classes, and then after you graduate? I could help you."

Happy now, Cassi said, "I'd be up for that. Think you could put in a good word for me with your boss when the time comes?"

"I am the boss now. And consider it a serious offer. What does your fiancé think about your aspirations?" Maria pointed at Cassi's engagement ring. "By the way, it's gorgeous, congratulations."

"Thanks. I love it." Cassi smoothed her fingers over the diamonds and then hid it like brides-to-be tended to do when they didn't want to appear to be gloating. "You have no idea how relieved he was when he found out I had my sights on being a lawyer and not a cop." Cassi laughed and waved away the questioning look. "Private joke."

"Well, helping me on this case will reinforce whether this ambition is really the direction you want to take. Let's Google your school choices in Las Vegas and find out what your next steps should be."

Before Maria could make her way to her computer, Gladys stepped into the office, the phone clutched in front of her ample chest and her face white.

"It's the jail."

Chapter
Forty-six

By the time Cassi got home that night, Trace had picked up Chinese food for dinner, a bottle of wine to go with the meal and was waiting patiently for her to arrive.

He hugged her close when she stepped through the door. "I'm so sorry, Cassi. I know you wanted to help Mary."

"We were discussing her defense when the call came in from the jail that they'd sent her to the hospital."

"Thank you for letting me know what happened. I'm sorry I couldn't get away to meet you there."

"That's okay. I had Maria with me." Cassi kissed him softly and then pulled back so she could see his gentle expression. It made her feel better. "She looked so tiny and frail, Trace. Surrounded by a multitude of machines in the acute care, all the flashing lights and beeping monitors, tubes coming out of her everywhere... it was frightening. They don't know if she'll survive the night, but one of the doctors informed us if she lives for the next twenty-four hours, she has a chance to survive the stroke."

"Was the damage severe?"

"Yes. When she came awake for a few seconds, she couldn't speak, though I had a feeling her eyes tried to communicate something before she slipped into unconsciousness again."

"What's going to happen to her court case?"

"Maria was going to file the appropriate papers to halt the proceedings until they know what the outcome of the stroke will be."

"If it's as critical as you think, they'll hold off until the doctors can predict her chances and the time line for her recovery."

"Between us, I truly don't think she wants to live. I believe she was trying to send me a message."

"What's that?"

"Good-bye."

Stepping back, he searched her face and suddenly his expression hardened. "You've got a bruise on your cheek."

Her hand flew up to cover it. She tried to step away only he wouldn't let her go. "What the hell, Cassidy. I thought all this kind of nonsense was finished, that you'd be safe. What going on now?"

She laughed, couldn't help herself. "It's Leni.

She snuck one past me."

Trace roared, his good mood completely gone. "Why the hell would she hit you?"

"'Cause we were sparring, goofy, and my sweet sister's turned into a frigging machine ever since Rusty got her a bout with Ariana Swift."

"What? When did that happen?"

"Just this morning. She's over the moon. If she took her training seriously before, and she always did, she's on a mission now. Ariana won't know what hit her."

"Maybe Ariana won't know, but I sure as shit do – she hit you, and I don't like it."

"She got lucky."

"I still don't like it."

"Oh, you big baby. What do you think we've been doing these last months?"

Trace lifted both hands to his hair and shoveled them through the soft thickness at the back of his head. "Hell, darlin', you weren't my fiancé before. Seeing marks on you makes me cringe. I get furious." He saw her irritation building and quickly added, "I know it's dumb. I just hate anyone pounding on my chick. Call me a chauvinist."

"You are a chauvinist. An adorable, loveable man who cares. I'm lucky to have you. I promise, I'll duck next time and block as much as I can, but she's driven. And she needs to be able to train hard. Between me and Adam, we have to keep her motivated, striving so she can win. And... she only has a month to get in top shape. After her recent infection, her hand's weak and she needs to strengthen it. I promised Rusty I'd be there for them. So, you'll have to accept it's my choice."

"Okay, oh-kay. I'll be good. Come, let me feed you. I'll get you a cold compress for your face and we'll behave like any old married couple."

"You're on." Cassi headed for the kitchen until she heard his next words.

"That's only until I get you into bed later. Then we'll be screwing like rabbits."

"Rabbits?" She broke out in a fit of giggles and loved that he joined in. She closed in on him so her breast nudged his chest, and her hands gently began to travel downward on his body. "Have I ever told you how much I love bunnies? How I like to pet them, kiss their sweet noses, hold them close, rub their furry little tummies—"

Trace threw her over his shoulder and headed for the bedroom, his voice muffled but she still heard his words. "Fuck dinner. Let's go play with the bunny."

Chapter Forty-seven

Leni reached with her wine glass across the table in the Italian restaurant Michael had chosen for their date. The scent of garlic and herbs from her half-eaten plate of spaghetti floated in the air and spiked her hunger for more. Relieved when he lifted his glass and tapped hers, she smiled. "Cheers and thank you for bringing me here. The food is scrumptious."

"You're just hungry after all that training." His appreciative eyes roved over her shoulders and goose bumps covered her skin. The admiration he managed to convey was a boon to her confidence. "Keep this up and you'll out-muscle me."

"Ha! I could take you anytime, just with the body I've got now."

He grinned. His dimples striking a chord inside so she had to force herself not to reach and caress. "One day, we'll have a match and see who ends up on top."

Flames started low in her belly. The image of her body under his turned her mushy. *Time to change the subject.*

"Do you believe it? In a little over four weeks, I get to fight for the US Featherweight championship in a title match."

"I thought these things took a long time to set up? That people trained for months for one of these competitions, yet you're saying you'll be fighting her that soon?"

"They normally do. But the poor girl she was supposedly up against was in a car accident and had to cancel. And when Ariana found out who I really was, a Santino sister, she jumped on the chance to regain her popularity after her fight with Cass. Beating Cass's sister will totally light her fire. And, trust me, this'll help her career."

"No doubt! She suffered some pretty bad publicity after the last bout. Cassi made her look foolish. It must have hurt."

Bristling, Leni added. "She deserved everything she got, dude. I've never seen a dirtier fighter. The bitch got away with that shit because the judges weren't penalizing her. They loved the energy in the crowd and the screaming, it made for good viewing. For them, it's all about the ratings."

"Calm down, little warrior. I wasn't dissin' Cassi. I cheered as loud as everyone else when she socked the chick. All I'm saying is – will Ariana pull the same shit on you?"

"Sure, she'll try some of her specialty moves, she's known for pushing the bar. But I won't let her get away with it."

"You better not. As it is, I'll have to get Trace to handcuff me to my seat."

Laughing at the vivid mind picture, she scoffed. "Why?"

"So, I don't jump into the ring and drive Miss Swift across the stage." Though his wonderful green eyes were lit with humor, breathtakingly soft, his expression showed how serious he was. He valued her, respected her and something else appeared that she was too nervous to try and decipher.

"I'm sorry. I've been doing all the talking. What happened in your world today?"

"You heard about Mary Devin? The old woman suffered a major stroke and the doctors aren't sure she'll make it through the night. Cassi called Trace a while ago and told him. She'd gone to the hospital where they were looking after the prisoner. She said Mary slipped into unconsciousness and they gave her medication to keep her sedated and make her comfortable."

"I'm sorry. Cassi cares about her."

"If she really cares, she might feel it's a blessing, a way out. The woman faces the rest of her life in jail. Not a very pretty picture."

"That's true. Don't you have any happy news to

share?"

He straightened in his chair and assumed a strutting kind of pose. "I'll have you know that Trace asked me to be his best man today. He's thinking they'll plan the wedding and have a honeymoon before he takes over as chief next month."

Happiness filled her. Okay, this was a lot better. "What did you say?"

He snorted and grinned. "I said – best man, eh? Was there ever any doubt?"

Leni's laugh brought a few stares their way. "Did he rescind the offer?"

"He called me a string of bad names, and then he tried to take the invitation back, but a deal's – a deal."

"Right."

"I'm thinking when Cassi asks you to stand with her, we'll be wedding partners. It'll be sweet. We get to dress up in matching outfits and spend the evening together. Could be good practice."

"For what?"

"For ahh... other weddings."

Leni searched his face; saw him looking sincere until a blush appeared to be working its way up from his neck.

What a sweetheart!

"If she asks me." Sudden guilt swamped Leni and it was all she could do not to throw up the beautiful meal they'd just consumed. How could she face her sister on her special day with this huge lie separating them?

She had to tell her the truth... soon.

Michael must have sensed her distress. Wanting to get her mind onto something else, he leaned over and whispered, "Come on, I'll take you home and we can sit in the car and neck for a while."

Wanting to be with him, spend the night with him, she urged, her tone serious. "Hell, why don't you take me to your place and we'll neck all night?"

He stood and waited for her to join him. Then he wrapped his arm around her waist and pulled her close. "Baby steps, honey. Slow is nice."

"Nice and safe."

"Yep."

***

Michael led her out into the night. The warm air surrounded them at once to remind them they lived in a temperate climate, hot and sultry. He smelled the heat from the day and appreciated the knowledge that Nevada had its own unique scent.

Helping her into the front seat, he let his hand rest on her small waist and had to stifle the urge to turn her into his arms and kiss her until she moaned and yielded.

Instead, he went around to the driver's side, clenched his fingers and prayed he'd be able to control his urges. To make her his woman and screw the consequences might be easy – except there *were* consequences.

He'd made himself a promise – this chick needed to be courted, to learn that she was beautiful and cherished. It shouldn't be rushed.

And before he could make her his, *he* needed to know his wife-to-be wasn't living a lie.

Chapter
Forty-eight

Days later, Cassi visited the hospital and stopped the doctor to get the update on Mary. "She's doing as well as can be expected. The damage from the stroke has immobilized her left side, which leaves her mostly bedridden. And without the ability to speak, she's very frustrated."

"Will she recover?"

"Maybe some. But not a lot. She refuses to eat and so we're feeding her intravenously. I've looked after a lot of stroke patients, and I can always tell those who want to get better from those who've given up their will to live. Your friend falls in that category. She's a very sad woman."

"Yes. You're right."

"Some of the reporters are saying that its retribution and well deserved."

Cassi recoiled. "I don't believe that."

"I don't either, but many do."

"For her, it was never about spite or hate. Every act she committed, she did from love."

"Then her passing might be a blessing. Excuse me, I have other patients. We'll take good care of her, Miss Santino. You have my word."

"Thank you, Doctor." Cassi watched the kind-hearted woman leave the room. She sighed and sank into the visitor's chair next to Mary's bed, reached for the thin hand and let her mind wander.

That very morning at the gym, she'd asked Rusty to take the place of her father and give the bride away. He'd been thrilled and had shown it. Cradling her cheeks, he'd looked into her eyes and let his love shine through. "I'd be delighted, monkey." Then he'd made a mock downturned face and added. "But no tuxedo for me, kiddo. I wear my own clothes or the deal's off."

"Hell, Rus, you can wear your sweats and that crumpled, woolly old tuke for all I care, just as long as you're there to hold on to me."

"What? You figure on running away when the time's close?"

"Not a chance. I'm more afraid I'd be rushing the altar before the music starts."

She'd spotted Leni arriving and went to head her off. "Hi, sis. I've just asked Rusty to be my wedding dad and walk me down the aisle."

Leni's face creased into a smile that started at her lips but eventually lit up her whole face. "What'd he say?"

"The old coot forced me to deal. No tux or he won't play."

Grinning, she added, "Does that surprise you?"

"Hell, no. I already ordered him a new black tuke from eBay."

Laughing together, Cassi followed Leni into the ladies' change room. Glad to see they had the place to themselves, she trailed Leni to her locker and patted the bench so the other girl would sit.

"Will you be my Maid of Honor, Leni? I want to share my special day with the people I care about most."

Shock flashed over Leni's features before she could hide her face. "You want me in the wedding party?"

"Of course. We're sisters now." Cassi's deliberate way of explaining her reasoning made sense to her. Guess it didn't to Leni. Cassi sensed her refusal and stopped her from voicing it by adding a word so hard to say. "Please."

Shoulders slumping instantly, Leni finally spoke, "Okay. I mean, if you're sure you wouldn't like to ask someone else – like maybe Faith."

"I want you."

"Then, yeah. Okay." Leni arched her back and unkinked her neck, a way she had of foreshadowing something she needed to get out. Not surprisingly, she blurted her next words. "Cass, I need to tell you something." Sensing it was important, Cassi waited. But when the door opened, and another girl stepped into the room, Leni balked and muttered. "It can wait."

Face closed up tightly, all gateways shut down, the troubled fighter snatched her gym clothes and headed for the shower. Cassi watched her walking; back bowed as if she carried one hell of a load. She wished she knew how to reach the other girl but when she'd mentioned this wall between them to Trace, his advice had rung true. *Give her time. She still needs to get to know you, to trust you. When she does, she'll tell you what's on her mind.* And so she would.

Next, she'd called Faith to say she wanted to meet. This time the cheery agreeable response lifted her from the morose feeling she'd sunk into.

***

She'd given Leni a good workout, always keeping in mind the way Ariana fought, her moves and her sly technique of sneaking in her elbows and knees. Both knew it was invaluable training for the other girl. But all through the session, Leni kept to business and before Cassi could reintroduce the earlier subject, she'd left.

Later, dressing with care, Cassi picked up Faith and Raoul. Once she'd switched over to Faith's vehicle and her brother's sweet namesake had been safely placed in the top-of-the-line car seat, they drove to one of the outlet malls full of shops and good restaurants.

Hands gripping the steering wheel, Faith burst

out. "I'm glad you called, Cass. It gets a bit lonely with just me and tiger here."

"Then you need to get out more and meet other women with babies, join some groups maybe."

Faith scoffed, her snort speaking for itself. "Yeah, right. Me, a former whore, hobnobbing with the nice girls. Sure. They're obviously eager to include someone like me."

"Don't put yourself down, Faith. Anyone would be lucky to have you. If you're upfront honest and they snub you, then fuck 'em. Go to another group whose attitudes are different. You'll eventually find people who care about the person you are now rather than what you did in the past."

"You think so, Cass?"

"Of course. Look how Steven forgave you. Others will too if they get to know you. Just be truthful from the beginning. Tell them you worked in a nightclub and entertained men for a living. Now, you don't. Two sentences."

"Steven hasn't forgiven me, as you so nicely put it. He was desperate and put the needs of his son first."

"Then you haven't cleared the air."

"If you mean by 'cleared the air' that he's stopped judging me, then no, we haven't cleared the air. We just agreed to move on. I'm good with that anyway. With your brother, it was love at first sight. I fell hard, Cassi. He meant everything to me. I'm still reeling from his loss."

"Raoul was a mixed-up guy, making bad choices. I warned him many times that he'd chosen to play a dangerous game. If I'd known you were together, I'd have pushed harder."

"I know. He told me. But you don't understand, Cassi. Once you're in, it's too late to change your mind. In the end, he was protecting both of us by not running away."

"You know, at the time, I never would have truly understood what you just said. Now I see so much clearer."

"He loved you a lot, Cass."

"I know. We always had a special bond and that's why I know he'd want you to move on and be happy."

"I am with my little Raoul. He's what makes the sun shine in my world."

"Your Steven is lucky to have you."

Stiffening, Faith's normally soft tones hardened. "He's not my Steven. I don't want him."

Cassi listened, and a little voice whispered that her friend's protest might be stronger than necessary. *Hmmm!*

After shopping a while, they settled in the family restaurant within the mall. Raoul, cuddled in Cassi's arms, stared as she created noises babies loved to hear, and held his bottle just right.

She waited until her friend ordered her lunch before she spoke. "I wanted to be with you today, Faith, to ask if you'll be my bridesmaid when Trace and I get married next month."

Faith's face dropped, and tears appeared. "You want me?"

"Of course. You're my friend and Raoul loved you."

"But what about the night he died. It was my fault—"

Cassi interrupted to save her friend the agony of having to relive those moments. "I know the story, Faith. You tried to stop him being killed."

"Leni told you everything."

Cassi just said yes rather than having to go into explanations about the police station and Rodrigo's arrest and confession. It was easier to let the poor girl believe it was Leni who'd told her the truth. After all, Leni had been present at the time.

"Yes. It's all been cleared up. We don't ever have to talk about it again. Let's just move forward. Say you'll help me to celebrate the most important day in my life."

Faith reached over and took Cassi's hand. "I'd be proud to."

Chapter
Forty-nine

Four weeks later:

"Where is she?"

Cassi heard the edge in Rusty's voice and she knew his protégé had driven him wacky for the last few hours.

"Rusty, she's fine. I suggested a shower, thinking it might soothe the savage beast." Cassi chuckled, knowing she was semi-serious.

"Yeah. She's jumpy as a sinner on judgment day. The crazy broad hasn't sat down for more than a few minutes. It's exhausting. Keeps shadow boxing until I want to handcuff her to a wall."

"It's her way. She's envisioning the match. There isn't anything else we can teach her."

"Maybe, kiddo, but she's strung up, nervous as hell, and I want her calm. Why can't she be like you? Hell, I never seen you lose your cool, not once."

"She'll settle down as soon as she's in the ring. You know that as well as I do. Was Dad this crazy before a match? Maybe she takes after him."

"Oh, yeah. He was worse. That's why I never let you kids near him the day of his fights. And when he lost, look out, He'd turn into the biggest jerk in the universe. It would last for a few days before he'd simmer down. Then he'd have to apologize to everyone he'd pissed off."

"You read Judy's diary – the one Leni's mother wrote. Do you think he ever apologized to her? If I remember correctly, she might not have let him before she took off."

"Hell, kid. I don't know." A knock sounded and Rusty opened the door to Adam. "What's happening out there?"

"It's crazy, man. The hordes are already crushing, and the fight isn't set for another hour."

Cassi remembering her mission, said, "I'll go get some ice, Rusty. The machine in here is broken and we'll need it for later. You and Adam can get her ready."

"No way. The hotel will bring ice, just call through." His grumbling continued. "I bet Ariana's ice maker works just fine."

"No doubt. She is the champ. Besides, Adam brought the wrong Gatorade. She wants the lemon stuff."

"Man, shoot me now. She's gonna drive me nuts!"

His words followed her down the hallway and out to the area where she'd parked the car. Smiling at Rusty's bitching, she relaxed the tension from her body and felt relieved to escape, even if it was just long enough to go to a nearby market.

Footsteps sounded and whoever approached in her personal space came a little too close for comfort. Not taking chances in a dark Vegas lot, she whipped around, had the man by the arm and with the force of her twisting movement, she pushed him against the wall, locking her arm on his throat.

Unfortunately, the gun in her stomach made a huge difference to her next move.

"Stand down, you little firebrand. Look and see who you've got pinned against the wall before my man's obliged to shoot and save his own life." Sergio spoke quietly, a smile in his voice.

Peering through the dark, she made out the features of her attacker and loosened her grip immediately. "Doug, you should know better. Call my name but don't ever sneak up on me in the dark. I could have hurt you."

"And he could have killed you."

"Nah. He knew who I was. I'm the victim here." Cassi rubbed Doug's back as he bent over, gasping for air. "Sorry, man."

Choking out the words, Doug managed, "S'okay." Then he stumbled to the Hummer she hadn't noticed and leaned against it.

"He's working with you now?"

"He's always worked for me."

Stunned, Cassi said, "No wonder you succeeded most of the time. Dani never stood a chance."

"She wasn't too smart."

"She was sick."

"So I heard."

"How come you're here?"

"I have one last debt to pay. I promised I'd tell you when I found out who killed your brother. But since it looks like you already know, I'm not sure what I have to share matters. Except, a deal is a deal."

Cassi smiled her agreement. "For you it is. But it's okay. I've laid it to rest. I just wish I knew whether Juan had made a cold-blooded decision to shoot him or not? I thought he liked Raoul, that they were friends."

"Okay, you don't know it all. You want the truth?"

"Of course. Why didn't you tell me when you found out?"

"I am. We had a celebration last night and a bunch of us got talking about the creepy moments over these last few months. That's when Doug started in about the night Raoul was killed."

"What? He was there?"

"No. But he heard about it first hand from Juan. They were partying together after Juan got out of the hospital and back into Dani's good graces.

Doug said as how the sick sucker was so pissed, he talked shit about how he'd finally gotten back the boss's trust, and he didn't want to screw up again. Doug said he'd acted really weird, kinda freaked him out. Juan revealed what happened – one minute he was bragging and then he was crying like a baby."

"What did he tell Doug?"

"He said that when the chick appeared with the gun, he almost crapped his pants. She pointed it at him with orders to stop hurting Raoul, and he lost his cool, grabbed her hand and swung the gun away. He didn't mean for it to go off and he certainly didn't purposely aim it in Raoul's direction, he just panicked. Next thing he knew the guy was dead."

"And Faith had helped kill him."

"Bullshit. I thought you said you knew."

"What?"

"That it was Leni there that night."

A cry of pain burst out. She doubled over. A punch in the gut wouldn't have hurt as badly as Sergio's words. She crouched and wrapped her arms around her middle.

"Shit, baby. You didn't know. Fuck. Cass. I wouldn't have blabbed it out like that if you'd told me the truth."

Tears blotting her vision, voice full of venom, she growled her words. "I believed I did know. But everyone's lied to me. Every fucking person I love has been lying to me all along."

"Shit me, honey, are you sure? Maybe you just had the wrong impression all along? Christ, you sure left me hanging like an idiot." He drew her up into his arms and rocked her while she cried out her misery, her whole world in pieces.

"I'm sick of everyone. All liars. They're all liars."

"No, dude. They love you. Especially Trace. He'd take a bullet for you, I know."

His words broke through her wall of grief. "How could you know something like that?"

"I just do. He's real, Cass, and the asshole loves you."

She listened and accepted his words to be true. But she didn't move, only sniffed and crept closer for protection, knowing, feeling, understanding he'd always look out for her. The knowledge soothed her.

"And what about me? I'm here, brainless sucker that I am, taking chances with my life for you, ain't I?"

Sensing he made a joke to get her to stop crying, she sniffled back the deluge and went along. "You're perfectly safe nowadays, bigshot. All the people who were gunning for you either work for you now or they've left town."

"How do I know some creep looking for vengeance hasn't snuck back to gun me down and take over the *Soldados*? Huh? Ever think of that? Stop bawling and get your shit together." His arms tightened for a few more seconds, and then he stepped back and used his tattooed hand to swipe at her cheeks until she cleaned them herself. "So, baby, you gonna let your sister be alone while she gets the shit kicked outta her?"

Prickly, hating his words, yet knowing they had substance, she explained. "I needed to buy some ice and lemon Gatorade. Leni hates the blue shit."

Sergio called out. "Doug, go to the store and get Cassi what she wants. Now you, my friend, get your pretty little ass into that building and look after the family you have left."

Suddenly, she straightened. "What time is it?" While she'd been wallowing in self-pity the fight would be starting, if it hadn't already.

My God, she'd left Leni alone when she needed her most. How could she have been so stupid? Did it really matter who had tried to stop the killing? Both girls had acted bravely and unselfishly.

She was the one who'd failed. Dammit, she'd frozen when her brother had needed her the most.

So how could she possibly judge Faith, or Leni, for that matter?

It was time to let it go once and for all.

It was time to forgive.

Leni.

Herself.

She'd done the best she could. Raoul would have understood. She'd solved the mystery and found his killers. They knew the truth, the whole truth.

It was over. She began to run...

Chapter Fifty

Cassi pushed her way through the hordes of people at the top of the stadium area and rushed to where Rusty stood craning his head, searching for someone. Her heart sunk, and anxiety tightened her gut.

Roars from the crowd added to her panic.

It had started.

Fuck!

How could she have had a break down on this critical night when they needed her? *Stupid, selfish...* Wriggling past the screamers, she worked her way to join Rusty and Adam in her place at ringside.

Trace and Michael were sitting in the first row, aisle seats. As soon as Trace saw her, his whole demeanor changed. Relief overcame anger as he accepted she was okay. He winked at her, but had no time to say anything. The racket exploded, and he had to reach out and haul Michael back to stop him from bounding out of his seat. She heard his words. "Back off, Mike. Relax. Cassi's here now."

As if he heard them too, Rusty reached for her, slammed his tuke back in place and bellowed, "Where, in all that's holy, have you been, Cass? Our girl's getting the shit kicked outta her, and you're missing." He raised his arms in frustration and added, "Jesus, save me from crazy females."

"I'm sorry, Rus. I'm here now." She looked at the two in the ring, both in deep concentration, but only one was bleeding; only one stumbled from a punch before she weaved at the last minute to avoid another. "What the hell is going on? She's not fighting the way we trained."

"Tell me about it. Something's stuck in her craw, I told you. She's not right. I caught her crying earlier." Tuke back in his hands, being mangled once again, he drilled his right eye into hers and blasted. "Where's her hustle, her killer drive? Do something, kid. With this kind of punishment, she won't last another round."

In seconds, the bell rang, and Cassi watched as Ariana snuck in her last dig in the ribs that had to hurt. Up to her old tricks, the fighter seemed cocky, assured enough to smirk at Cassi before she turned and headed for her stool.

Leni, acting as if she didn't even know where she was, stumbled in their direction. She flopped down on her seat as if all the energy in her body had disintegrated.

Cassi grabbed her face and made her look into her eyes.

"Cass. You're here."

"Fuck me, where else would I be? I got sidetracked, but I'm here to tell you now that I know what you did for our brother. That you were there with him in the end, trying to save his life. I'll never be able to thank you enough for what you did. I love you, girl. Now you listen to me good."

Leni's eyes, glued to Cassi's, cleared and they filled with happiness. A sob escaped, and she nodded.

"Raoul's riding your back in that ring, him and Dad, and they want you to beat the shit outta that bitch, or they'll never rest in peace. You got that?"

As if she'd received a blood transfusion of grit and determination, Leni straightened her shoulders and back. Bumping her forehead against Cassi's as her way to say thank you, she accepted a drink and her mouth guard. Then she flew to her feet a second before the bell rang.

From that moment on, the crowd never sat. For every punch Ariana tried and failed to get past Leni's blockers, and for every dirty move she fell back on, Leni had a response and each one weakened the other girl so much, it was *her* stumbling to her trainer after the next bell. And the next. Points were now being tallied for Leni.

Rusty, screaming in her ear, had lost all sense of decorum. "What the hell did you say to her, kid?

I've never seen her fight like that before. She looks like her dad at his best."

"I told her that both Raoul and Dad were in the ring with her and not to let them down. She's using our game plan now, Rusty, what you trained her to do. She's focused and strong."

Dancing in place with excitement, he added, "And she's beating the crap outta the US Featherweight champion."

A roar filled the arena, and Cassi swiftly turned back in time to see that Leni had snuck in a jab that had connected. As she watched, their beautiful fighter hauled back and drove another uppercut, following through with a punch to the jaw that made every Ariana fan in the place wince.

And the people who'd hoped to see history remade for the Santino family tonight, cheered with delight.

Ariana hit the canvas. Down for the count.

The referee grabbed Leni's arm and raised it above her head.

Leni had won. She'd be wearing the belt that would give her the desired status in the woman's world of boxing.

Michael beat Rusty under the ropes to lift his girl high and twirl her 'round and 'round while the spectators went crazy and the reporters rushed to ringside so they could get their close-ups of the new champ.

Cassi and Rusty joined them, watching as Leni

laughed through the blood dripping off the side of her battered face. She reached down to wrap her arm around Rusty, yanked his tuke off to kiss his head to the delight of the boxing fans who knew and respected the old man.

Then she wriggled to be lowered and flew into Cassi's hug. "Thank you."

Cassi pushed her away roughly, grabbed her by the arms and with tears streaming, she asked, "We good?"

Leni's tears flowed, too. Happiness, a glowing halo around her face, she nodded and reached to be let back in close. "We're good."

Chapter
Fifty-one

Opening her eyes to the sun streaming through the blinds, Cassi breathed a sigh of relief. Since it seldom rained in Vegas during this time of the year, she'd have thought it a bad omen for it to happen on her wedding day.

Especially when it had taken them hours, too much beer and many petty quarrels that ended in laughter to set up the tent and decorations in the newly landscaped backyard.

Glancing at the other two in her bed, she slithered out from the middle of the mattress where the three of them had finally dozed off in the middle of the night. She looked back at Leni and Faith, both cuddling the quilt on each side and smiled.

It had been a blast the night before. After the guys left, the girls had drunk too much and played Truth or Dare until their faces were sore from laughing. When they'd run out of crazy ideas for the dares, they turned on the music and danced up a storm.

In the distance, the ringing of Cassi's cell phone had her rushing to grab it before the noise of Trace's ringtone woke the others.

"Hi, love." Her voice sounded husky even to her. Must be from the singing...

"Hi, baby. You didn't skip town?"

"I planned to but got too drunk last night at our girls' party and passed out. Now I'm here, I might as well go through with the wedding." She giggled and continued to play. "What about you?"

"Oh, I'm calling from Mexico. Michael escaped with me."

Laughing softly, loving the playfulness, she whined, "You mean you intend to leave me waiting at the altar?"

"Baby, there ain't a chance in hell I'd miss our big day." Serious now, he added, "I can't wait to make you my wife. You know how much I love you. I just wish..." The hesitation let her know something vital would be following.

"You wish what?"

"That my mom could be here with us today."

"Oh, Trace. Me, too."

She heard his deep breath to gain control and then his next words. "As long as you're there, that's all that matters. It took me hours to write my vows and after spending all that time, I want to share them with you."

Now worried, she tried not to let it show. "I kept mine rather simple, Trace. I hope you don't mind. Just know they're very heartfelt."

"Okay. See you soon, honey."

***

Her dress had taken the three girls hours, and a trip to Carson City, to find, but the search had been worth it.

In the palest pink, the long, silky skirt full of ruffles floated behind in billows like soft, cloudy, cotton candy. And the strapless rhinestoned top highlighting her tanned shoulders brought gasps from everyone at the church. With a tiara of roses to keep back the mass of curls around her face, Cassi felt more beautiful than ever before.

Holding onto Rusty's arm, she beamed at him with delight. The old man had surprised her by wearing a black tux to match Sam and Michael. "They talked you into joining them, eh, Rus?"

"Trace said he wouldn't name your first son after me if I didn't cooperate, the bast-brat."

Laughing happily, she hugged his arm. "Well, I have something for you and it'll make you feel more like yourself. She reached into a waiting box on the table nearby and pulled out his new tuke, a tiny pink rose decorating the brim.

Beaming, he plunked it on his head, shmushed it down and let her check it out.

"Now we can go."

The ceremony went perfectly. And the picture of Kathleen she'd arranged to have placed nearby delighted Trace, and he hugged her hard when he saw it, upsetting the whole routine they'd practiced.

She didn't care. It was spontaneous and wonderful. Even the priest sensed it mattered and had stepped out the way for a few seconds until pandemonium had settled and they could begin.

When it came time to read their vows, Cassi went first. Trepidation filled her when she remembered his earlier words about how he slaved for hours over his offering.

She only hoped she hadn't left anything out. After listing all the nouns she could think of about the man she loved so desperately, she'd formed her vows around them and felt her total adoration for her new husband would be covered.

She read every word to him, looking into his eyes, and watched as he accepted her words, silently sending her his loving thanks and faithful commitment.

When it was his time to speak, she flinched when he didn't take out a paper like she'd been forced to do so she wouldn't forget anything.

Instead, he reached for her hands, looked deeply into her eyes and said, "No woman will ever be loved more than you."

***

Dinner and speeches over and the dancing

beginning soon, the time had come for her to throw the bouquet. Trace helped her to stand on the stage they'd organized for the head table. She looked over the crowd of friends who circled the area and scanned the faces.

Wanting to memorize the moment, her gaze floated from couple to couple. She saw Steven with a sleeping Raoul over his shoulder standing next to Faith, his empty arm around her waist and smiles filling their happy faces.

Then she saw Leni with Michael behind her, his arms wrapped around her as if he'd never let her go. Not that it looked like she wanted to be let loose.

Rusty stood next to Sam and both lifted their glasses of beer in her direction as a salute. She saw Sergio and Doug, slipping to the back of the crowd, making their getaway. As if he felt her eyes on him, Sergio turned, and he nodded, accepting the kiss she blew his way as her thank you to him making an appearance, for braving the crowd of people he'd never feel comfortable with, especially the police presence from Trace's list of friends.

Trace whispered in her ear and she listened to his words. "It's been such a strange few months. So much has happened. It all started the night you lost your brother."

"And ended when I found my sister."

"Yes." He hesitated. "So, baby, you've gotten retaliation, justice and in the end, some resolution. How does it feel now?"

"There's only one word I can think of."

"What's that?"

"Sweet!"

He chuckled. "Whenever I hear the word sweet, you know what comes to mind?"

"What?"

"You."

The noise from the waiting crowd yelling *throw the flowers* stopped their smooching and got her attention. She turned and lifted her arms. The flowers flew...

And landed right in Faith's hands.

Afterword

Thank you so much for reading – *Endings* – Book #4 of *Her Sweet Revenge Series*.

When I came to the end, I decided Faith had a story that needed to be told and so the next in Her Sweet Revenge Series will be: *FAITH* – *Available on AMAZON*

If you liked reading this Romantic Suspense series, you might like to check out my Undercover FBI Series of stand-alone books.

l loved writing this story and I hope you enjoyed reading it. If so, I would ask you for a favor. Wherever you purchased this set, please take a few minutes and leave an honest review. Authors enjoy hearing that readers like their stories, and hopefully, others will read your words and choose to buy the book because of your sentiments.

If you want to be notified for all my new releases, visit my website at **http://mimibarbour.com** which has all my books listed with links to the various publishers to make it easy for you find my other work. While there, be sure and sign onto my newsletter where I like to have special giveaways, book sales and lots of info about me and what's coming soon. It's nice to stay in touch...

http://bit.ly/mimibarbournewsletter

***You have my word that your address will never be shared.

Hugs, Mimi

Faith

Her Sweet Revenge Series Book #5
by
Mimi Barbour
NYT & USA Today Best-selling author
AMAZON

~*~*~

Hooker turned nanny, Faith Whitely, known to her johns as Sunshine, has struggled to be a decent person all her life. And her options were never the same as the good girls in town. Growing up with a sick mother and limited resources, she does the best she can until a man she loves dies in a violent, intolerable situation where she blames herself. Then her world crumbles into drugs and self-hate. She's saved by the sound of a baby's cry, an unmanageable child who she bonds with and then needs as much as she wants his daddy.

Any luck Steven Corella has with the women in his life has been all bad. Sensitive, a man who works in a job unsuited to his inner nature, he manages to fool the world. When he finds he's to become a daddy, the tough-guy personality he's been portraying all along turns real. He hardens his heart and hides behind thick walls of protection he's carefully erected. And then Sunshine enters his world, and nothing makes sense anymore.

Faith - Chapter One

"Your man is one damn good-looker, Faith."

Laughing at the way her best friend's Aunt Barb strung together a compliment, Faith shook her head, depression settling in. "He's my boss, Barb. Not my man."

Unfortunately. The thought popped in, and as quickly she shut it down.

"You can't kid me, honey. When Sam greeted you by calling you Sunshine and swirled you in his arms, your guy's head swivelled like a hawk sighting prey. Until it seemed he recognized Sam, then he just looked confused."

Faith let the image play out in her head. "It was probably the name he didn't like. That's what the idiot at the casino called me when he tried to hire me for the night."

"Oh, you mean the idiot that Steven pounded the shit out of so that three bouncers had to pull him off – that idiot?" A grin played around the edges of Barb's smirk and her eyes twinkled.

"He'd learned my history in a shocking way, Barb. He'd thought of me as a normal woman who he'd just hired to be his precious baby's nanny. It would throw any man."

"You could be right, sweetie." Aunt Barb patted her cheek in a loving way. "Seems to me that if all he sees when he looks at you is his nanny, then he's not just stupid, he's blind, too." The older woman, dressed in a pantsuit that showed off her slim, medium height and colored blond hair, headed to the doorway and as Faith watched her leave, she saw both her friends, Cassi and Leni, leaning into the room. Both faces wore teasing grins.

Cassi entered first and headed for the champagne bottle, poured two drinks, added ginger ale to her own, then handed the girls their glasses.

A flowery whiff of perfume hovered around her, stronger than what one normally smelled as she walked by, but a scent Faith associated with her friend.

Cass's lovely wedding gown took up the biggest space in the smaller, old-fashioned kitchen. Soft ruffles of silk fluttered, rhinestones sewn into the material around her bare neck and shoulders glittered, and her black hair, with small roses woven throughout, shone in the overhead light.

As bridesmaids, Leni and Faith had chosen similar dresses just not identical. Both wore long gowns in the same tone of stunning, baby-blue sparkling silk. But, Leni, her thick dark hair worn in draped curls over her shoulders had opted for a low-cut number that hugged her body, whereas blonde-haired Faith had gone conservative until she turned. The backless to her waist style suited her creamy pale skin. While the front lovingly hugged her chest, and swirled from her hips, it flared out with each step she took.

If her intention had been to downplay any hint of sexiness, she'd failed miserably. The material clung to her breasts, showing in detail their fullness and the swirling silkiness below the waist melded to her lush body every time she moved. Meanwhile, the gleaming softness of the skin on her back became an invitation to touch.

Since most of the guests were in the lit garden, hovering around the tent where masses of food kept them occupied, the girls had the room to themselves.

Cassi broke the silence and had their attention. "To us – three misfits who love each other!"

Leni lifted her goblet and added, "Sisters of the heart!" A clearing of Cassi's throat, made Leni chuckle as she added, "And half-sister to one weirdo who won't let the other forget."

Not to be outdone, Faith took it a step further as she contributed to the toast, "My adopted *sisters* who are both nutcases, but whom I adore and will always support."

Laughing, they all downed their drinks and then Leni dropped a bombshell. "Cass, you've been drinking non-alcoholic drinks yesterday and today. I bet you thought your sneaky maneuvering went unnoticed. Is there something you want to share with your sisters? Hmm?"

Cassi's blush had Faith reaching for her hand. "Oh my Lord, girlfriend, are you pregnant?" She waited, breath abated, praying that the news would be what they all wanted to hear.

"Shush. Don't breathe a word to anyone. I'm late. That's why I slipped out this morning. So I could buy some pregnancy tests just in case. On the off-chance that I could be, I'd never take any risks to harm Trace's baby."

Faith sighed, her smile huge. "It's your baby, too."

Leni exhaled, but with a slight groan thrown in, disgusted at their sappy, feminine expressions. "Oh, for heaven's sake, Cass, you mean to tell us you're hesitating. What? You afraid you're pregnant or you're not?"

Cassi put her arm around her bristling half-sister's shoulders. "Hold on, Leni. What I've seen between you and smitten Michael; you might be in need of a test too. I bought three so there'd be no doubt. You wanna use one?"

Laughing, Leni answered. "I'm too smart for that kind of shit. Ever heard of the pill?" Shaking off Cassi's arm and turning the conversation back to the original subject, Leni grumbled. "Bet you intend to make us wait for the news."

"Yep. There'll only be two of us at the peeing

ritual... or maybe three if it shows positive."

Laughing, Leni and Faith moved in for a group hug. Before Faith could escape, Cassi hit her with the question she'd been dreading. "Steven seems to be having a good time. He's been hanging out with Sam a lot."

Leni piped in, "Didn't think that would happen when Sam greeted you with your nickname, Sunshine, and that enthusiastic hug. I bet if Steven hadn't been carrying Raoul, he'd have made a fool of himself. The look on his face when he heard the nickname could freeze molasses."

Faith giggled. "You know why he reacted. He's so worried another slimeball will make a move on his nanny that we never go anywhere together except the grocery store and the mall.'

Bristling, Leni questioned. "You sayin' he's ashamed to be seen with you?"

"No, not ashamed as much as scared someone else will recognize me. Or at least that's what I believe."

Cassi put a calming hand on Leni's arm. "Back off, tiger. Remember Faith told us his casino manager's sick. No doubt, as the assistant, he's taken on all the extra work. Right now Vegas's crawling with tourists so it could be that he doesn't have the time to take her and Raoul out." Cassi turned to Faith. "Does he still come by and see the baby before he goes to sleep for the night?"

"Oh, sure. He's only missed once, and he

phoned to apologize. They'd had a situation at work, some people passing out counterfeit bills or something."

Cassi held out both hands in a way that showed them she felt vindicated for supporting the man.

Facing Faith, Leni erupted, "Have you two had the talk, yet? The one where he's supposed to forgive you? Bastard." She held up her fist and pumped it in front of Faith. "I'd beg his forgiveness alright."

Laughing, Faith put both her hands against Leni's flushed cheeks. "You are my biggest fan, and I'd give you my best pair of Jimmy Choos if I had any. Truth is, ever since you overheard us saying we'd forgive each other that word has stuck in your craw. But... what you need to know is this. I do need his forgiveness or we can never move forward."

Cassi broke in. "That's just it, babe. Leni understands the same as I do. You've done nothing... NOTHING that requires his forgiveness. He has no right to judge your past. He either understands that life happens, lets go of the shit and moves on, or you leave him."

A tear snuck out before Faith could stop it. Her hands clasped together prayer-like, and the fear in her eyes wasn't faked. "That's just it. I could never leave him because that would mean I'd have to abandon Raoul. That baby is my lifeline to sanity and my path to a future. I'm clinging on as hard as I can, and if I have to take a little prejudice and judging then bring it on."

Leni bowed her head, her tone kind of joking. "I have an idea. Just get the prick to marry you and then make his life miserable."

Before they could stop giggling, the prick entered the kitchen with a squirming baby and a hard gleam in his eye. "Raoul woke up and misses you, Faith. And, Cassi, everyone is looking for you. It's something to do with your bouquet."

***If you'd like to continue reading this story, click here for my Amazon Universal link: http://mybook.to/sweetfaith

***All the books in *Her Sweet Revenge Series* are free in Kindle Unlimited.

Special Agent Kandice

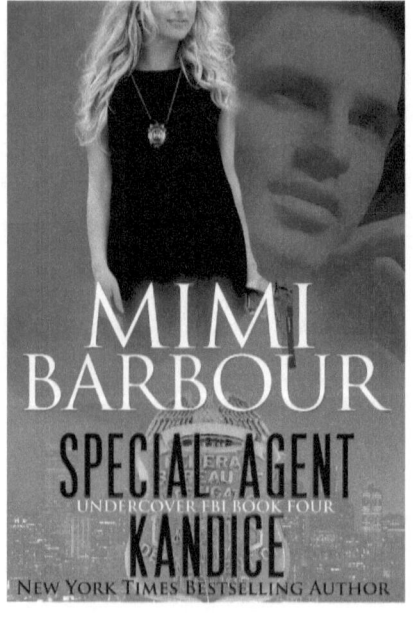

AMAZON
Book #4 – Undercover FBI Series
by New York Times Best-selling author Mimi
Barbour

Powerful, thrilling and character-driven, this romantic suspense is a real page-turner.

Special Agent indeed, Kandice Warner is everyone's best friend. Talk about a Barbie doll! This female might have the same pretty-girl looks but even though she has a tender heart, she also has the resilience needed for a very successful FBI Hostage Negotiator. Feelings of inadequacy constantly force her to prove that she's tough, and she demonstrates her courage when dealing with a murderous bank robber, a desperate jumper, being stalked, kidnapped and beaten. But her tender heart can get her in trouble and she needs to grow a thicker skin. Almost impossible when her obstinate new boss, for reasons of his own, interferes in everything she does.

Assistant Director of the Criminal Investigative Division in Washington, Dan Black is as hard as they come. With the grit of a street youth stiffening his resolve, he's worked his way up through the ranks, his personal space shields as strong as ever. Until he sees the sweetest things on two legs! A girl from his past. The one he's never been able to forget. Working undercover in the Seattle bureau, he tries to protect his childhood fantasy but she refuses to stay put or take orders. Faced with a woman like that, what's a mere man to do?

Praise:

"Kandi has a way about her that draws people to her; her heart is so big, it's hard for her to sound like a tough FBI Agent, but she tries. Kandi is well suited to her job as a crisis negotiator. When their office gets a new ASAC, Dan Black, Kandi feels drawn to him and doesn't really understand why, as Dan seems not to like her from the moment they meet. Dan was supposedly demoted from AD of the Criminal Investigation Division in Washington and sent to this Seattle Branch of the FBI. He had forgotten Kandi was assigned to the same office. Now he's in trouble! This is really a heartwarming love story with an interesting "cops and robbers" storyline!" ~ *reviewed by Susan*

"Can't wait to read more by this author. This was the first book I read by this author so my expectations weren't too much, but they should have been. I really enjoyed this book. I can't wait to read more of her books. I even joined her newsletter." ~ *reviewed by SusieQ*

"In my opinion, the Special Agent series by Mimi Barbour just keeps getting better and better. I loved this story, the humor, the characters and the plot...especially the things I didn't see coming. Wonderfully entertaining read!" ~ *reviewed by Anne C*

The Vegas Series

AMAZON
Romantic Suspense at its best
by
New York Times Best-selling author,
Mimi Barbour

This sizzling box set for the Vegas Series starts off where we meet up with hardworking, hard-assed Detective Aurora Morelli. Attempting to arrest a rapist who attacks her colleague then continually thwarts her attempts to bring him to justice—to a horrific nightmare where her new baby is kidnapped—this scrappy detective does everything in her power to control these events. Kai Lawson, a partner she doesn't want, fights against and in the end accepts (in her job and in her bed) is the hero in these first few stories. The bald-headed, purse-carrying hotshot knows just how to pull her crank and the outcome is entertaining. Their blockbuster story will get you totally invested in this series.

In the last three books, along comes Lisa Jordan, a kick-ass kinda gal who loves wearing the shield as a Vegas detective and enjoys the more strenuous aspects of her job. She steps in for a while as Aurora's partner while Kai is MIA. Her story begins here and ends the series as she fights her attraction for wealthy casino owner, Jeff Waters. After one wild night, the charismatic charmer digs his way into her heart and that of the three-year-old nephew in her care. The fact that he leaves her speechless, literally, detracts from his appeal for Lisa since as a self-professed chatterbox, it's the first time ever. On the other hand, everything else about the man is fascinating. She can no more fight her memories than stop herself from rescuing him from two killers holding him hostage in revenge for the mistakes of his father.

~*~*~

Praise for the Vegas series:
"Cops & drama, absolutely loved this series!" ~
reviewed by luvbooks
"Good action and great stories. What a
bargain!" ~ reviewed by Johnny Rotten Apples
"Great story lines, wonderful characters!" ~
reviewed by Rachel Larson
"Bloody fantastic!" ~ reviewed by Bernadette
Boyce

A word about the author, Mimi Barbour

Mimi is an incredibly busy New York Times, USA Today and award-winning, best-selling author who has nine series to her credit.

She lives on the beautiful east coast of Vancouver Island and fills most of her day with writing and promoting her work. The rest of her time is spent in her garden, doing minimal housework and planning weird meals to ward off starvation.

"The favorite part of my job is meeting the characters from each new book. Creating them the way I want and having them act however I think they should. It's thrilling. Especially when most of my make-believe folks are interesting, witty and in most cases, people I would love to know."

Contact Me

Write to me, I truly love hearing from my readers!

~ ~

My website: http://www.mimibarbour.com/
Follow me on Twitter, Facebook, Pinterest
Amazon, Goodreads, BookBub, LinkedIn